THE VILLAIN

DR. REBECCA SHARP

The Villain (The Vigilantes, Book 3)
Published by Dr. Rebecca Sharp
Copyright © 2024 Dr. Rebecca Sharp

All rights reserved. No part of this book may be reproduced, distributed, or transmitted in any form or by any electronic or mechanical means, including information storage and retrieval systems, photocopying, or recording, without permission in writing from the publisher, except by reviewers, who may quote brief passages in a review and certain other noncommercial uses permitted by copyright law.
This is a work of fiction. Resemblance to actual persons, things, living or dead, locales or events is entirely coincidental.

Cover Design:

Sarah Hansen, Okay Creations

Editing:

Ellie McLove, My Brother's Editor

Printed in the United States of America.

Visit www.drrebeccasharp.com

THE VILLAIN

Book 3

DR. REBECCA SHARP

Chapter One

Dare

He was here somewhere. *He had to be.*

I scrolled through the images on the screen. Names and faces becoming a blur of pixels in front of me. *I would find him. I had to.* We were too close to have him slip away again. I leaned closer for a better look, and the surveillance footage started to swim and then split in two.

Dammit. A deep exhale carried a rough sound of frustration from my chest as I pulled out my earbuds and pinched the bridge of my nose, closing my eyes for what felt like the first time in hours. I was turning into a zombie—a creature consumed by the need for one thing: justice.

My hand strayed to the jagged scar on my left cheek, tracing the raised, mostly healed flesh. A potent reminder that there was work to be done. A criminal to catch. *Ray Ivans.* Up and down, my finger traced and retraced the path of the blade in a newfound tic. Ivans might not have wielded the knife that sliced open my face two months ago, but he was the man responsible, and I was determined to find him.

I forced my eyes open and back to the glowing screen, fresh resolve steeping my focus.

Appear, dammit. Just for one fucking second so I can find you.

The knock on the door jarred my concentration, and my head snapped up. The office took a beat to sharpen. Shelves of security, surveillance, and computer equipment surrounded a small table in the center. This office was the center of our operations for both our motorcycle garage, the Sherwood Garage, and our motorcycle club, the Vigilantes.

"Yeah?" I called just as the door opened, my gaze narrowing on the intruder: Rhys Garrick—a friend and fellow Vigilante. "What do you need?"

If he didn't need anything, then I needed him to leave; I had work to do, and so did he.

There were five of us total in the club. Four of us—myself, Rhys, Tynan, and Harm—were former Special Forces. Green Berets. Fifth *Special Forces Group, Third Battalion.* Brothers by fire, we said, but in my case, the leader of our unit, Harm, was also my older brother by blood. The fifth member of our club was Rob—Robyn. My older adopted sister. She was the reason we existed in the first place: to get justice for what had been done to her and to those like her.

"I came to check on you." Rhys shut the door firmly and flashed me his too-easy smile.

Dammit.

What we'd seen, what we'd lived through, and what we'd lost...they were the kinds of things that had both broken and bonded us forever. We understood each other in a way no one else could—a way forged from unbreakable trust and unimagin-

The Villain

able tragedy. And it was exactly that perceptiveness I didn't want to deal with right now.

"I'm fine. Working—"

"You've been cooped up in here working for weeks now. I've never seen you like this, man. Let me—let Ty—*let someone take over for a little,*" he drawled, approaching the desk.

I stilled and bit into my tongue, the taste of blood keeping me from snapping back. *And do what instead?*

I'd finished my last engine rebuild early for a client's vintage Harley—no surprise there since I'd spent my days and nights in the garage working on it, and I wasn't scheduled to start another bike until next month. If I didn't focus on this, I knew exactly where my thoughts would go: to him and Harm. *How they both had someone to go home to.*

Fuck.

For some reason, I thought things would stay forever the way they were. Our unit, together, fixing bikes and seeking justice. It had been that way for so long. But then Harm found Daria, and Rhys fell for Merritt...and it wasn't jealousy that hit me, it was reality.

After everything we'd been through, they'd found happiness. Love. *The one thing I'd never allow myself to have.* So, to take a break or *let someone else take over* meant having to face the truth: instead of a life here with the only people who knew me, I could end up facing forever alone.

"I'm handling it."

"Dare, if this is about me and Merritt—"

"It's not."

"No?" Rhys moved closer, his presence like a pin against the thin skin of a stretched balloon.

I glared at him, words balling on my tongue like a balloon inflating to the point of rupture. Carefully, I let the breath hiss out.

"I'm happy for you, Rhys. Honest to God," I rasped, and it was the fucking truth. I was happy for him and Merritt. It wasn't their fucking fault their happiness reminded me of my failure.

"But you wanted to be happy, too," Rhys said, seeing more than I wanted him to see.

It wasn't their fault the woman I'd fallen for betrayed me—betrayed us. Love had been a costly mistake for me, one whose price I still continued to pay. *And who the hell could blame me for not wanting to sit around and dwell on how my attempt at happiness had almost cost us all our lives?*

"No," I said and scoffed. "I mean, I am happy. I have enough."

I had the club. Freedom. Security. Life on the open road. And purpose. Holy hell, did purpose change a life—*save* a life. I looked back at the images on the computer, our purpose plastered all over them: *vigilante justice*.

Our ex-military motorcycle garage and club were equal parts good business and a good cover. By day, we worked on expensive motorcycles, and by night, we used our unconventional skill sets to bring hundreds of criminals to justice by unlawful or lethal means. The criminals we hunted were the ones who used money and power to shield themselves from punishment. The ones who hid in plain sight, bribing the law for its protection.

"You can want more." Rhys spoke, bringing my attention back to him, his hands propped on the desk as he tipped forward. "She already took enough from you, Dare, you don't have to let her—"

"Don't," I warned in a low voice. "Just...don't."

She was like fucking Voldemort—I didn't want to talk about her, didn't want to hear her name. *Ever*. She'd taken Ryan's last breath—the only one of us who hadn't made it home from that last mission, and I wouldn't let Rhys or any of the other guys waste a single breath on the woman who'd betrayed me.

"You should take a break."

"I will when we find him," I gritted out.

Dr. Ray Ivans had worked at GrowTech, a biochemical engineering giant, and was involved in the cover-up of Rob's parents' deaths almost two decades ago—a cover-up that climbed a ladder of criminals right to the top of the billion-dollar company.

Magnus Sinclair. Les Wheaton. Ray Ivans. Lloyd Wenner. Bernard Belmont. They'd all been involved in concealing the cancerous flaw in one of their new pesticides. Rob's parents became sick while working on the project, and Ivans downplayed their concerns and falsified their medical records to hide that the chemicals were killing them.

After their deaths, Ivans vanished. Belmont claimed the doctor had fled the States with all his documentation—leaving behind no proof of his crimes—but we knew better. Belmont paid him to disappear and start over. Paid for him to have a new face, a new identity, and a new life. But after so long, Belmont got tired of paying to hide a ghost.

I scrolled back to the beginning of the hotel's security feed from two months ago, zeroing in on the few seconds that had captured Ivans entering the lobby and making his way to the mezzanine.

Dressed in a tux, he headed for the ballroom, where a black-tie fundraiser for GrowGood, an NPO associated with GrowTech, was being held. I followed his path to the door, where he disappeared into the crowd and off the cameras completely. If only we'd known then who he was.

Instead, Harm, Rhys, and I were there to track down a band of international jewel thieves who'd targeted and kidnapped Rhys's girlfriend, Merritt. We thought their ring leader was the man who sliced my face when we captured him. In a twist of fate—and a bullet to that man's chest—we realized that their leader was none other than Ivans, who'd been using an alias and who had surgically altered his face to look nothing like the man who'd fled the States two decades earlier.

Rhys made a low sound of disapproval, but I ignored him and the odds stacked against me. I didn't care if the footage I searched through was two months old, there had to be something on it—something I could use to figure out where he was hiding.

I pinched the bridge of my nose, needing Rhys to leave so I could focus. "I don't want to talk—"

Another knock sounded on the door. "Rhys?"

Dammit. Merritt's voice was unmistakable even before she opened the door and poked her head through, her bright eyes finding Rhys in an instant.

The way she looked at him...the way he lit up...my chest tightened. I'd never have that. I wouldn't let myself. *I didn't deserve it.*

Love was dangerous. *Deadly.* It was the goddamn bullet you didn't hear until it was buried in the center of your chest.

"What's wrong?" Rhys stepped in front of Merritt, blocking my view.

Good. Maybe they'd both leave now.

"Nothing, I—" Merritt said and peeked over at me. "Something came for you." She moved around Rhys and extended her hand. "Sorry, I grabbed a bunch of envelopes from the mail, and this was stuck between them."

Interesting. I took the envelope from her and muttered my thanks, but she was already back in conversation with Rhys.

I stilled when I looked at the front. There was no address on it. No return address. No address to the garage. Only my name. *Darius Keyes.*

The Villain

My heart collided with the front of my chest. *Shit.* The last time a letter had been delivered like this to our garage, it had come from the Most Wanted criminal on the FBI's list. *Damon Remington.* Former FBI agent turned fugitive. A broker for the criminal underworld. *If he was sending me a message...*

Fuck it. I ripped open the seam of the envelope and yanked out the contents. A single paper. *No.* Not a paper. I flipped it over. *A photograph.*

Air pierced my lungs like a bullet, stopping my heart on a damn dime.

No.

It couldn't be.

My mouth went dry, and I brought the image closer like I could step right into it, absorbing every detail of a face I'd never forget.

Blond hair like soft wheat. Cornflower-blue eyes. But it was that smile. *Fuck me.* I pressed my fingertips to the image, tracing the gentle sweep of her cheek to the dimples pinned at the edge of her wide, beaming grin.

Athena Holman.

God, I'd never forget how that smile felt like the sun when it had shone on me—or the way I'd sentenced myself to a life of darkness when I'd broken her heart.

Fuck.

In almost two decades, I hadn't let myself think of this woman. Hell, she'd hardly been that the last time I'd seen her standing on her mom's front lawn with tears in her eyes. She'd been heading off to college, and I'd been heading off to war.

We were young. Hopeful. Foolish to think it could last. I'd ended it before someone got hurt.

And after I came back from war, trying to think about who I was, the people I'd known and cared for...*hurt.* There was no going back—no making it right. To try would be like trying to open a door with no knob. So, for two decades, Athena Holman had remained safely and securely behind that door, untouched by any more of my trauma and tragedy.

Until now.

Until this photograph, where she sat at a restaurant smiling at the very man I was hunting—smiling at him the way she once smiled at me.

Fuck. My blood turned to ice, hard and sharp as it sliced through my veins. *What the hell was she doing with Ivans?*

In less than a minute, I'd searched her information and found her current address—ironically, it was her old address, too. Her mom's house, which was only about twenty minutes from here. All this time, and she was that close…*and so was he.*

I dropped the photograph and shoved up out of my chair, ignoring Rhys and Merritt's stares as I headed for the door.

"I'll be back," I shouted, not needing to be stopped by one more of Rhys's welfare checks.

I made it down the hall in a blink, the door to the garage banging open into the wall before it slammed shut behind me. It couldn't have taken another ninety seconds to make it through the massive ten-thousand-square-foot garage to where my Harley was parked. My leathers stretched over my shoulders like a second skin. I didn't bother with the clip on my helmet before revving my bike to life.

I flew down the miles-long length of the tree-lined drive, the overcast sky turning everything gray. The irony of the shadowless day mocked me at every turn, as if it were the shadows of my past looming heavily over me.

Twenty minutes.

Twenty minutes to figure out what I was going to say to a woman I hadn't seen in twenty years. A woman I'd promised forever back when we were too young to understand everything forever could mean. *A woman whose heart I'd broken.*

The Villain

Twenty minutes to figure out how the hell I was going to tell her that her new boyfriend—an assumption I made on her smile—was a criminal. A murderer, thief, and liar. *Twenty minutes to figure out how to get a woman who surely hated me to believe I was telling the truth.*

The house was a small, single-level structure at the end of a cul-de-sac. Brick with worn red shutters and a bright red door.

... I don't want a house with a white picket fence, but I do want a red front door. Do you think that's too much? I just want to look at it and know I'll never have to watch you leave through it again. I miss you. —Athena

The smallest smile started to curl at the corner of my mouth, remembering her words from the very first letter she'd sent me after I left. *God, those letters.* Pain seared through my chest, my small smile dying like an ember tamped out before it could turn into a flame. Remembering what I had—what I could've had—would only make this worse.

Those letters...that woman...she didn't belong to me anymore.

I slowed and parked in front of the neighbor's yard, letting my bike rumble so I wouldn't have to be alone with my thoughts. There was a car in the driveway; hers, I presumed, and it was still running. I'd gotten here just in time.

I peeled my fingers off the handlebars. Fuck, this was going to be difficult. But that didn't matter. I would protect her even if she didn't want me to. Even if she hated me. After everything, I would always protect her. *Even if she wasn't mine to protect.*

"Hey, Athena. It's me, Darius. I know we haven't spoken in a long time, but I had to find you and tell you you're dating a killer." No—"Hey, Athena. Sorry to come back into your life like this, but you're dating an internationally wanted criminal."

Fuck. My fingers went to my scar, feeling the ragged flesh.

How was I going to get her to believe me? Tell her the truth? The truth was hardly believable—a criminal doctor who had a full-face reconstruction and turned into a thief was taking her to dinner. A short, bitter laugh escaped. The alternative was I could beg her to trust me—*to trust the man who'd broken her heart.* My laugh turned into a groan, weighing the options of bad and worse.

What if she already knew who he was?

No.

I cranked off the engine and got off my bike in a swift, angry movement. There was no way she knew Ivans was a criminal—no way she'd smile like that at him if she knew the truth. Not a damn chance. A lot of things could change over the course of decades, but not that. Not the way she valued integrity.

The red door opened, and through it stepped a sight that stole my breath. Almost twenty years later, and she looked the same as the day I'd left her. All willowy grace, smooth skin, and hair spun of sunshine. There were all kinds of beautiful, but for me, there was only ever one definition of breathtaking. *And I was looking at her.*

I stood dumbstruck, watching her fumble to lock her door and then move toward her car, a small duffle over her shoulder.

She must've either forgotten the bag inside or had only stopped home for a minute to grab it. It looked like a gym bag, but she was already wearing gym clothes.

Was she taking clothes to Ivans's house?

Goddammit. A surge of emotions that I lacked both practice and a right to feel swept over me, and I quickly channeled them into my pace, closing the space between us.

"Athena!" I called, my voice deeper than usual.

She stopped and turned just a few feet from her car. Her eyes met mine, and air rushed from my lungs like I'd been punched in the gut.

The wind dragged a strand of hair over her face, catching on her parted lips. She might look like an angel, but she had a mouth made for sin. Full, pink lips, the bow on top promising they were as kind as they were soft. Heat injected into my veins, melting away the cobwebs and cold that had lingered there for a decade. *Damn, those lips.*

Lips I'd tasted. Lips I'd dreamed of. Lips I'd fought over when other guys talked about her in a way I didn't like.

Time didn't stop; it turned back. It spiraled like a top out of control, winding back the clocks, unraveling the fabric of decades until we were just teenagers. Until the moment I'd last seen her, standing here on this very lawn.

"Don't say goodbye," she'd begged, her hands clutching my shirt and tears streaking her cheeks.

I jolted, and the memory dissolved into the present moment.

Athena's jaw went slack, the first touch of recognition sparking in her gaze and reaching for her mind.

And then everything went to hell.

A loud boom. A force that threw me back. *Fuck!*

My head slammed into the ground, pain erupting as everything went black. The blast knocked my consciousness straight out of me for a split second.

I came to with a heavy breath, consciousness returning full force as heat and debris sprayed over me in a way I wished I wasn't familiar with. My eyes opened to a violent show of flames and fragments and destruction, her car an exploded mass of tangled metal.

Fuck!

Ears ringing, I forced myself to move. Years of training and even more years of experience that no training could prepare for had me on my feet and looking for her. *Looking to protect her.*

I found her in an instant, all that sunshine streaked in ash, curled in a heap on the lawn. *No.* My heart dropped into my stomach, beating like a bird in a cage. I stumbled toward her lifeless form. She'd been close to her car—closer to the source of the blast that was now a flaming metal cage, plumes of black smoke blotting the gray sky.

"Athena!" My voice was raw, breathing in too much of the thick smoke as I kneeled beside her.

Soot, but not a lot of blood. Nothing glaringly broken. I carefully took her wrist, releasing a breath I hadn't realized I'd imprisoned when the faint thump of her pulse met my touch. *Unconscious, not dead.*

Instantly, a second truth struck with even more force. *She was alive, but someone had just tried to kill her.*

"Athena..."

Distantly, through the ringing, I heard the sounds of sirens and calls for help. I scanned the surroundings, starting to see people approaching the scene. Neighbors. Random cars stopping along the road.

Shit. I had to get her out of here.

Her soft whimper broke through the noise—it broke through everything. I froze, watching her eyes work their way open. It was only for a split second that she looked at me. A split second where she looked right at me, but didn't see me.

"Help...me..." Her whispered voice cracked, and then she faded once more.

The Villain

"Dammit," I muttered, carefully lifting her and carrying her away from the burning car.

She wasn't heavy, but the weight of my guilt was. She was in danger—had been in danger. And I hadn't been here quick enough to stop it. *The second time I'd failed her.*

Taking Athena anywhere on my bike wasn't an option. She wasn't conscious and almost definitely concussed; it was too dangerous. So, I headed toward an old man standing by his pickup truck; he was wearing an Army sweatshirt, and therefore my best bet.

"Are you alright, son? What the hell—"

"I need to borrow your truck. I need to get her to the hospital." I went to the passenger door and opened it, placing Athena in the front seat before he even had a chance to protest.

"Someone called an ambulance—"

I hooked her seat belt and then faced him. "It's not enough, soldier." I addressed him low so only he could hear. "I'm Special Forces, and I have to get her out of here. Her life is in danger."

Instantly, his spine straightened, duty transforming skepticism into steel. His chin clipped. "Of course—"

"I'll return it," I promised as I took his keys.

Ignoring the pound in my own head, I went to the driver's side and got behind the wheel. For being at least two decades old, the pickup moved with surprising pep as I put my foot to the floor.

Chapter Two

Dare

> *It's only been one day, but I missed you too much not to write. Last night, I laid outside on a blanket and watched the stars. I thought it would help to look at them and know you see them, too. So far, it's not working like I hoped. - Always, Athena*

"You know her."

I glared at the man who'd been by my side during the hardest times of my life. Dr. Rorik Nilsen.

Rorik had been the medical attaché assigned to our Special Forces unit—the sixth member of our team. After our final—failed—mission, he'd returned and became a medical examiner for the city for a good couple of years before taking a private contract with a local security firm, Covington Security, as their

The Villain

on-site doctor and medical consultant. He consulted on cases and did things like this—patching up the team, friends, and anyone else brought into his domain.

"Did her test results tell you that?" I ground out, dragging my stare back to Athena, who lay unmoving in the hospital bed, tied and tethered to a dozen machines inside the medical bay at Covington.

I felt Rorik's sharp stare flay me open before he replied calmly, "No. The way you look at her does."

Instantly, I turned to him. His cold blue eyes glinted as though with one look, he'd cut right to the center of my secrets and saw what—*who*—Athena had been to me.

"It was a long time ago."

"Ghosts don't age."

My jaw locked, barricading my protest rather than opening a can of worms.

Rorik had reconnected with his high school sweetheart a few years ago—over an autopsy table no less—and their former spark rekindled into the kind of flame Harm and Rhys had found. I wasn't about to encourage him to find any similarities with my situation because they were nothing alike.

"No, but people do," I rasped, my fist balling against my side as he took the last vial of blood from her arm.

People aged. Things changed. *And some things would never be the same.*

"Why don't you sit?"

And why don't you go back to figuring out why she's not waking up? I swallowed down the rude response, knowing he was doing everything he could for her. For me. And all at the drop of a hat.

I'd given him only a few minutes notice that I was on my way to Covington with an emergency. They had a state-of-the-art medical bay, and I wasn't about to take Athena to the hospital. I didn't trust them—I wouldn't trust anyone else with her except Rorik.

"I'm going to run her labs and check on her scan results. I'll be back in a few minutes."

I managed a grunt just as the door swung shut behind him, its haunting swish sweeping away the last distraction that buffered me and the unconscious woman from my past.

Athena.

I didn't realize I'd moved to the side of the bed until my legs pressed against the edge.

She didn't move, lying just as lifeless as when we'd arrived. The monitors beeped, an incessant—necessary—reminder that she wasn't lifeless. *Stable* was the work Rorik used. *What the fuck was stable when she wasn't waking up?*

I gripped the bed rail like I could channel my frustration through it to the floor. Even though I was safe—even though she was safe—the drum of my heart wouldn't let up.

Wake up, I willed like I had the power to make it happen. I didn't. I was powerless to help her, and for some reason, the thought gutted me.

Someone had tried to kill her. It wasn't enough for her to be caught up with a criminal, but now her life was on the line, too. *And I hadn't been able to protect her from either.*

"Wake up, Athena," I murmured under my breath, letting my eyes roam over her. This was the first moment I'd had to look at her—the first moment I felt safe enough to let myself really look at her since the blast.

God, to see her again... It had been sixteen—almost seventeen—years since the last time. But while I was tattooed with ink, scars, and trauma, Athena Holman looked just as she did when she was eighteen. All soft sunlight and warm curves. Even banged up, bruised, and covered in dirt and ash, she was still the most beautiful woman I'd never seen. An angel.

The Villain

And an angel shouldn't be this dirty.

I turned and went to the sink on the other side of the room, grabbing a fistful of paper towels and wetting one end. Returning to her side, I didn't think twice about what I was about to do until it was too late—and I was wiping her face clean.

Maybe I should've had Rorik take a look at my head, too. No sane man would knowingly open Pandora's box and reach right in.

Pain and pleasure wove like vines through my DNA, sending everything from my blood to my bones into a kind of electric frenzy I couldn't control.

I cleaned the stretch of her forehead, careful to avoid where Rorik had already taped over two nasty gashes. Then there was the soft crest of her brow and the slender bridge of her nose.

"Dammit." The word came out under my breath, my hand shaking as I tried to gently dislodge some ash from her eyelashes.

I wasn't even touching her skin, and my body felt like it was coming out of itself for more.

I gritted my teeth and wiped the gentle slope of her cheeks, my throat tightening at how pale they were underneath the soot. There was more tape on the bottom of her chin where it had slammed into the ground, and I carefully cleaned around it as though I could wipe away everything. Every hurt. Every injury. The whole incident—*including me.*

"You're going to be okay, Angel," I murmured roughly, the slow stroke of my finger pausing when it got close to her mouth.

I shouldn't. My mouth went dry, but I couldn't pull away. *Fuck.* It had been so long since I touched a woman. Even this— this *not touching*—had me about to come out of my skin.

I started at the corners, tracing the edge of her pink lips like there was still time for her to wake up and stop me. The beeps of the monitors droned louder in my ears, like the ticking of a bomb set to explode. My finger traced the perfect arch of her top lip, and I stopped breathing.

She didn't deserve this. Athena Holman had been the kind of girl to put wildflowers in her hair and dance in the rain and make up her own constellations. She'd exuded light and love in spite of the loss life had thrown at her. She didn't deserve to be tangled up with Ivans—*or me*.

Wake up and hate me.

Her lips parted, and my pulse raced, hungry for something I couldn't have.

Wake up and curse me.

My body thrummed, feeling a thousand things—*everything I shouldn't.*

Wake up and tell me you never want to see me again.

A ragged groan broke from my chest. She deserved so much better than this after everything she'd been through—

The door swung open, and my hand fell to my side as I turned.

"Harm." I exhaled and met my brother's frenzied stare.

He'd been the second call I'd made on the furious drive here. I'd hardly given my brother a chance to speak before telling him there was a situation and to meet me here ASAP.

"You alright?" He let the door close and took a step toward me.

I turned, shielding Athena from his view. There were things I needed to tell him first—things I needed to explain. "Fine—"

"What the hell is going on? First, Rhys texts me to check on you. Next thing I know, Ty is getting reports over the police scanner of an explosion, and a few minutes later, you call and tell me to meet you here."

"There was a car bomb that went off," I said, knowing my

black jeans and black leather jacket weren't enough to hide the black ash that seemed to be everywhere.

"Who was the target?"

"Remington sent me information. A photo—a lead on someone connected to Ivans."

"What?" He growled his displeasure. "How? What did it say? Did he give you a name?"

A man like Remington would always have more answers about the criminal underworld than we did, but that was the key to his criminal empire. He brokered information—bought and sold connections when it suited him. And right now, it didn't suit him to give us Ivans's new alias—*if he knew it.*

"It didn't say anything. There was only a photo in an envelope addressed to me." *And barely that.* "The image was of Ivans—his new face—and he was with a woman; they were sitting at a restaurant. Looked like they were on a date." *Dammit.* I tried to clear the irritation from my voice before continuing. "I looked up her address and went to confront her—was about to when her car exploded."

"Jesus..." He shook his head and started to move toward the bed. "Who is she?"

"Harm—" I grabbed his arm, but it didn't stop him; he reached the side of the bed, his swift inhale marking the moment he recognized her.

His gaze whipped to mine. "Is that...Athena?"

There was not a man on this earth who could see this woman and forget her—or not recognize her even after almost two decades. Even when she was lying in a hospital bed, bruised, concussed, and covered in ash, it would be like seeing the sun and then forgetting its light.

I gritted my teeth and nodded. "Yeah."

He let out a long breath and ran his hand along his jaw. He was always the best of the team and of the two of us at keeping his emotions in check. Meanwhile, I still hummed with adrenaline and anticipation...and something else I wouldn't admit to.

"She's...here? Living here, I mean?"

My muscles tensed. "At her mom's house."

"Did you—"

"No." The word smacked down between us. *No,* I didn't know she lived there until today. I didn't know anything about her life now—nothing except all the reasons I had no right to be in it. Our past—what happened between us—had nothing to do with this. "I didn't get a chance—didn't even get to her before her car exploded. She's been unconscious ever since."

I'd given up my chance with this sleeping beauty a long time ago. Now all that was left—all that was honorable for me to do—was what I'd been trying to do all along: protect her. And for that, I'd risk her hate—and her hurt—if she'd only wake up.

"So, Remington sent you a photo of Ivans and Athena?"

My eyes flicked to the door, willing Rorik to walk back through it with some kind of fucking assurance that she was going to wake up and be okay.

"Yes." My jaw locked tighter, and I looked back at her.

"And you have no idea if she and him—"

"No," I clipped, not wanting to hear the end of that statement. "All I have is that photo until she wakes up and can answer questions."

He made a low noise, but I refused to look at him. Not that staring at Athena was any better, with the way my brother read into my focus.

"When I got there, her car was already running in the driveway, so the bomb wasn't triggered by ignition."

"On a timer?"

"Or a remote." I focused my gaze on the steady rise and fall of her chest, letting the rhythm hypnotize me.

"Maybe Ivans was the target."

"He wasn't there." Not that I could see. Not that I wanted to consider.

"But he's the more likely target if she's involved with him—"

"It was only one photograph." I interrupted. "When she wakes up, we'll ask her about Ivans. Explain who he is—what he's done. Figure out what she knows. And then take her back home."

"Take her back?" He gaped, and I could practically feel the way his brows lifted like a hold around my throat. "She was almost blown up."

"And we'll find the person responsible," I clipped, shifting my weight. "The police can protect her. Hell, Covington Security can protect her. We don't do protection." I said it like it wasn't total BS. Harm had been hired to protect Daria, and Rhys had protected Merritt when she was targeted by criminals from her past. But *typically*, we didn't deal in private security; we were hunters, not guardians.

"Then why did you bring her here instead of a hospital?"

Dammit. Air hissed through my lips.

"Because I wasn't thinking," I said, grabbing for whatever excuse I could find. "The explosion happened, and I acted on instinct—save her. Bring her here. Have Rorik look at her. But you're right, I should've taken her to the hospital instead."

My brother made a low noise that I was all too familiar with after thirty-six years. *His rumble of disbelief.*

"You were the one who said Ivans was most likely the target," I offered just as the door swung open, drawing both our attention to Rorik.

"Harm." He greeted my brother with a deferential nod and a firm handshake.

"Is she going to be okay?" I didn't have time for their pleasantries.

"Other than the cuts and bruises, she has a concussion and some swelling in her brain, so she'll need to rest for a few days—physically and mentally. She may have some amnesia about the blast, but we won't know until she wakes up. If she does have some short-term memory issues, it's nothing that shouldn't clear up with a little time."

I let out a long breath.

"You said you got her attention right before the bomb went off?" Rorik probed.

I nodded.

"If she'd been any closer to the car when it exploded, we'd be having a different discussion right now," he said low, banding his arms over his chest.

Any closer... She'd stopped because I'd called to her. If I hadn't, she probably would've been at the car when it—

"I'll see if Ty can pull any home security feeds from the development. In the chance it was remote detonated, we may be able to find a lead." Harm thought out loud as he pulled out his phone, sending off that message to Ty.

I didn't care about the bomb right now; I cared about her.

"When will she wake up?" I demanded, hating how my voice cracked.

Rorik stared like I shouldn't be asking that question. "I don't see any reason she won't wake up soon," he said tightly. "But when she does, her brain needs to rest. You can't jump right in to interrogating her—"

"You think that's what I'm going to do?" I demanded, moving toward him as anger lashed through me. "After someone tried to blow her up?"

"Dare." Harm grabbed my arm, his hand like an anchor, stabilizing me through the surge of emotion.

I'd do anything to spare this woman pain. Hell, I'd broken her heart and mine to keep her safe, and in the end, she'd ended up entangled with Ivans. I couldn't stand it. I'd fix it—tell her the truth and protect her. It wasn't like I could give her any more reason to hate me than she already did.

I started to apologize, but a soft noise from behind me derailed my good intentions. A whimper. *She was awake.*

My heart slammed into the front of my chest, air exploding from my lungs. Suddenly, I forgot all the things I'd planned to say—all the explanations and apologies I'd worked up in my head. All the ways to start a conversation with the woman I'd abandoned.

"Athena..." *Fuck, why was my voice so fucking hoarse?* In an instant, I was beside her, Rorik and my brother forgotten in the background. "You're okay. You're safe."

It was instinct to reach for her and torture all the same. I took her hand, heat rushing through my veins like lava. Her skin was warmer and softer than I remembered—than I imagined. Memories, desire, desperation—they all consumed me. Like an earthquake, a massive fire, and the swell of a tsunami ravaging me all at once. I forced a breath through my lips and squeezed my eyes shut for a beat, afraid if I didn't, I'd come apart at the seams.

"You're okay," I repeated, lower this time. "I'm here."

She whimpered again, her lips breaking apart for the sound as her brow scrunched.

"Athena..." I braced myself for what would come next. That recognition. The remembering. The hurt I'd caused.

I deserved what came next.

Her eyes fluttered and then finally pulled open, and I held my breath. She looked straight at me—straight into my eyes, and it felt like all the way into the broken shards of my soul.

And then she blinked, and her body tensed like she'd been physically shocked.

"What happened?" her voice rasped, unsteady but determined. "What is this—where am I?" She jerked her hand back and reached for her face.

Shit.

"You're safe—"

"What's going on?" she repeated, the pitch of her voice rising in panic as her fingers felt her forehead and pressed to her eyes. "Who are you?"

My mouth snapped shut, my instincts immediately on alert. Something was wrong. She knew me—she should recognize me. *Scars and all.* But she didn't.

Rorik stepped to the other side of the bed. "Ms. Holman, I'm Dr. Nilsen—"

"What's wrong with me? Why is it dark?" She completely ignored him—didn't even look at him as she pressed her hands to her cheeks and then to her eyes—she rubbed on the sides of them, over them, wiped at them like there was something irritating them. "Oh my god." Her head started to shake. And then her shoulders. But it was the way she kept rubbing her eyes that worried me.

"Athena—" I forcibly took her wrists, but then her whole body started to shake. "You're okay—"

"I can't see—" she whimpered, her chest starting to heave.

What? My head snapped to Rorik, and when I saw surprise on his face, I knew this wasn't good.

"I can't see. Oh, my god. *I'm blind—*" She started to hyperventilate. "Where am I? Why can't I see? What happened?"

"I'm Dr. Nilsen, Ms. Holman. You have to calm down, please." He tried, but she wasn't hearing him because she was fighting me—shaking and pulling herself away even though I was only trying to reassure her.

The Villain

"Calm down, Angel," I begged. "It's okay—" She wasn't hearing me. She was panicking, and I couldn't stop it. "You have a concussion—" It was of no use. She pushed back into the bed, her head whipping side to side.

"No! What happened to me? Who are..." Suddenly, all the energy went out of her, and she slumped down, her eyes drifting shut. *No!* My heart cracked against my chest, fearing the worst and looking to Rorik to resuscitate her.

And then I realized he was responsible, and I growled at him like an animal.

"I had to sedate her," he said firmly, pulling the syringe out of her IV line. "She couldn't stay that agitated. Not with her concussion. She would've done more damage."

Fuck.

For a second, I couldn't move. I couldn't do anything but process the look on her face when she'd come to—the pure panic and fear that consumed her. I should've just told her who I was. *It wouldn't have mattered,* a voice inside my head responded, forcing me to accept that Rorik had introduced himself as a doctor, and she still couldn't process it. I knew—I understood. I'd been around plenty of people who survived explosions and came to with a consuming kind of panic.

"What the hell was that?" I rasped and carefully straightened, balling my arms to my chest as Rorik leaned forward and peeled her eyelids open. He ignored my question, examining her eyes with a small light before letting them close again.

"You said she was fine—that her scans were fine—"

"And they are." He cut me off, his cold stare daring me to question his expertise. I wasn't, but fuck me, she wasn't fine, and that was all I could think about. "Her scans are clear; her pupils respond normally to light—"

"Then why is she fucking blind?" I growled.

"*I can't see.*" Her panicked cry still haunted the room.

He shoved his little flashlight back into his scrub pocket and folded his arms. "I believe she has what's called cortical visual impairment—used to be called cortical blindness."

My brother made a low noise and nodded.

"You know what that is?"

"Used that to describe what happened to soldiers who were shot or had other injuries to the back part of the brain," he said with a grunt.

Rorik nodded and further explained, "Basically, her eyes are fine but the part of her brain that processes information from the ocular complex is injured."

"Can you fix it?"

"No, but the blindness is most likely temporary—a side effect of being too close to the blast and hitting her head. As her brain heals—as the swelling goes down—her vision will start to return."

"How long?"

"Days, weeks, maybe a month." He reached for his iPad, tapping notes into Athena's chart. "Just depends on how her brain heals."

A month. She could be blind for an entire month.

I dragged my gaze back to Athena, her body calm and her breathing steady. *Beautiful but vulnerable.* So fucking vulnerable. This changed everything. There was no way I could question her and let her go. Not when she was wounded. *Not when she needed me.*

Fuck.

I exhaled.

Fuck!

"We're bringing her back to Sherwood," I turned and declared to Harm, my voice low even though Rorik had stepped away.

My brother tipped his head, curiosity dripping from his

The Villain

stare at my sudden change of course. "Are you sure that's a good idea?"

A feeling I didn't like slithered over my spine, cold and subversive.

He wasn't asking because we didn't typically bring outsiders to the compound beyond the garage. He wasn't asking because he was worried she'd learn about our lawless vigilante work. He asked because of me—because of our past.

Because he knew what this woman had meant to me all those years ago.

"It has nothing to do with that," I told him, my breaths so strained, every inhale felt like I was trying to inflate a stone.

"Then what is it?"

My jaw hardened to stone. "I don't trust anyone else to protect her."

Something flickered in Harm's stare—something I ignored as I went to talk to Rorik, needing to know how long he was going to keep her sedated. When we could move her. *How long I had before I had to explain...*

Harm could think whatever he wanted about my choice. I didn't care. After what I'd done. How I'd hurt her—abandoned her. Protecting her was more than the right thing to do; it would be my penance. She might hate me when this was all over, but it would be worth it if she was safe.

Just like it had been all those years ago.

Chapter Three

Athena

In the darkness, there was a hand that held mine. An anchor in the foggy thoughts and stormy nightmares. A security in the shroud of uncertainty. My mind drifted somewhere between thoughts and dreams and memories, obscuring all of them together, but when the strong fingers wrapped around mine, I felt safe as the darkness swallowed me whole.

"...*Are you sure this is a good idea? She could stay in the guest cabin...*"

"...*Keep her eyes covered and let her rest...*"

"...*What are you going to tell her?*"

"*The truth.*"

The warm hand tightened on mine, and I relaxed back into the darkness.

Beep. Beep. Beep.

The sound pierced through the dark bubble. *Beep. Beep. Beep.* Then came the scent of smoke and pine and...alcohol.

Not drinking alcohol—rubbing alcohol. It was faint and pungent at the same time, burrowing deep in my lungs.

I winced, feeling a sharp pang in my head and then a dull pain everywhere. I curled my fingers, expecting to feel that strong hand in mine, but instead, something soft folded into them. A sheet—*I was on a bed.*

My entire body ached like someone had beaten me with a bag of oranges. I hadn't felt this sore since my roommate in college, Josie, dragged me to a CrossFit class my first semester.

Beep. Beep. Beep. A timer. Or alarm. Or monitor. But beyond it, there was a low rumble of voices. Close, but not close enough for my foggy brain to decipher what they were saying.

Where was I? Why was my brain so muddy?

I tried to think of the answer—it felt like I *knew* the answer, but what I wanted to know sat like the sun behind clouds. I could see the glow of the truth, feel the warmth and comfort of understanding, but I couldn't clear the clouds away to get to it.

A heavy exhale pushed through my lips. I needed to see what was going on. Maybe that would clear away the fog. But forcing my eyes to open took effort and seemed to take minutes rather than the split of a second, my eyelids having a weight to them I'd never felt before. But even when they were open—or when I thought they were open—everything was still dark.

The darkness.

I sucked in a breath, dragging my hand to my face, my fingers colliding with fabric. *There was a bandage wrapped around my head.*

Why?

What happened to me?

Had I been kidnapped?

Beep. Beep. Beep.

Monitors. Men's voices. *Darkness.*

My heart pounded so loudly, it chased away every other

sound in the room. Everything except the rush of blood to my head, awareness and panic leaching through the sluggish calm I'd been feeling.

I whimpered, my throat feeling like it had forgotten how to make sound as my fingers fumbled for the edge of the bandage. I had to get it off. I had to see where—*who*—

"Don't," a rough voice begged, but it was the warm hand that gently pressed to mine that stopped me.

I knew those fingers. That touch. That voice. *He was the calm harbor in my dark storm.*

"*You're going to be okay,*" he murmured in the darkness. "*You're safe. I'll protect you,*" he promised through the shadows.

I turned, feeling his presence beside me. I couldn't see him, but I could sense him. His closeness.

"What happened? Where am I?" My voice hardly sounded like my own as I let him pull my hand down from my head.

"Safe," his rough voice replied, giving me another chance to absorb the fullness of its tenor. Deep and husky, as though sound could have a scar, the single word wrapped around me like a shield.

It wasn't an answer I'd been expecting, but between that and the warm embrace of his fingers, I felt a wave of heaviness through my veins again. *Safe.*

"What happened?" I swallowed, resisting the urge to reach for my face, and instead focused on the large fingers wrapped around my hand.

They were long. Calloused. Strong, but knew their strength —knew the boundary between firm and painful.

"There was an accident. What do you remember?"

I opened my mouth and realized I didn't have an answer. *What did I remember?* I remembered driving in my car. I remembered needing something, needing to get away from something, and then...nothing. Memories felt like a deck of cards strewn all over the floor that he wanted me to pick up and put back in order, except they were all blank.

"I don't..." My voice cracked. "I don't know."

My brow creased under the bandage. Trying to remember was even worse in the darkness. I couldn't look around for clues. I couldn't hold onto something recognizable. There was nothing—nothing except him. The man attached to the rough voice.

"It's okay—"

"Can I take the bandage off? Did something happen to my eyes?"

He didn't respond right away—he didn't have to. I could feel the slight burst of tension ripple through him where his hand held mine, and in the pause, I heard his quick inhale. It was quiet—taken through his nose rather than through his mouth. The kind of inhale that would've made his nostrils flare.

He didn't need to verbally respond because my other senses had already picked up on his answer.

"What happened to my eyes?" I probed softly, trying to swallow through the grip of fear around my throat.

There was another pause, and a sensation spread over my skin. Like there'd been a blanket over me this entire time, and for a moment, that blanket was removed.

"Your eyes are fine," he said, and the warmth over me returned, his hand tightening almost imperceptibly on mine. Supportively. "The accident gave you a concussion, and the swelling in your brain has created a temporary blindness."

Temporary...*blindness.*

"*I can't see.*" I heard my own voice inside my head, bits and pieces of a memory coming back like the ashes of a former flame. "Are you the doctor?"

"No—"

"I am." A new voice spoke from the other side of the room,

and my head turned on instinct, my stomach bottoming out again when there was nothing to see.

Breathe, Athena. He said it was temporary.

"I'm Dr. Rorik Nilsen, Ms. Holman," the second voice continued, and it was so different from the first. Deep and calm and doctorly. I imagined his white coat and expressionless face. "You sustained quite a few bumps and bruises, but overall, there was no major damage to any organs or bones, which is good—"

"Except I'm blind," I repeated thickly, trying to wrap my head around this new reality.

Blind.

Cold panic seized my chest. I was an artist. Yes, I was just starting out with making my art my business, but I had good opportunities. Several of my paintings had been featured at events in San Francisco. I had a gallery show coming up in a few weeks, and several other opportunities that...my throat tightened. The phrase was *starving* artist. There was nothing said for a *blind* artist.

"You have cortical visual impairment due to the traumatic brain injury you sustained in the accident. As your brain heals, I expect your sight, along with your memories, will fully return, but it could take some time and will require you to rest and remain monitored," he explained succinctly, and then added, "Your eyes themselves are fine, but I've bandaged them so you don't inadvertently do them any damage."

Translation: Don't take it off.

"And if it's not temporary?"

"It will be." He sounded so sure, it should've comforted me more than it did.

Beep. Beep. Beep.

"I understand." I let out a deep breath. "So, I was in an accident—where am I? A hospital or outpatient facility?" I pushed aside the worry about my sight and instead let the other million questions I had rush to the forefront. "Should I call—" I broke off, giving my head a little shake. I didn't have anyone to call. Not anymore. Not here.

Carmel Cove was supposed to be a fresh start. Well, as fresh of a start as someone could have moving into my childhood home. *Thank God, I hadn't listened to Brandon when he'd demanded I sell it.* It was hard enough to move to Sacramento with him and leave my hometown—the place with all the best memories of Mom behind—but when he'd ordered me to sell it, that was the final straw.

Final straw made me sound stronger than I was. The final straw should've been five months into our marriage when he shouted at me in front of a bunch of his work friends because I hadn't made wings for them the way he liked—*legs only*. But I'd let that slide, like I'd let a thousand other verbal abuses be downplayed and glossed over. Like I'd talked myself out of thinking for too long about the way he criticized me because it was always little comments...about everything.

The way I cooked. The way I cleaned. The way I picked out his clothes every morning—*"Just pick me out a shirt."* But then every shirt I picked was unacceptable. *"No, that one is too long. No, I don't like how the collar is. No, that one is too dark."* He criticized the way I dressed. The way I wore my hair. Always little things—things that seemed so easy to fix and, therefore, so easy to please. But it never worked. As soon as I did what he wanted or asked for, it became the wrong thing.

It wasn't like that when I met him in college. He'd been there for me when Mom died. Held me. Let me soak through countless shirts with my tears. He'd been a constant at that lowest moment, and that was why it had taken me so long to see the truth of how deceptively abusive he was.

Eight years of marriage before I'd finally asked for a divorce

—I fought for it. Used all my savings. Lost everything except Mom's house and my paintings.

Lost my health insurance.

Oh god... how was I going to pay for this? I'd sold several of my paintings, but not to the tune of a hospital bill.

"When can I be discharged?" Blind and concussed, and I was asking to be put back on the street. I was sure the doctor—Dr. Nilsen—was going to add "crazy" to my diagnosis.

"Discharged?" the rough and tumbled voice croaked.

"I don't have insurance," I said firmly, noting that not being able to see their pity-filled reactions made it a whole lot easier to speak the simple truth. "I can't afford—"

"You're not at a hospital, Ms. Holman. You're at a safe house."

"Safe house?" I didn't know which shock was worse, hearing that I was temporarily blind or that I was at a safe house. "I don't understand. I thought I was in a car accident..." I started to shake my head. A safe house inherently implied danger. "Who are you?"

He made a low sound. "You...what do you remember?"

I opened my mouth to answer, except nothing came out because...I couldn't. I wasn't only blind to the present, I was blind to the past, too.

"I was driving home, and that's the last thing I recall. Did I crash into something—someone? Did someone hit me?" I couldn't suck in air fast enough. "Why am I at a safe house? I don't remember what happened after. I don't know who you are. I can't see—"

"Athena, please," he begged, and the way he said my name was like a speed bump to my spiraling anxiety and runaway train of thought, forcing it to slow down. "Just breathe."

I tried to swallow through the tightness in my throat. *Goodness, that voice...* it was like hot coals under my body, warming me so unexpectedly—especially for a man I couldn't see.

He released my hand, and heat rose in my cheeks, afraid my face had given away the effect his voice had on me.

"Ms. Holman, it's very important for you and your brain to stay relaxed right now. Any stress could intensify the swelling and cause further damage," the voice of the doctor said, and my head swiveled—pointlessly—in its direction. "I can give you something to relax you, if you want—"

"No," I croaked and gently shook my head and let out a self-deprecating laugh. "I'm already down a sense. I'd rather not dull the others." I shivered. "What would help is the truth, please."

As if everything they'd already explained wasn't enough, I could sense there was more. Maybe because I couldn't see. Maybe because everything was dark and uncertain, I could sense other things more acutely.

Like that the woodsy pine scent was coming from the man beside me. It wasn't the smell of the room or the sheets—it was the scent of him. Earthy and rich and rough. I should ask his name—*should've* asked his name—but it suddenly seemed an inconsequential question compared to—

"You're at a safe house because the accident...it wasn't an accident, Athena," the man at my side said.

My chest caved with the release of my breath, my ears starting to ring. "What do you mean, not an accident?"

I thought those kinds of things only happened in movies, but apparently, I was wrong.

He cleared his throat, but it didn't affect the rough timbre of his voice. Nothing would. "Your car was running in your driveway. You walked out of your house to get back in it, and I called to you. Not even a second later, it exploded."

"Exploded?" *Oh, my god.* "My car exploded. In my driveway..." I repeated, everything feeling numb as well as dark. *How could I not remember this?* "Why? How? Was something wrong with my car?"

It was old, but I kept up to date with the inspections and maintenance. Even still, cars didn't just blow up, except in movies—

"Athena."

His voice stilled me again, but it was the pause after that made my stomach drop. It wasn't filled with facial expressions or nuanced movements; in my blindness, all the distractions were gone, leaving only the giant, cavernous space that spanned an extra second. A space that held a thousand sentiments—all of which he hesitated to tell me.

"What was wrong with your car was that there was a bomb attached to it," he said finally, his voice impossibly lower.

A bomb. Goose bumps washed over my skin. "Someone *blew up* my car?" I barely got out the question, my throat impossibly tight.

"Another step closer, and it would've been more than just your car," the doctor's voice rumbled from the other side of the room. *Another step closer...* "You're very lucky he got your attention when he did."

My lips parted, and I hated the darkness the most in that moment, wishing I could see the man who'd saved me.

"You saved my life," I breathed out, feeling tears well against the bandage over my eyes.

He responded with a low noise that sounded remarkably like a growl. Was he angry for saving me? Or angry I was now aware of what he'd done?

"I took you from the scene, got you medical attention, and then we brought you here for your safety."

Who was we—who was he?

"So, you're with law enforcement..."

"Someone tried to blow you up. You weren't safe—aren't safe, especially in your condition," he said, and I heard him shift his weight. "That's why you're at a safe house."

I tried to swallow, but this time it was impossible. Blind. Almost blown-up. In danger. *And I'd thought divorced, starving artist moving back into her mom's house was rock bottom.*

"Why would someone try to kill me? I'm not...I don't have money." My heartbeat turned erratic. Heavy thuds and low flutters. The pulse in my head became insistent, and suddenly, it felt like it was the sheer number of questions themselves that started swelling my brain.

"I just moved here. I know maybe three people in town. I'm an artist." I rambled through the sad facts of my life, desperate to find even the semblance of one that could serve as an explanation.

"Athena." *Speed bump.* "I'm going to find out who did this and why—I'm going to make sure you're safe."

It wasn't a question. It wasn't a request for permission. It was a promise. To protect me. To take care of me. My lips parted, and the unsteady beat in my chest started to calm. No one had promised me that in a very long time, and the last person who did had lied.

"But for me to do that, I need you to focus on resting and getting better. Do we have a deal?" His hand slid around mine as though we were going to shake on it. This time, it hit me how large his hand was and how small mine felt in his grasp. *The man himself must be huge.*

"A deal?" I murmured. "How can I make a deal with you when I don't even know your name?"

Again, that pause. That canyon. That vast space filled with all the things he wasn't telling me.

"My name..." He trailed off like he was waiting for something. "You can call me Dare."

Dare.

My teeth bit into my bottom lip, tempted to ask if that was short for something else. *Darren? Darrel? Dar*—No. It wouldn't be that—it couldn't be. I refused to think that the man who'd saved my life had the same name as the one who'd first broken my heart. There were a lot of things I wished I could remember right now, but none of them had to do with Darius Keyes. There were enough hurts I had to revisit coming home, I refused to let him be one of them.

I released my lip and let the name be just that. *Dare.*

"It's nice to meet you, Dare," I murmured, my voice cracking again. "Thank you."

"Don't thank me," he insisted, his voice taking on a different quality, the rough notes stretched taut like my gratitude physically hurt him.

And then his position changed. He'd been kneeling or sitting beside the bed, but now he stood, and the movement forced all the atoms of oxygen in the room to rearrange. I felt the tension of them between us—like I could sense his distance from me rather than see it.

"But you saved my life." I wished I could see him—could see his face. I wished I could understand why he didn't want to be thanked.

Cavernous silence.

"You should rest," he replied. "I'll be back in a little with food and your medications." Something cold and hard pressed into my palm. "If you need anything just press this button, it will call right to my phone."

I let out a sad laugh. Thirty-six, broke, and almost blown to bits, and I was now the less-than-proud owner of a Life Alert.

"Okay." I nodded, listening for a moment to the indistinct shuffling amid footsteps as the two men went to leave the safe house.

Was it really a house? Or an apartment? *Did it matter?* I was stuck here until I was better—until I was safe. And it wasn't like I could complain about the view.

"Dare?" I called when I heard the door open. At first, I didn't even know if he had still heard me—if he was still here. I didn't think about how unnerving that was because if I did, I would need some of the medications that the doctor had offered.

"Yeah."

I shivered, his voice filling the space.

"Thank you." I held my breath and released it when I heard his grunt, which was quickly punctuated by the door closing and a chill consuming me now that I was alone with my thoughts.

I was blind.

And someone had tried to kill me.

I closed my eyes and tried to do what he asked—rest—but the scent of him still lingered. The woodsy pine and the coarse warmth of his fingers along mine. *Dare.* The man who'd saved my life. The man whose voice was as husky and warm as hot coals. *The man who promised to protect me.*

And then the dark canvas of my mind took liberties with my memories, blending present with past, reality with imagination. It took the face of the boy I'd once loved and attached it to the musky scent, strong feel, and rough promise of the man who'd saved my life.

It was more than a fantasy. It was evidence of my brain injury.

Chapter Four

Dare

Darius—I miss you. I miss Mom. I wish I could tell you I was settled, but I haven't even really unpacked. I'm sure my roommate thinks I'm either a vampire or just plain crazy since I spend every spare minute in the art lab and come back covered in paint. I wish I could tell you I was excited, but all I can think is that I shouldn't have left Mom. Not that she would've let me stay, but she's not doing well, and...I wish you were here. I wish we were eating grilled cheese and finger painting and I wish I could hear you tell me one more time that it's all going to be okay.—Always, Athena

The Villain

. . .

Nice to meet you.

Athena had no idea who I was. I almost couldn't wrap my head around it, but it had been almost two decades. A lifetime, really, considering everything I've been through since then.

Even if she could see me, I no longer looked like the eighteen-year-old boy who'd kissed her one last time on that very lawn. Injury and trauma made it so my voice no longer sounded like that boy either—the boy who'd promised we'd be together in the end. For all our sakes, it was better she didn't recognize me because anything she recognized would be nothing more than a fossil of someone I used to be. *Someone I no longer was.*

"She needs rest, Dare. I'm serious. Don't push her too hard," Rorik said as soon as the elevator doors shut.

The Sherwood Garage compound had two personas: what was seen and what was unseen.

What was seen—what was public—was the motorcycle garage where we took on all kinds of high-end projects. It was the massive garage bay, expensive and rare motorcycles stationed throughout the pristine floors in preparation for various work. It was the club room with its TV, bar, and pool table. Ty's office filled with computers and monitors, and last, the kitchen.

What was unseen was everything hidden beyond the garage space in the woods—the connected cabins tucked into the thick forest where we lived. There were six of them. One for each of us, plus an additional guest cabin for any friends in need of shelter.

That sixth one was where Athena should be right now. Instead, I'd set her up in mine. *Another indication I should let Rorik check out my head for injury or temporary insanity.*

"That was exactly what I told her." I huffed and punched the button for the main level.

This elevator was what connected the seen and unseen, descending from the back of the garage to an underground tunnel that branched out to the individual cabins.

"I know." His stare didn't flinch.

"Don't look at me like that."

"I'm not looking at you." But he saw me, and that was the fucking problem.

Rorik saw the way I looked at her. He saw the way I went to her, the way I held her hand, and the way I promised I would fix this. *I was only doing the right thing*, I wanted to argue, but he wouldn't be blinded by the symptoms of duty, not when he saw the disease underneath. The disease of guilt and the disease of desire.

The guilt I could take, but the desire...my jaw locked tighter. I'd get over it—I had to. My desire was what had cost Ryan his life—what had almost cost all of us our lives. There was a reason I'd sworn off women since his death; I wasn't going to let myself make that same mistake again.

"You didn't tell her who you were."

"No, I didn't." I held my breath, releasing it a second later when the elevator door opened. I managed a mumbled thanks and a promise to update him on Athena's condition tomorrow before stalking away from him and toward Ty's office.

I already had to answer to my brother, I didn't have the energy to answer to Rorik, too.

I opened the door to the smaller room, prepared to find Harm and Ty inside working. Instead, I came face to face with my adopted sister.

"What are you doing here?"

Robyn DuBois was the fifth and final member of our motorcycle club. She hadn't been Special Forces, and she wasn't exactly a big fan of motorcycles, but there were none of us who fought for justice—who fought for the weak and wounded and betrayed—like she did. The work we did was dangerous, but the way Rob hunted criminals bordered on reckless.

"Good to see you, too, Dare." Rob smiled and rose from her chair to greet me.

Clothed in all black, her swash of bright red hair cut through the darkness like fiery vengeance through the shadows. Sometimes, that rich red was the only thing that gave away the true depths of the fury at what had been done to her parents—to her.

"I heard you got a letter," she said as she hugged me.

So that was why—*Remington*.

Lately, the notorious traitor had involved himself in our club's business, targeting some of the criminals we were after. It was strange—like we were missing some bigger picture. But Rob seemed to be the most unsettled by it. Sure, he was a criminal—the kind we hunted who'd escaped justice for far too long—but for Rob, it felt like more than that. And there were times, like now, where it felt like the two of them were planets in the same orbit, rotating around the same sun, but in a path of collision.

"What else did you hear?"

"The letter brought you to a ghost."

I frowned. "Yeah. Something like that." I banded my arms over my chest and looked at Harm before settling my gaze on Ty. "Where's Rhys?"

"He left with Merritt for the day."

It was a small miracle that I wouldn't have to endure Rhys's probing stare, too, when he learned the truth.

"How's Athena?" Rob probed, hoisting herself back onto the table where she'd been sitting.

I glanced at my brother, his heavy look warning me that harder questions were coming.

"Blind. Confused. Afraid." *All the things she should be.* "She doesn't remember anything about the explosion—doesn't even remember being at her house."

"And she doesn't remember you?"

Here we go.

"No, but it's been a long time, and she can't see me."

"But when you talk to her..."

"If a voice was that identifiable, The Masked Singer wouldn't be a damn show," I ground out. "Can we move on—"

"Are you going to tell her?"

Dammit. Guess not. "No."

"Dare—"

"Is it relevant to her safety? To our duty? *To anything?*" I ground out, the frustration and anger of the last twenty-four hours draining into my voice. I hadn't done anything—ate, slept, *moved*—because I wanted to be there when she woke up. *As though it mattered.* For some reason, it mattered to me. "Unless you can prove that telling her who I am will make her *safer,* this discussion is over." My fist balled against my side, and I looked to Ty, hoping I could count on him for a rational discussion. "Did you get the security feeds? Any update on the bomb or who planted it?"

"I went back yesterday to return the truck you borrowed, and local PD was at the scene with Hadrian," Harm began and stepped forward, extending his hand with my motorcycle keys, which I quickly took.

"Good." The band around my chest loosened a little.

Hadrian Mills was an explosives expert and was currently employed by Armorous Tactical, a large, elite private security company just outside San Francisco.

"He said, based on his initial sweep of the scene, it looks

like it was an amateur bomb. Something about the pattern and radius of the blast," Harm continued. "He also said he's pretty confident the bomb was remote detonated, but he won't know for certain until he examines all of the debris and will call with an update when he does."

"Doesn't make sense," I said gruffly and dragged my hand along my jaw until I found the ridge of my scar. "Why not trigger the bomb when she was back in the car?"

"Maybe killing her wasn't the bomber's intent," Ty suggested.

"Or there was a timer," Rob said.

"Hadrian thinks it was a remote—"

"A remote that triggered a timer," she interrupted and shot me a glare that warned me to let her finish. "Think about it. Amateur bomb with a remote detonator?" She shook her head. "The transmission radius was probably small—forty? Fifty feet? —from the trigger to the bomb. If he couldn't trigger the bomb from farther away, the only other way to compensate and give himself time to get away before the blast would be to have it activate a timer."

"So, Athena exits her house and heads for the car. The bomber starts the timer, thinking she's getting right into her car and giving himself time to get away..."

"But then you stop her," Harm finished. "Even if the bomber could disarm it, he would be too far away at that point, possibly to even realize his plan was going awry."

I grunted. It was a solid theory, but I wouldn't be satisfied with anything less than certainty. "What about the footage?"

Ty answered this time. "Doorbell cam from across the street only saves the last forty-eight hours, and the footage is pretty limited. There's a good shot of Athena's car, so I can tell you no one planted the bomb while she was at home, so either it was planted before that window or—"

"It was planted somewhere else," I finished, tracing my scar again until I caught Rob staring, and I quickly lowered my hand.

"There are a few other cars in the footage I can track down, but the camera is still blind to a good portion of the street," he said and then winced at his word choice. "Sorry."

"Yeah," I said, staring at the video feed of the house on the screen. The wreckage of the car had been removed, but there was a giant stain of soot on the asphalt and a radiating spray of ash on the lawn. Except where Athena had been. There, the grass was still green and bright.

She'd always left everything around her brighter and for the better—except me.

"What are you thinking?" Rob asked, capturing my attention.

I tensed and told her what I *should've* been thinking about. "That this all has to do with Ivans."

"Interesting." Her face completely masked her thoughts, which only made my suspicions about them run rampant for a second.

"Not interesting. Logical." I met her stare. "What other reason would someone have to target her? For what gain? Ivans is the only thing that makes sense." *Though her relationship with him still didn't.*

"If someone wanted to blow Ivans up, then why not put the bomb on his car?"

"Maybe they couldn't find or get access to his car. Maybe whoever did this only wanted to send a warning—" I broke my stare from Rob's and swallowed down a curse. *Shit.* I shouldn't be arguing about this. *I should fucking know better.* I quickly pivoted to Ty. "Unless you found out something about her that I don't know? That would put her in danger?"

I'd been with Rorik, scrutinizing everything he did, every

breath Athena took, until she'd woken up. I was sure by now that Ty had done at least a cursory background check on my high school girlfriend, and sure he found years—a lifetime—of things I didn't know about her.

His eyes briefly flicked to Harm, and my fist tightened. *Jesus Christ,* I didn't need to be protected from Athena's past. Sensing my sentiment, Harm nodded, and Ty shaded in the last two decades of her life with bold strokes.

"She graduated with a fine arts degree. Got married to a Brandon Martins and moved to Sacramento."

Married. The air whooshed from my chest, and I swayed back. *She'd gotten married.* The idea was like a second detonation, but this one was contained inside me. *Of course, she had. What the hell else did I expect from her? From the world?* Athena Holman was a gold mine. Brains. Beauty. Beneficence. Any man who let her go would be the biggest fool.

"Not too much of note there until she filed for divorce a year ago. Took about six months and looks like it was pretty bitter. Brandon ended up with everything," he continued, and I fought to maintain my composure.

Bitter? And he'd taken everything? I didn't know who this guy was or what happened, but I already hated him. Nothing about Athena would ever be bitter, and knowing her, she wouldn't have fought for anything; she would've given it all up to make the other person happy because that's what she always did—*put everyone else's happiness before her own.*

"Utility bills started being paid at her current address six months ago."

"Her mom's house," I said low.

After a second and a few clicks of his mouse, he nodded. "Yeah. She inherited it...eighteen years ago."

"What is she doing here?"

"Part-time work at museums..." He trailed off, scrolling over the screen. "Looks like she's starting to show and sell her artwork. She has a local gallery show coming up in about a month."

"But nothing to indicate a connection to Ivans or Grow-Tech?" My pulse thudded heavily.

"Nothing except that photo, but I'll keep looking. Her artist gig is pretty freelance, so it's hard to track down where she's been and when. If we knew Ivans's new alias…"

"We have to ask her, it's the fastest way," Rob chimed in.

A surge of protectiveness whipped through me. "No." I glared at her. "She needs to rest. Doctor's orders."

"Enough." Harm broke in. "Until we have more information, all options are on the table. We'll see what Hadrian has to say about the bomb, check on video footage in the development and traffic cams *leaving* the development. In the meantime…" He trailed off and looked at me.

"Rorik said she needs to rest."

"I understand, but right now, she's our best shot—our only lead. All we need is his name," my brother countered firmly.

"I'll sit and talk with her," Rob offered, sliding off the table and looking between us. "Might be easier for her to open up to me anyway. Not being able to see…I'm sure she's feeling very vulnerable right now."

I swallowed my gut reaction to protest. I knew Rob would be gentle—careful—with Athena; one of my sister's many projects in San Francisco was sheltering women—victims of violent men in power—and then bringing their abusers to justice. I didn't doubt her compassion—it was as boundless as her vengeance. The problem was I wanted to know the answers, too.

"Fine, but I'm coming with you."

"Dare—"

"She just woke up to the news that she's blind because her

The Villain

car fucking exploded. I don't think random new people confronting her is fucking ideal," I ground out. I also wanted to know what Athena's relationship with Ivans was—how far her involvement with him went—and I wanted to know for all the wrong reasons.

Rob's brow lifted, and I should've felt good—relieved—when she then nodded; instead, I was afraid I was only proving the very thing I insisted wasn't true: *that Athena was here because I still cared for her the way I once did.*

"Okay."

A few minutes later, I'd grabbed the evening meds Rorik instructed me to give her and was whipping up a grilled cheese sandwich in the kitchen. It was quick and easy—and they'd been a favorite of hers back then.

"Smells good."

I didn't turn when Rob joined me.

"I'm almost done, and then we can go." I flipped the sandwich in the pan one more time, wanting the bread to be golden.

"You put her in your cabin, not the guest one," Rob said, not bothering to make her change of topic a smooth one.

"My cabin is more open—easier to get around." The excuse was lame; the layout of all the cabins wasn't much different between them, but compared to the guest cabin, my space was a little easier to navigate.

"Because you hardly have any furniture."

I gritted my teeth. Since all of us lived more or less at Sherwood, except Rob, though she still had her own cabin, we didn't really frequent each other's homes. There was no point. We had the rec room and communal kitchen in the clubhouse. I couldn't remember the last time anyone else had been inside my cabin until Rorik, Harm, and I had brought Athena there earlier.

I'd ignored my brother's hard look when he realized I only had a bed and a single chair to break up the modest space.

"Like I said, easier to get around." I slid the grilled cheese sandwich onto a plate and covered it with a piece of foil. "Let's go."

I moved around her and went to the elevator, jamming my finger onto the button.

"Dare..."

Dammit. Air hissed through my lips, and the door opened.

"You should tell her the truth."

"Why?" The word fired like a warning shot. "It doesn't matter who I am." *In fact, it would only make things harder— worse.* "It's bad enough asking her to trust strangers, let alone asking her to trust someone who hurt her; it'll be easier for her this way."

Rob lifted her chin, having no intention of leaving this conversation alone. "For her, or for you?"

My spine snapped straight, and I replied with a low, firm voice, "It doesn't change what I'm doing...or what I've done."

"You're afraid of her...of what she meant to you."

"It was a long time ago. We were practically children." *Not even close, but for the sake of this conversation, it had to be.*

"So, you feel nothing for her now? Nothing but duty?"

I turned and loomed over her five-foot, fire-haired frame. "I feel nothing. Period."

That made her eyes widen. A small crack in an otherwise impenetrable facade.

"If you felt nothing, you wouldn't have brought her here." Her accusation was hardly loud enough to top the elevator doors sliding open, yet even the smallest noise resounded in a hollow space, and so her words boomed in a loud echo around the empty cavern of my chest.

Sherwood was a secret—sacred for a reason. Not the garage itself, but the real work we did here, and anytime any of us brought an outsider in, it risked exposing the lawless way we exacted justice. I'd criticized the others for doing so in the past, and here I was, without a second thought, to bring Athena here for her safety.

"Dare—"

"Wonder again why I won't tell Athena the truth, and I'll start to wonder what it is about Remington that brings you running the second he's involved," I interrupted before she could ask anything else—saying the only thing I could think of to get out from underneath her microscope.

Remington.

Rob's steps faltered, and her nostrils flared. "I came because there was a lead on Ivans and a fucking car bomb. Not because of Remington."

I held her eyes for a long second. So stubborn and strong, but there was a kernel of hurt buried behind it all. A hurt that had nothing to do with what happened to her parents or how long Ivans and Wenner and Belmont had gone unpunished. A hurt I recognized: betrayal. I was the only one who understood it, which was why I couldn't bring myself to ask her to explain it.

We reached my door moments later, and I punched in my code, unlocking access to a lengthy hall shrouded in dim light. We walked in silence to the end, where a short staircase led to another door.

The pressure in my chest built as I gave a soft knock so we wouldn't scare her, and then I let us inside.

My breath released in a rush when I saw her lying there.

Wounded. Vulnerable. And even though she was safe, I felt no relief, only the hollow hunger of anger left in my gut and the self-loathing for thanking God she couldn't see me—couldn't see the way I'd burn down the world to punish whoever had done this.

"Hello?" She made a soft noise and then pushed herself up to sit. *In my bed.*

"Athena?" I rasped, my voice getting farther and farther from its normal tenor each time I saw her—each time the strain on my body got worse. "It's Dare."

After Rorik had sedated her back at Covington, he'd called in a favor from a local nurse and friend of the Covington team, Gwen McIntyre, to come in and help clean Athena up. Gwen had gently and diligently sponged away much of the dirt and ash, and then exchanged her equally dirty and torn clothes for a loaned pair of red scrubs.

The glorified pair of pajamas were the only burst of color in the space. Everything else in my cabin—which wasn't much—blended into varying shades of gray. Black bed frame. Gray sheets. White towels. A lone black chair in the corner that was dragged in from the kitchen.

"Hi." She reached for her face and then let her hand instantly fall—like she'd forgotten about the bandage for an instant.

Her head dipped, and I felt the whole weight of it on my shoulders. A lock of hair slid over her shoulder, and tension rippled through me. The ash in her hair was the last remaining remnant from the explosion. Soot streaked the waves of sunshine, and I wanted nothing more than to wipe it away.

"I brought you a sandwich if you're hungry," I offered, approaching the bed cautiously but with enough noise for her to follow me.

"Thank you." Her tongue swiped over her lips, and a bolt of heat went straight to my groin.

I reached her side and gently placed the paper plate on her lap. "Grilled cheese."

Her lips parted, and I caught the slight dust of pink on her cheeks underneath the bandage. "Thank you." If it was still a favorite of hers, she kept it to herself. *Of course, because I was a stranger.*

She slid her hands along the sheet, needing to feel her way to the sandwich, and a fresh dose of world-burning rage packed inside me.

"I also brought someone else with me—a friend," I murmured, feeling my sister move closer.

"Hi, Athena. I'm Rob. I'm a private...investigator from San Francisco. I specialize in working with women who are hurt or...in trouble."

Athena swallowed, her fingers retreating into a fist, before she nodded. "Hello."

"Dare has brought me up to speed on what happened. How are you feeling? Are you comfortable?"

"I'm...okay." A whisper of a small smile appeared. "I understand it could've been much worse, so I'm grateful."

I tensed. I didn't want her damn gratitude. Didn't deserve it. But to explain that to her was impossible.

"I know you've been through a lot, but I was wondering if I could just ask you a few questions, if you're feeling up to it," Rob said, her voice taking on an almost melodic tone. I rarely heard her talk except in that unyielding, matter-of-fact, and relentless way—but that was because when we talked, it was always about work. About club business. *About the men who'd killed her parents.*

But this was a different Rob. A persona that felt like warm velvet, soft and soothing in the way it encouraged trust.

"Of course." Athena's hand furled and unfurled like she was checking to make sure the rest of her still worked. "I'm a little groggy from the medication, and I don't...I'm sorry, I don't remember much about that morning."

"Don't apologize, and don't worry, I'm not going to ask about the explosion."

I took a long, deep breath, slowly letting myself come around to this...questioning.

"Could I...could you take off the bandage over my eyes?" Athena murmured and then let out a sad laugh. "I know it doesn't really make much of a difference, but I'd just—I'd like—"

No. It was my knee-jerk response, but Rob answered quicker. "Of course, we can."

My head whipped, and I glared at my sister as I explained, "Since your brain isn't reading the signals from your eyes, the bandage protects you from accidentally physically damaging your eyes. You could stare straight at the sun and not realize."

"But since the sun already started to set and we're inside," Rob began, approaching me and ignoring the daggers in my gaze. "I think we can remove it for a few minutes while you eat."

I didn't care how rational an argument my sister made, I wouldn't risk—

"Thank you."

Athena's soft gratitude broke me—the desperation consuming it. Like it was the first breath of air she'd taken since she'd woken up. And I wouldn't be the one to rip it away.

I stared Rob down for one long second and then muttered, "I'll remove it for you."

It was one of the more idiotic things I'd done, but when it came to taking care of Athena, I couldn't stop myself. It was guilt and duty, I told myself. That's all. Guilt for the way I'd treated her and the foolish belief that caring for and protecting her now made up for it.

I turned and placed my hand on her shoulder to let her know I was here. She didn't even flinch. *Because she trusts you.* The irony there tightened my jaw to the brink of snapping, and I quickly buried the anger—easy to do when the feel of her quickly consumed my thoughts.

Heat flooded underneath my fingertips in a familiar yet unmistakable warning: *don't touch.* But I had to. I shouldn't, but I had to because the thought of anyone else touching her—even Rob—created a much darker version of the same warning from somewhere deeper inside me. *Don't. Touch.*

"Athena, do you have any idea who would want to hurt you?" Rob asked gently as I undid the hook on the bandage.

"No, I don't." Athena shuddered slightly as I started to loosen the wrap. This close, I could see the flutter of her pulse against her neck. "I don't know many people here; I just moved back to the area. I'm an artist—a struggling artist. I don't have family or money..."

Fuck. It took everything I had—every bone, every muscle, every artery, every vein, every nerve, and every single breath—to not pull her into my arms. The weight of watching her bear something like this alone almost crushed me.

But to comfort her would be wrong, too.

The rules were simple around Athena. What was wrong was wrong, and what was right was also wrong. I shouldn't touch her, but I couldn't let anyone else touch her. I should stay away, but I needed to be close to protect her. I should tell her the truth, but she deserves better than an apology.

"What about your ex-husband?"

Athena sucked in a sharp breath and instantly choked on it.

A curse welled on the tip of my tongue, and my head

whipped to my sister, about to lash out, when Athena spoke and stopped me.

"Brandon? No. I mean—no. I can't imagine…"

I looked back at Athena, watching the crease in her brow appear as I reached the last layer of the bandage. I hesitated for a split second. There was a chance some of her sight had returned. *Slim—very slim.* And I would face the consequences if it did.

"He wouldn't do this. He's not…he wouldn't even know how to…"

I pulled the bandage off and rolled it in my hands. *Dammit.* I forgot Rorik had taped gauze over her eyes, too.

The bandage was one thing. I didn't have to touch more than her hair to unwind it. But this…I forced my exhale out and reached for the one end of the tape—right as Athena lifted her hand.

Our fingers collided. Like matches and gasoline, a riotous unwieldy flame burst through me. She pulled away, but the whole of my arm seemed to have already turned to ash.

"I'm sorry."

I grunted and focused on my task, acutely aware that Rob stood at the end of the bed, assessing every move and breath and sound of mine for evidence to support her claim.

"But you are getting a divorce, correct?"

My finger flinched as it pressed to her skin so it wouldn't hurt when I pulled the tape. *Married. She was married.* I still couldn't process it. As though, all these years, she'd only belonged to me—like a star in the sky only I could see.

"Yes," Athena said and nodded, making my fingers brush more of her skin than necessary. *Or recommended.*

"And was the divorce amicable?" Rob asked, even though she knew the opposite to be true. Even though the answer was written all over Athena's face.

"No." The word was a defeat. *A loss.*

"Turn toward me," I murmured, breathing deep as her head tipped in my direction so I could work the tape around her left eye free. This time, I moved faster.

With the second patch gone, I made the mistake of lingering for a split second to stare at her upturned face. Even with the cuts and scrapes and the scabbed gash on the edge of her chin, she was still the most beautiful woman I'd ever seen. Too beautiful. Unearthly beautiful.

And then her eyes opened.

Athena's bright blue stare collided with mine—*just like that morning.* My breath stilled in my lungs like I'd stepped on a land mine, unsure if moving was safe or would send me to pieces.

"Thank you." Her soft voice released the danger, and I felt myself breathe again; *she still couldn't see.*

It was the most unnerving thing I'd ever experienced—to have Athena look at me and know she wasn't seeing me. To know I could stare at her, drink my fill of her cloudless cerulean eyes, soft cheekbones, and the perfect bow of her pink lips, and she had no idea. I'd be disgusted with myself if how much I enjoyed it wasn't matched by the pain it caused me.

I never thought I'd see her again—I never planned on it. And here she was. In my life. In my home. *In my bed.* Hadn't fate had enough fun with my life?

"You should eat." I pulled away and moved the grilled cheese closer.

The band around my chest tightened again as her hands crawled toward the plate like twin spiders, needing to feel their way to her dinner.

I didn't realize I was holding my breath until she took the first bite, and the look on her face—the soft sound that barely escaped from her lips—was enough to make me feel like I couldn't survive on oxygen alone.

"This is delicious," she murmured after devouring half of it in just a few bites. "It's just like—" Her head dipped for a second. *Just like the ones I used to make us.* "I'm sorry. I haven't had grilled cheese in a long time. I think I forgot how good it is."

Right. Air hissed through my lips.

"So, your ex..." Rob trailed off, her stare vacant like she hadn't just layered in one more subtle reminder.

"Brandon?" Athena felt for the napkin and brought it up to wipe her mouth. "I don't think Brandon would hurt me. He took everything—will have everything once the divorce is finalized. He's...done enough."

Done enough. What the hell did that mean? What had he done? Why had she filed for divorce?

I jerked my head away, focusing on the nearby door to the bathroom because the rush of rage through my veins was so acute I couldn't see straight. I didn't want answers, I just wanted to murder the asshole who made her look and sound this way.

As if that wasn't the pot calling the kettle black...

"Sometimes even everything isn't enough for someone who wants to hurt you," Rob said, reaching for the necklace she always wore around her neck.

We all had things that helped us remember. Mementos that grounded us to the person or thing that drove our purpose. For the rest of us, it was tattoos of Ryan's dog tag number; his loss inked permanently to our flesh. For Rob, it was the thin gold band on the chain around her neck—her mother's wedding ring.

It wasn't odd that she wore it; it was odd that this conversation made her reach for it.

As soon as Rob realized I was watching her, she let the

chain go and continued. "Is there anything in your new life that Brandon wouldn't like? People supporting you? A new relationship, maybe? Since the divorce isn't finalized?"

My eyes widened for a split second. *Smart.* This was why Rob was so confident about talking to her; the way she was going to get answers about Ivans was so subtle. I was impressed. But only for an instant before I had to brace myself for the answer.

"Not really. Not seriously," she murmured, unable to see nor hide the color that deepened in her cheeks. "There was a man I met at a show I did a few weeks back. We've gone out a handful of times, but it's not...official."

"Would Brandon be angry if he knew you'd been on dates?"

"I...don't know. Maybe?"

She struggled to fathom the possibility. Then again, the ability for people to be cruel was something Athena always struggled to see, even back then. It was one of the things that drew me to her. She always looked for the good—for the positive. Maybe it was the artist in her, finding the beauty in everything, but I'd never met someone who had the capacity for compassion like her.

"What's his name?" Rob asked calmly, like this wasn't the piece of information we'd been looking for for months. "We want to make sure he's not in any danger."

He wasn't in danger, he was the danger.

Athena paused, and a veritable pin-drop silence descended. "Richard," she said. "Richard Iverson."

Rob and I turned to each other when Athena began to eat. *Ray Ivans. Richard Iverson.* We assumed he was using another alias with the same initials, and we were right. Blood pumped in my ears.

We were right. *And we had a name.*

"And what does he do?" Rob asked while I immediately fired off a silent message to Ty with the alias.

"He's an investor and an art collector."

And conscienceless doctor and jewel thief and murderer.

"Very nice. Charming," Athena continued with a small smile. I hated that his memory made her smile when mine would surely bring her to tears. *My own damn fault, I knew.* "Kind. Generous. He wanted to invest in my art—a gallery even."

Rob paused, giving Athena a break to take a few more bites of her sandwich.

"Were you going to let him?" I asked, earning a glare from Rob that practically shouted, *Not important.*

Except it was important to me.

"Yes—no." She stopped, her brow furrowing. "I mean, I'm not even close to opening my own space yet, but I was happy to have investors in my work. I'm just starting over—starting out, so any support was welcome."

"How did you meet him?"

"Actually"—Rob interrupted before Athena could answer and pointed a warning finger at me—"we just need to know if you have a contact number for him?"

"Yes—no." Athena's shoulders slumped. "I had his number in my phone."

Which was in the passenger seat of her car and completely eviscerated in the explosion.

"That's okay. Do you know where he lives?"

"No—ahh." She broke off with a small cry and reached for the side of her head.

I let out a low snarl in Rob's direction; *we'd asked too much too soon.*

"It's okay." Rob moved around me. "Here, let me take your plate." When she reached for the dish, she also placed a comforting hand on top of Athena's, and when she squeezed, the tension melted from Athena's face.

"I'm sorry."

"Please, don't apologize. You've been through so much and have been so helpful already. We're done with questions for the night." Rob shoved the plate at me like I was the problem. "We have your medications for you to take, okay? And then we'll have to put the bandage back over your eyes."

Now, it was my turn to shove something at Rob—the bandage. I'd touched...enough for one night—enough to fuel my fantasies for another couple of decades. *God, just the feel of her soft skin was enough to have me crawling out of mine with desire.* I thought years without had killed this hunger. I was so fucking wrong.

"Do you think...I'm sorry," Athena started and then broke off with a shake her head.

Goddamn, I wanted her to stop apologizing. And then I wanted to kill whoever it was that instilled in her this idea that she was always at fault—always the problem.

"No, please." Rob sat on the edge of the bed, still holding Athena's hand, and I realized this was right—having someone to comfort her, to be able to be there for her, to be close to her—that was the right thing to do. Not having a man protect her who was tortured by every moment in her presence. "What can I do?"

When Athena replied, her voice was softer, and I could tell by the way her head turned and tilted that she wasn't sure where I was standing and hoped it wasn't close enough to hear.

"Would it be possible for me to take a shower?"

A shower.

Her.

Naked.

In my shower.

Naked.

My processing capability devolved into that of a four-year-old. Short strings of stark reality hitting me like bullets from a gun. *Athena. Naked.*

Rob turned and looked at me, and I wished I could disappear. I wished I hadn't heard her—and more, I wished I wasn't the one who had to agree to it. But I'd made myself the gatekeeper to Athena's recovery, only deferring to Rorik when he was on the premises.

"Carefully," I croaked, feeling like the executioner sending the guillotine for my own neck, and then left before I heard any more.

I'd made my bed—*with the woman I'd once loved in it*—and now I had to figure out how the hell to never sleep again.

Chapter Five

Athena

Doorframe. One step into...the bedroom. Three steps until...the bed. Two steps around—"*Crap!*" I let out a hiss of pain and sank to the floor, clutching my calf, which I'd just caught against the corner of the bed.

"Crap," I repeated, defeatedly, and felt for the end of the bed. Carefully, I maneuvered so I could rest my back against it.

Steeling myself, I pressed my fingers to my ankle and slowly moved them higher until I reached the spot that triggered pain, and then I continued to probe and assess my newest injury. There was no wetness, so I hadn't broken the skin. Unlike my poor big toe that I'd caught on the lip of the shower yesterday.

Thankfully, Rob had been there. With the water from the shower, I wouldn't have even known I was bleeding everywhere if she hadn't told me before carefully bandaging it up.

It had been four days since that first shower. An entire week since the explosion. And I was convinced I'd acquired enough bruises to start a museum. A bang here. A tap there. The worst part was I didn't go far—*I didn't have far to go.*

In a matter of moments, my entire life had been whittled down to the space between a bed and a bathroom. In a safe house.

I thought back to nights when I was married to Brandon, when I would get up to use the bathroom and turn on the nightstand lamp. He hated that. My side of the bed was farthest from the bathroom with several obstacles in the way, but he didn't care. The light woke him, and that was unacceptable, so after many trials and injuries, I'd learned to maneuver the path in darkness.

Ironically, that was what this felt like except there were no lights to turn on, and I was in darkness all the time.

Every morning, I felt my way to the bathroom, flicked on the light switch, and pulled off my eye mask. Every morning, I hoped that the flip of a switch would turn my vision on again, and every morning, all I saw was the same stretch of black.

They all assured me it would come back—along with my memory—but every day I stared into the darkness and cracked off a chunk of that hope.

The worst part was that my head felt better. There were still holes in my memory. *And I still couldn't see.* But the pressure and headaches had decreased. The only time I took any of the pain medication from Dr. Nilsen was before bed to keep the throbbing pain away, and that was when Dare came and held my hand.

I didn't know if it was him—I couldn't be sure if it was anything more than a delusion from the meds or a consequence of the trauma to my brain. Or it could've simply been a fantasy I wanted to hold onto—the one good thing I looked forward to during the dark days.

Strong, warm fingers. A massive palm covering mine, firm and tender, assuring me he would protect me.

I would almost swear that hand had held mine every night since the explosion—even the ones I'd been unconscious or sedated for. But it all could've been the drugs.

And that was a small part of why I kept taking them—because I didn't want to lose that hand to hold onto. *My gorgeous guardian ghost.*

"Get back up, Athena," I murmured before I dwelled on the feel of his fingers all day.

I had big plans this afternoon. Big, walking-to-the-front-of-the-house plans.

I flattened my palms to the floor, my fingertips feeling the crease between the individual wood planks, and then pushed myself upright. This time, I reached one hand to the bed, exploring along the end and charting out the tip of the corner before navigating with cautious steps around it.

I'd only ventured to the front of the safe house when Rob was with me, but I couldn't just sit back in bed and listen to music or another audiobook. I needed to be...up. I needed to move.

I needed to feel sunlight.

So, I did, at the pace of a snail. Around the corner of the bed, and then out straight until I felt the wall. From there, my fingers crawled like a spider until I found where it turned into the short hallway, and then I followed that all the way to the front room.

In my case, this safe house was more than a safe house. It was the *safest* house because, aside from the bed and a chair I'd only heard move around, there wasn't any other furniture in it. Rob had apologized for it, but I couldn't understand why. No one lived here, why would the small house be filled with furniture?

I gripped the corner of the wall like I was about to step off into the deep end. I'd only been out here once yesterday because I'd asked Rob for a walk—something more than the safe several feet between the bathroom and bed. She'd agreed, tucking my hand into her elbow, and we'd joked about how we were "taking a turn" about the room, like we were characters in an Austen novel rather than...whatever this twilight zone was.

She'd verbally mapped out the space around me. The light gray walls. The windows along the front that faced a small clearing bordered by a dense forest. There was a kitchen with a small island. And then the door she always entered from that she said led to a kind of satellite workspace and garage for them so they didn't disturb me; her tone had barbs when she'd mentioned that—like it was a topic not to be trespassed on.

Another change I'd noticed. As the pain in my head dimmed, my other senses started to sharpen, especially my hearing. The rustle of the sheets. The breeze that hit the front of the house. The splatter of rain drops on the windows. Even the bottomless exhales from the man who sat beside my bed each night and held my hand.

My hearing was so good now, I'd started hearing dreams.

I'd never questioned the idea that someone with a deficit of one sense had heightened responses to the others. But to know that fact was entirely different from experiencing it. It was like understanding the principle of gravity...and then being tossed out of an airplane without a parachute.

I was in free fall and trying to hold myself together.

My head spun at the first sound of the doorknob.

"Rob?" I faced the direction of the sound—of the door.

She usually came by around this time. We'd sit and talk. Eat dinner. She'd tell me about her work in the city, helping abused women find shelter and justice, while I showered. And then...back to darkness.

The Villain

My inhale coincided with the soft opening of the door and the rush of sandalwood into my nostrils; it wasn't Rob.

"Athena."

Dare.

The man who'd saved my life had disappeared with the same harsh abruptness as my sight. *Except for in my dreams.*

"Hi." I pressed my hand to my chest, feeling warmth creep into my cheeks as I kept my head turned toward his voice.

I willed my eyes to work. Willed the darkness to turn to shadows and the shadows to morph into a man. I wanted to see the man who'd saved my life and who made me warm just by being near me. The one who'd taken care of me...made me comfortable...promised to keep me safe.

But all my willing didn't work; no matter how hard I stared, there was only darkness instead of Dare.

"What are you doing?" His voice rumbled over me, warming me like the heat of a fire rasping in the hearth. Each word got slightly louder as he came closer, and his footsteps got heavier where they landed on the floor.

Rob was about my size, but this man...was bigger. I heard the weight of him, and I could almost feel the change in pressure against my skin. Like there wasn't enough space in the room for both all the oxygen and all of him.

"I wanted...I needed to get out of the bedroom," I said, trying not to let my voice waver.

Six years was a long time of being trained not to stand up for myself—of constantly breaking down my own needs in order to satisfy Brandon's. *But Dare wasn't Brandon.*

"I'm sorry. Just with everything"—my fingers subconsciously lifted to my face—"it sometimes feels a little like a cage."

I hated how ungrateful it sounded. I was safe. Protected.

Guarded, here. But I was also trapped in my own mind. Alone in a dark, windowless, wallless cage.

"What can I do?"

My lips parted, a wash of tingles racing over my skin. His nearness was almost as breathtaking as the dedication in his voice. It was as though I could ask anything of him, and he'd do it.

"Take me outside."

I felt his hesitation. The ripple in the air from his harsh intake of his breath. This wasn't what he'd come here to do, but it was what I needed.

"Please."

A bottomless exhale. "Okay," he husked. "But you have to cover your eyes."

My shoulders sagged with relief. "Of course," I agreed eagerly. "My eye mask is in the bedroom." It went unsaid that he'd be able to grab it faster than I would.

A coldness accompanied his retreating steps, and then the heat returned along with his presence.

"Here."

My heart stumbled when he returned, as though his body carried its own charge—a kind of magnetic field that pulsed and drew me toward it—toward him—whenever he got close.

Because I couldn't see him, the rest of my senses went into overdrive. My skin blanketed with goose bumps. My ears fixed on the heavy tumble of his breaths. The soft flutter of silk in his hands. And the scent of him…my nostrils greedily breathed it in. Drowned in it. All potent and rich. Even my tongue, through my parted lips, could taste its raw masculinity.

And then the cool silk of the mask draped over my eyes. Instinctively, I reached up to adjust it and bumped his hands in the process.

"Sorry," I murmured, feeling him pull away instantly.

"Don't apologize." His order made me shiver.

All Brandon ever wanted from me was apologies. Each of them reminded me what a failure I was to him and how generous it was for him to still love me.

But not Dare. He wanted no apologies. He seemed to want nothing but to take care of me—even if it was at a restrained distance.

"I'm ready." I pressed the mask gently to my cheeks, making sure it was secure.

"I have your shoes."

"Oh, right." I nodded. *How could I forget those?*

The air moved as he lowered in front of me, and since my hand braced on the wall, it must've been the entire world that tipped when his strong hand wrapped around my ankle. *God, his skin was so hot.* Each of his fingertips was like a small flame where they touched, burning an unspoken ache onto me.

"What happened here?" His deep voice was rough, distracting me until a burst of pain announced the touch of his fingers on my injured calf.

"Is it cut? I didn't feel blood—"

"Bruised."

Breathe, Athena. Just breathe. I coached myself silently, grateful that my eye mask also covered most of my heated cheeks.

I forced myself to swallow. "I ran into the corner of the bed."

"And here?" He rubbed over the bandage around my big toe.

"Caught my toe on the edge of the shower," I answered, his sharp inhale piercing the silence a second later.

At that, the questions stopped as he put my sneakers on, my brain foggy and drunk by the time he was finished.

"Ready," he grunted low and straightened, bringing a wave of electrified air up my body with him.

I managed one solid breath before large palms cupped my shoulders to guide me forward. And instantly, I was adrift in the darkness.

His nearness disorients me. Even without my sight, my brain tried to map my surroundings as I felt my way through them. The bedroom. The bathroom. The front of the house. It took a lot of focus, and the bruise on my calf evidenced how hard it was, but when something interrupted that focus, it was like the part of hitting a piñata where they spin you around after blindfolding you.

Any direction could be right. Any direction could be wrong. *But as long as it was those strong hands that held me, I'd let them lead me anywhere.*

One of his hands disappeared, replaced by the sound of a handle turning, the soft glide of a hinge, and then...I inhaled, and his unmistakable sandalwood was replaced with cool, crisp air—the kind that was scrubbed clean by trees and then steeped in salt.

My chest tightened. *Freedom*. Or as much of it as I could have right now.

"Careful, there's a lip," he warned low, guiding me slowly over the doorframe and out onto the distinct softness of earth.

"Are we close to the ocean?" I said between massive breaths; I really underestimated how much I needed some fresh air.

"Yeah." He led us a few paces forward, and I soaked in every sense of my new surroundings. The earth under my feet. The cool air in my lungs. The slight prickle of sunlight on my skin. The faint taste of salt on my tongue.

We stopped, and the second his hands let go of me, a whip

The Villain

of cold raced along my spine, and I couldn't stop my body from jolting slightly.

"I'm okay," I said quickly, somehow sensing he'd seen me shiver and afraid he'd insist we go back inside.

"Here." His gruff word was followed by a weight on my shoulders. A jacket. A *heavy* jacket that was warm and soaked in his scent. I felt for the edge, smooth leather greeting my fingertips.

A leather jacket.

"Thank you." I curled deeper into the masculine cocoon, and when he stepped back, the vacuum of darkness swallowed me again. Biting my lip, I tried to imagine our surroundings. The shape of the leaves catching on the wind. Their color brimming with the sun-saturated summer green. And the ocean—would it be visible on the horizon? Blue and glittering against the sky?

There, I lost the image. All the threads I'd woven together tangled back into a knot of darkness.

"Do you think my sight will come back?"

I tried not to dwell on the alternative because it wouldn't make anything better, but sometimes I couldn't stop myself. I couldn't help but worry if this was it—the end of the career I'd envisioned before it had hardly started.

I'd survived so much to be back here—to be painting and drawing again. And to think that could be irrevocably altered...

"Dr. Nilsen believes so." His low voice chased away my thoughts.

"Do you?"

"I'm not a doctor."

I shivered. "You're very black and white, aren't you?"

"Makes things simple," he grunted.

A small smile curled up my cheeks. "I knew someone like that once," I said, and just as quickly, I shoved the memory away. "I thought I'd notice some change by now—some improvement. But every day is the same. I know I should probably be worried about other things, but I'm an artist. My whole life...is what I see."

My throat felt thick. To say it out loud, to hear what could be gone forever, it felt like the air had been taken right from my lungs.

"I understand." His deep voice grounded me.

"I feel like I can't trust anything." *Oh no.* Heat lifted to my cheeks, realizing how that sounded. I clamored to correct myself. "I didn't mean you. I know I can trust you," I said quickly, feeling like the biggest, ungrateful jerk. "I feel like I can't trust myself, if that makes any sense. It probably doesn't—"

"No," he interrupted. "It makes perfect sense. Losing trust in your own instincts...is one of the hardest battles to fight."

He spoke like he knew firsthand, the tenor of his voice cutting a measure lower, the inflection of his tone hanging at the end of certain words like he had gathered strength to speak the rest.

I wondered if I were able to see him, if I would've noticed those small changes, or if this was some superpower silver lining to having been robbed of sight.

"It feels like I'm losing myself," I admitted softly, my voice cracking.

There was no reason to hide my vulnerability. How could I when I relied on them for everything? Food. A place to stay. A babysitter while I showered. How could I when it literally covered my body in bumps and bruises and was written across my face in the form of an eye mask?

I felt the solemn assessment of his gaze penetrate through me, but I fought the urge to fidget, instead tightening my hold on his jacket like it was a life vest. "Even now, how do I know what time it is? Is it even daylight? Are the stars out? To think it could be anytime, and I could be anywhere—at the edge of the ocean or on the edge of a cliff—is mind-boggling."

He didn't reply, but I knew he was looking at me. At least the eye mask hid from him the well of tears that burned in my eyes.

"I have no picture. All my life, I've had a picture..." I trailed off, and the silence that lingered was just as heavy as the darkness encasing my world.

What if this was my future?

It would be okay. *I would make it okay.*

"To your left is the safe house. A small, dark wood cabin with big windows framing the gray front door. It's built up against a grass-covered hill, which camouflages it from the back."

His rasped words brushed bold strokes through my mind, painting right over the darkness. I sucked in a warm breath, feeling the safe house come to life before me. A modern hobbit's house framed into a grassy knoll.

"In front of the house is a small clearing in the forest where we're standing now. Grass and daffodils all the way to the trees." Sentence by sentence, the darkness cowered and retreated in the face of his firm tone. "The evergreen trees are thick, so you can't see too far even in winter, but now, with the rest of the trees in bloom...it's impossible."

"I can smell them. Pine and ocean," I murmured. "And I can hear the way the wind rustles every needle and leaf." My head tipped back, feeling that same breeze on my face.

"The sun is playing hide-and-seek above the clouds," he went on, shading in more of the picture. "But it's mostly a tired and gray sky."

"From all the rain." I'd heard the patter on the windows for two days straight.

"They're calling for sun by the weekend."

I wondered if I'd be able to see it by then. I swallowed, feeling a knot form in my chest. A reminder. "Thank you for bringing me out here. I'm sure this wasn't what you'd planned on when you came to see me."

He paused. "No, it wasn't."

I felt the edge in his tone, and guilt washed over me. They were already doing so much to help me—protect me—and here I was, begging him to describe the sky.

"Do you know what happened? Do you know who..." *Tried to kill me.*

"The explosives expert finished his investigation and confirmed what we believed—that the bomb was on a timer activated by a remote." His weight shifted, the subtle crush of foliage underneath his feet. "It means the bomber had to be close. First to plant the bomb, and then to set it off. Do you remember anything about that morning? Did you have a regular routine you were following?"

My shoulders slumped, and I gripped his jacket tighter.

Routine?

It was hard to find a routine when it was more than boxes to unpack being back here.

"I remember...leaving my house that morning. I was in a rush. I even forgot a jacket, but I was carrying some of my paintings—" I broke off with a small cry.

"What? What is it?"

My paintings.

"I'm sorry." I wished I could turn away from him, but there was no turning away from someone you couldn't see. "I just...do you know if they found any artwork in my car?" I'd worked on those landscapes for months. To think they were gone...

"I don't," he answered after a beat.

I lowered my head in a nod, wishing the whole of me could disappear inside the shell of his jacket.

"Where were you taking them?" he asked next, giving me something to focus on rather than the tightness in my throat.

My brow scrunched, my mind suddenly treading in the deep end. "The gallery..." I bit my lip. "I think that's where I was going—I don't know where else I would be taking them, but..."

"But what?"

I tried to remember. I dug for what happened next, but it was like trying to dig myself out of quicksand. "I don't know," I admitted defeatedly. "I have a gallery show in four weeks—three weeks. That has to be where I was going."

"What gallery? And can you describe the paintings?"

"The Tableau. It's on First Street in Monterey." I breathed out slowly. "They were two cityscapes of Downtown Carmel Cove."

"I can have someone check and see if they're there."

"Thank you." My shoulders slumped. "Someone should let Glenn—the gallery owner—know. She gets back from vacation tomorrow." And considering I stopped there almost every day, it wouldn't take much before she started asking questions.

"We'll speak to her."

"I wish I could remember. I hate that I can't." I lifted my hand to my temple, only to be met with the silk of the mask, which frustrated me even more.

"One day at a time."

Even as he spoke, my brain hooked on a thought that seemed out of place yet hadn't come from nowhere. "Did you speak to Rich? Is he okay?"

There was a shift in the air, but I couldn't tell if it was a breeze or if Dare had suddenly stilled.

"We haven't talked to your...Rich yet. We've been...ahh... more focused on your ex."

Brandon?

"I can't imagine Brandon would be angry about Rich—or how he would know. It's only been a few dinners," I insisted, giving my head a small shake.

Even with everything he'd put me through for the divorce, deep down, I knew it wasn't because my ex still wanted me—wanted to be with me. He just didn't want to feel like he'd lost. Brandon always had an incessant, obsessive need to win.

"Athena..." The low gravel of Dare's voice made me shiver, like a rumble strip that brought the conversation to a heavy pause. "Were you aware your ex-husband took out a two-million-dollar life insurance policy on you last year?"

Two million...

The world didn't tilt this time, it washed out from underneath me.

I stepped back in shock—and right onto something that was uneven. A rock—a branch—whatever it was rolled my ankle. I let out a cry and started to topple backward. But gravity didn't have a chance. Not against this man.

"Shit." His low curse dissolved as he grasped my arms and steadied me against him, an anchor in the storm. "You okay?"

"Yeah." Physically, at least, but even my voice didn't sound like my own. "Are you...sure?" I gave my head a shake. *What an idiotic question.* "Of course, you're sure. This is your job." I let out a quick breath. "No...I had no idea he had a life insurance policy on me."

Two million dollars.

It was insane. So insane, I still didn't want to believe it—couldn't believe it. Why so much? Why right when I told him I wanted the divorce? It wasn't like he was going to leave me with anything anyway.

"I'm sorry, I just can't believe Brandon...I can't imagine why..."

I couldn't finish the thought—I couldn't get farther than the audible breath Dare took. It wasn't from the exertion of catching me...it was a *bracing* breath. And I felt that familiar black hole in my chest—like some part of me knew there was more to this.

"What is it?" My heart stumbled and slowed, preparing for whatever the other shoe was that was about to drop.

"Were you aware that he liked to gamble?"

At least Dare was already holding me this time when my knees gave way.

"I...yes, Brandon liked to gamble, but he wasn't...he hadn't..." I trailed off, taking a second to pull apart the stitches of my past in order to tell him the whole truth. "It started when we were in college. Frat party games. Sometimes the stakes were decent, but nothing too crazy."

It was college. There were people doing crazier things on campus than a backroom game of poker once a week. It was how Brandon relaxed, and sure, sometimes he lost more than he was expecting and asked to borrow money from me, but I didn't think twice about it. By that point, the number of times I'd leaned on him for support after my mom...they were countless. Priceless.

"I didn't realize it was a problem—or, I guess, how big of a problem it was for him—until we went to Vegas for our honeymoon. He couldn't...I couldn't pull him away." My cheeks felt on fire. I shouldn't be embarrassed—I wasn't the one with the addiction—but I guess I still had a ways to go in breaking the habit of blaming myself for all my ex-husband's faults. "We had to come home halfway through our trip because we couldn't afford to stay. He'd lost all the money we'd brought with us and maxed out his credit cards."

Dare released my shoulders, but not before I felt the jolt of anger that went through him. But after anger would come pity, and I didn't want pity. I'd gotten out. I'd lost almost everything in the process, but I'd gotten out, and that was something to be proud of.

"It stopped after that," I continued. "I was so hurt and he felt so guilty that we agreed to no more casinos." *That was back when Brandon was agreeable.* Time had changed him slowly, the way a weed creeps up around the trunk of a tree in slow suffocation.

And then the pressure in my chest started again.

"I'm guessing by your line of questioning that that was a lie, too."

I'd never not notice the way Dare hesitated before telling me something he knew was going to hurt me. The kind of care this stranger took with me was something that could easily overwhelm me to the sweetest of tears if I dared to let it.

"From what we've uncovered, your ex-husband is significantly in debt. Some on online gambling sites, but we're pretty confident he owes a significant sum to a loan shark in Sacramento."

A year ago, the news would've brought me to my hands and knees. To know the man I thought I was going to spend my life with—the man who promised he'd forever pick me over the thrill of a card game—betrayed me would've broken my already breaking heart. But now...I wished I was surprised.

I wished...but I wasn't.

"What is significant?"

"Well, the biggest online site blocked his account fifteen months ago and started pursuing legal action for debts owed."

A year ago... "The house..."

The Villain

"He refinanced your home twice to fund his habits—"

"No." I stopped him. "I mean where I live now—my mom's house. A year ago, he wanted me to sell it. Demanded, really. He said we were never going to live there, so it wasn't doing anything for us." I swallowed through the tightness in my throat. "That was the final straw. That argument. He was so cruel, but now I see..." It wasn't cruelty, it was desperation. "He needed the money."

"We're still trying to get a final figure that he owes the loan shark, but it's at least seven hundred thousand."

"Seven...hundred..." It was the extent of his addiction—his betrayal—that shocked me. The sheer sums of money he tried to win...and couldn't fathom he'd lose.

"Athena." His husky voice corralled my thoughts. "Did you tell him you wanted a divorce before you filed?"

"Yes, that day. I told him I didn't recognize him anymore, and I wanted a divorce."

"When was that?"

I thought for a moment. "The end of August?"

Another pause. "Brandon took out the life insurance policy on September first."

Air whooshed from my chest. "And I filed on the fourth."

The implications of the timeline hit me like a hurricane; *he'd taken out the policy in the gap between when I told him and when I'd filed.* My heart hammered in my chest. I was literally blind, but I could see the truth so clearly: he knew what I was going to do, and he'd been desperate.

"The policy only pays while you're still married."

"Which is until this coming Friday." I sounded hollow. *I felt hollow.*

Two days.

"Athena..."

"How long—" My voice cracked, so I started over. "How long was he gambling online?"

There it was again—the rough rumble as Dare cleared his throat. *His tell.* I'd first noticed the sound right before he'd told me there was a bomb planted in my car, intending to kill me. It happened again right before he'd shared that Brandon was a degenerate gambler who placed a wager on my life. And now...

"Two months after your wedding."

Years. My husband—ex-husband—had been gambling for years and had started only weeks after promising me he'd never do it again.

Asshole. My eyes welled with tears. Not for Brandon. Screw Brandon. Tears because I'd been so blind—a painful irony given my current circumstances.

"I'm sorry." I reached for my cheek, feeling one tear that escaped underneath my mask. "I'm just..." *Shocked. Hurt.* "A fool."

His hands on my shoulders slid to my face, holding my chin up as though I were looking straight at him. One after another, his thumbs swiped away my tears. His tenderness was overkill for my pain—like knocking down a sand castle with a wrecking ball.

"You're not a fool."

"No?" I choked on the question. "I married a man—trusted a man who just tried to kill me to save his own skin."

At this point, I'd have to be more than a fool—I'd have to be brain-dead to not make the connection between his gambling debts, the insurance policy, and the car bomb.

"This isn't your fault," Dare growled, his deep insistence painting something else in my mind—a different story than the one I was trying to tell myself.

"Have you found him?"

"Sacramento PD has been looking for him for the last day and a half, but nothing yet."

"When they do, I want to see him." I winced. "Talk to him."

"We're going to get to the truth, I promise." He paused and then added in a rough whisper, "Trust me."

Trust him. It should be easy, right? He might be a stranger, but he'd saved my life. Except knowing now that the man I'd loved and devoted my life to had betrayed the years of trust I'd built in him...

"How can I trust anyone anymore?" I asked brokenly, my mind as tangled as my strained voice. "I'm sorry. I just wish..."

My throat wouldn't work to swallow. *What did I wish? What did I need?* It was all locked in darkness until he spoke.

"Tell me."

My lips peeled apart, and somehow my tongue found its way over my words. "I wish I could see you." *An impossible wish.*

The heat of his exhale reached my cheeks, quick and coarse. And then his big hands found mine, capturing them and lifting them higher and higher until he pressed my fingertips to his face.

Dare.

The ground solidified. The air stilled. The sounds—all of them—silenced. Nothing was left for me to focus on except him.

Stubble and warm skin pressed to my fingers. I splayed my hands, feeling the muscles of his jaw fire instantly under my touch, but he didn't pull away—and neither did I. Slowly, with the precision of a surgeon, he drew my fingertips over his face, letting me chart his harsh cheeks and square jawline.

I managed to hold back a sound of surprise when I felt the puckered ridge of a scar running down his left cheek.

What happened? When? Who did this to you? Questions filled my mind. *How many times have you been hurt? What other scars do you have?*

I searched out the spot where the scar originated, right underneath his left eye, and followed it all the way along his cheek, and then it cut sharply toward his mouth. My pulse picked up, and suddenly the weight of the jacket on my shoulders felt too much. Too warm.

But that was as far as Dare's guiding hands let me go. I didn't realize how much I wanted to feel his mouth until he wouldn't let me.

Instead, he repositioned my hands at the edge of his nose and then lowered his away, allowing me to explore as long as I obeyed his boundary. *And I would, because I didn't want to lose this.*

I mapped the slope of his nose up to the ridge of his brows, higher over his forehead. *Was he bald? Buzz cut? Did he have long hair? Was it curly? Short?* Thick, I realized when my fingertips breached his scalp. His hair was thick and soft, collected in unruly waves on his head.

Scarred and unruly. That was who this man was. And it was something that was as equally safe as it was dangerous to me.

I threaded my fingers into his hair as though I were going to pull his head to me—his mouth to mine. His kiss wouldn't fix this, but somehow I knew it would at least let me forget.

Dare made a low noise—something between a plea and a warning—and I realized just how close our faces were.

My heart thudded wildly, and I quickly returned my hands down to the slash of hair marking his eyebrows and then lower to his eyes. The soft brush of his eyelids as they closed teased my fingertips. Men always had the nicest lashes, and Dare was no exception.

I wondered what color they were but didn't ask. It was too much. Too...intimate.

With every touch, I created a portrait of him, one I painted with my fingertips on the blank canvas of my mind. Shading in the handsome, rugged contours of his face until I reached the perimeter of his lips—lips that let out the low voice that haunted my dreams.

"Athena," he rumbled in a warning I thought I could obey, but I couldn't.

So, I first traced the valley that bracketed his mouth, giving him plenty of time to pull away and stop me himself. But he didn't. My heart did laps inside my chest, circling this moment again and again and again until I had myself in knots. Air vaulted into my lungs as I slid my hands toward each other, feeling the corners of his mouth and then the fullness of his lips.

My jaw went slack, and brushing over the soft swells made my body feel all the things it shouldn't.

Dare had lips made to do damage. Full and firm, I imagined their press on my fingers was on my palm. And then my neck. And then my mouth. I shivered, wanting more than to know their shape; I wanted it memorized. I wanted him to be more than a voice inside my head when I slept at night—I wanted to imagine those lips rumbling my name even if I'd never see it.

The shallow rush of his breaths greeted my fingertips when they landed on the seam where his scar met the border of his lip.

Who hurt you? The question was right there on the tip of my tongue—but so was the urge to kiss it. To kiss him. To trace my tongue along the tiny ridge and make it better.

Oh god. What was wrong with me? Was this a new symptom of the blast? A fresh indication of my broken brain—lusting over the man who'd saved my life?

Dare groaned low, the sound pure pain.

I stilled. "Are you okay?"

"Stop licking your lip." The order was gruff and filled with hunger.

I bit down on the side of my tongue, not even realizing I'd been doing that while I'd imagined licking him. "I'm sorry."

He shackled my wrists in his grip and carefully peeled my hand from his face as though he were pulling a knife from his body. *Necessary but painful.*

"I...thank you." Maybe if touching his face had been as simple as creating a blueprint, that would've been the right thing to say, but it wasn't. I knew it wouldn't be. One touch and I knew I'd been crafting a fantasy.

And he knew it, too.

Embarrassment seeped into my cheeks. His face—his expressions might be hidden from me, but mine were an open book to him. He'd watched the blush form in my cheeks. He'd watched the swipe of my tongue over my lips. He knew he saw the moment the veneer of exploration—the need for information—dissolved into something far less appropriate.

"It's going to rain. We should go back inside." His gruff command seemed to have power over nature because, an instant later, the cold splat of a raindrop landed on my nose.

He released my arms and brushed my side as he stepped behind me. Like a puppeteer with his marionette, he held my shoulders and guided me to the only place left to go—back inside the safe house.

At least now, the darkness there was a little less dark—Dare's handsome, scarred face burned into my mind so bright it was impossible to ignore.

Chapter Six

Dare

> *I'm worried about you—about why you haven't written. I'm sure you're going through a lot, so I'm trying to ignore the worry and be patient. But I miss you.*
>
> *I'm looking at the stars again, and is it just me or do they not shine like they do when we're together? —Always, Athena*

Fuck. I pressed the door shut to my cabin, leaving my palm flat on the surface as I hung my head.

What the fuck was I thinking? Letting her touch my face like that? Forget the risk I took that she'd recognize me—however small it might be—the greater risk was that touch—*her touch.*

The last time I'd been touched by a woman...I shuddered,

feeling as though an earthquake had let loose from deep inside me. The last woman to touch me aside from my sisters was the woman who'd betrayed me—broke me. *Amira.* What the hell kind of twist of fate was it that the next woman to touch me after that was the woman whose heart I broke?

It wasn't a twist. It was a goddamn torpedo.

Fate didn't deal with my life in games, only weapons and destruction. And I didn't know what was more destructive—the pain in Athena's voice or the desire flushed to her cheeks.

Either one should've been reason enough for me to stay away, but when we'd learned about her ex and gambling and the policy he'd taken out on her life, I couldn't let anyone else break that news; it had to be me.

Maybe I wanted to protect her from the pain as much as possible, but more likely, I sadistically hoped she'd shoot the messenger. *I deserved it.*

I'd been the first to betray her, and now, her almost ex-husband...

"Fuck," I muttered and scrubbed my hands over my face like I could remove every trace of her soft fingertips, every last trace of heat, every remaining tingle of electricity.

She wasn't a fool—*I was.*

"Dare?"

I dropped my arms and looked at Ty. I hadn't heard him approach, but it was obvious by the look on his face that he'd been watching me for some minutes.

"What's up?" There was no hiding the bite of frustration in my voice.

"You good?" The very fact he was asking the question implied that he knew I wasn't.

Shit.

"Yeah. Fine," I clipped. "What is it?"

"Sacramento PD just called. They have Brandon Martins in custody—"

"I'll go—" His arm barred me from walking by him.

"Wait," he said steadily. "They're bringing him to Armorous for questioning. Harm's going to go with you."

Armorous was better than a precinct; there were more rules I could…bend. But to have my brother there…

"Fine." We walked to the elevator together. "We'll go up and interrogate him. In the meantime, Athena said she had paintings in her car the morning of the explosion. I don't know if Hadrian found evidence of them, but I told her I'd check the gallery she was bringing them to; it's the Tableau in Monterey."

"I'll look into it."

I grunted my thanks. "What about Ivans? Still nothing?"

Ty shook his head.

The way Ivans managed to hide himself under layer after layer of deceit was nothing short of surgical. I'd hunted through every database and resource at our disposal to find anything linked to one *Richard Iverson*—property, business, hell, I would've taken a fucking parking ticket—but there was nothing. And by the time I came to that conclusion, Ty had uncovered Brandon's gambling debts and the life insurance policy he'd taken out on Athena.

No matter how unlikely it seemed that Athena could be involved with Ivans and it not be the reason for her attempted murder, the facts pointed in a different direction. So, I held off telling her the truth about Ivans—*Iverson;* maybe if this truly had to do only with her ex-husband, I could spare her any additional pain.

"We're missing something," I said under my breath.

"I feel the same way, but talk to the ex-husband. Maybe that will shed some light."

"Yeah."

"Harm. Darius. Good to see you." Hazard Foster, the owner of Armorous Tactical, greeted us at the door that seemed extra wide just to be able to fit him. He stood a good couple of inches above my six-foot-one and at least an inch above my brother's six-foot-three.

"How long ago did he arrive?" I asked once we'd made it through pleasantries.

Harm's pointed stare snapped to me.

"Twenty minutes," Hazard said, leading us down the hallway.

The building was like a military barracks. Halls of rooms equally spaced. Everything was either metal or painted various shades of gray. Even the massive team—*there had to be fourteen or fifteen of them now?*—all wore a kind of standard uniform: black pants and black and gray camo tees, the Armorous logo just barely visible in shiny black.

Armorous was like Covington Security, but on steroids. It made sense; Hazard tended to recruit only military elites, most of his team were retired Army Rangers, and their focus was split between tactical training as well as high-value target protection and asset retrieval.

"I held off interrogating him. Figured you'd want to handle that." Hazard stopped in front of a metal door, the plaque on the front said *Interrogation One*.

"Yes." *Questioning Brandon Martins was only the beginning of what I wanted to do to him.*

"Sacramento PD said we could have an hour to get the information we need before they'll have to release him."

"Got it." I wouldn't need an hour.

Harm grabbed my arm. "Dare—"

"Give me ten minutes, then come in," I ordered, belatedly wondering when the last time I'd given orders to my older brother and former commanding officer was. *My first guess was never.*

His nostrils flared. Harm didn't like the idea of me going in alone.

"Five minutes," I growled and shrugged my arm free, shooting him one last look before I walked in the room and closed the door behind me.

"What the hell am I doing here? You can't just fucking hold me like this. I have rights," the man whined—*actually fucking whined*—from the chair he was cuffed to.

Short, dark hair. Dull brown eyes. Quivering jawline. Brandon Martins. Athena's husband. *Piece of shit.* His clothes were a mess, and he looked like he hadn't slept in days. *Yeah, this guy was guilty.*

I hated him instantly. Not because he was guilty. Not because he was a degenerate gambler. Not because he whined like a fucking coward. No, I hated him instantly because he'd had her. He'd had her smiles. Her laugh. Her talent and compassion. He'd had her love, *and this was what he'd done with it.*

I walked up to the table, my palms landing on the top like a goddamn crack of thunder, and he jolted.

"What the hell, man? Where am I?" he snapped petulantly.

"Did you try to kill your ex-wife?" The words bubbled like acid between my lips.

He shook his head and fidgeted in the chair. "She's not my ex yet."

My hand launched forward and clamped around the front of his throat. Instantly, he gasped and choked for air.

"And you're not dead...yet," I countered, letting him fight for a sliver of breath before I let go. "Did you try to kill your ex-wife?"

He glared at me, face red, nostrils flared. But there was nothing he could do.

"Don't make me ask again." I tipped forward. "Because when I try to kill people...I don't try."

"You can't kill me," he said hoarsely. "You're law enforcement."

I chuckled. "No, I'm not." I turned my arm so he could see the patch on my jacket. "Vigilante. So, I answer to no one."

He tried to hide it, but he started to shake in the chair. *Fucking coward.*

"I didn't kill her. You have no proof." He jostled the cuffs.

"I have a laundry list of gambling debts that you owe and the life insurance policy you took out on her after she told you she wanted a divorce, and the fact that divorce is supposed to be finalized this week. That's all I need," I said low, lifting my hand in front of his face and stretching out my fingers, just waiting for him to give me an excuse to strangle him again.

"Alright." He turned his head and ducked as I reached for him. "Alright. Just stop."

"Did you plant the bomb on her car?"

Slowly, he looked up at me, pure rage leaching over a face that looked increasingly gaunt before he snarled, "Yes, okay? First off, she deserved it for what she did to me! Trying to keep

The Villain

that house—for what? And then leaving me? She was *nothing* without—"

My fist finished his sentence, sending him and the chair flying back into the wall before toppling over. Behind me, I heard the door open, but I was already on Brandon, hauling him up against the wall with one hand and landing my knuckles into his cheek with the other.

"You never deserved her." *Crack.*

"Dare—"

"You don't deserve to live." *Crack.* "I'll spare you prison—"

"*Enough.*" Harm bodily hauled me back, his arms hooked under my shoulders. I struggled for a second, my chest heaving as Brandon crumbled to the floor.

"Get him away from me," he shrieked, his nose broken and bleeding as he tried to worm closer to the wall. "He tried to kill me! He tried to—"

"You're fine," I spat. *What I'd done was nothing compared to what he'd done to her.* "*I'm fine,*" I muttered to my brother who reluctantly released me.

"Calm down, Mr. Martins." Hazard appeared and dragged the other man back into his chair. "Tell us exactly what you did."

"I want a deal." He turned and wiped the blood from his nose on his shoulder.

"The deal is that prison spares you from those loan sharks taking a limb."

"Fuck," he muttered, his head swiveling mindlessly. "*Fuck.*"

"Thirty seconds, or they leave you alone with me again."

His head jerked to me and he stared for a long second—too long. "Is this a setup? Who are you people?" He looked wildly at Harm, then Hazard, and then me. "Is this because I failed?"

Failed?

"Enough." I slammed my fist on the table, making him jump again. "You have thirty seconds to answer my questions, or the next thing my fist hits will be you." My temples pulsed with rage. "Did you plant a bomb on Athena's car to kill her?"

"Yes."

My fist curled like a loaded gun, but before I could ask my next question, he started rambling wildly.

"I had to do it. I didn't have a choice—"

"You were in debt, not sitting with a fucking gun pointed at your head."

"They were pointing a gun at my head."

"Who?" I tipped forward, scrutinizing his face for the slightest indication that any of this was a lie.

"I don't know! I don't know. He was waiting for me in the back seat of my car one night when I left the casino. It was dark. I couldn't see him."

I grabbed my phone and pulled up the only recent photo we had of Ivans. "Was it him?"

"No," he said too quickly, and when I glared, he looked again. "No. I could hardly fucking see anything, but no, I really don't think it was him—whoever the hell that is."

"What did the man say?" Harm asked.

Brandon let out a tense breath. "He made it clear I didn't have long."

"To pay?" Hazard asked.

"To live," he snapped.

"Go on."

"He knew about everything. The debts. The insurance policy on Athena. I'll admit I got it...as a backup plan."

"To kill her to collect on the money?"

He glared at me. "Yes." He wiped the blood from his face again. "But I hadn't decided to...until he made me. Said he'd double the payout of the life insurance policy if I went through with the plan. Left the damn bomb in my car. The remote. Told me how to activate it."

"Why?"

He sputtered. "Did it matter? I had people practically beating down my door for money I owed them—one loan shark in particular..." He trailed off and shook his head. "This was my answer."

"You're a piece of shit—"

"I wasn't in any fucking position to ask questions—"

"Well, you've certainly asked plenty here," I snapped back.

"Did he say anything else?" Harm stepped in—and stepped in front of me—before I did something stupid.

I backed off, giving myself a beat to let the rage come to an even keel.

"No."

"And what proof did he give you that he'd pay you?" I asked.

"The fucker was sitting in the back of my car, a gun held to the back of my neck and a bomb on the seat. I didn't need proof that he'd kill me if I didn't—"

"Liar." I narrowed my gaze. "You're lying."

He snarled. "Fine. Fuck—*fine*. He left cash for me in the trunk. A ten percent deposit. When the bomb went off, he wired me another fifty percent."

"But she didn't die."

His lips curled. "Which is why I thought you might be working with him, wanting it back."

Oh, fuck no. "Where's the money now?"

His silence was the answer I needed.

"You gambled it away." I shook my head in disbelief. "You're a fucking idiot."

"Fuck you—"

"Stand up, Mr. Martins." Harm didn't give him a choice. "You're under arrest for the attempted murder of Athena Holman. The police who brought you here will be escorting you back to Sacramento, where you'll be booked."

"I want protection—extra protection. This loan shark, you don't understand—" He stopped speaking abruptly when I stepped in front of him.

"They'll give you protection in prison," I assured him. "It's called bars."

Harm passed him off to Hazard, and even once the door closed behind them, I could hear his cries all the way down the hall. *Fucking coward.* I didn't know what was worse—knowing the truth...or knowing I'd have to tell Athena.

"Fuck," I muttered, dragging both my hands along my skull.

"You're in too deep."

I whipped around and glared at him. After what we'd just heard, *that* was the first thing he said to me?

"I don't know what you're talking about," I said tightly, my body light as a tightrope of anger stretched too thin. "We needed answers, and I got them. I'll call Ty—" My brother grabbed my phone from my hand, and I snapped.

A sound erupted that I didn't even realize I'd made until I'd pinned my own brother to the wall, my forearm over his throat.

My chest heaved, and our stares collided. His was hard and shocked and hurt. And shame washed over me like ice water. *I was fucking losing it.*

I stumbled backward, driving both hands along my scalp. "Fuck." I turned back, scrambling for some kind of apology.

"We'll talk later," he said before I could say anything. "Call Ty."

Gritting my teeth, I swallowed hard and pulled out my

phone again. My heart pounded so hard, Ty's name tremored on the screen when I tapped on it.

"What did we learn?" he answered.

That I'm fucked.

"The ex was paid to plant the bomb on Athena's car," I rasped.

"*Paid?*"

"Promised double what the insurance payout would be. Ten percent cash deposit, fifty percent deposited into an offshore account when the bomb went off."

"I'm guessing the last forty was supposed to come when her death was confirmed."

"Yeah."

"So, he was getting paid twice to kill her?"

I flexed my fist, my jaw so tense I couldn't get out an answer.

"He was approached in his car. Didn't get a good look at the guy or a name. Denied recognizing a photo of Ivans." Harm rattled through the details. "He seems to be under the impression the man is someone he borrowed from coming to collect—"

"He's a fucking idiot," I interrupted. "It makes no sense. First, why pay him more money when he already owes them? Second, even if the job he was doing for them was worth the investment, why Athena?"

That was the part of this that made no goddamn sense. At least before, Brandon trying to kill her for the insurance payout was a solid motive. But for him to have been paid additional money to do it by someone else...*who? Why?*

There was only one answer my mind would let me consider.

"It has to do with Ivans." I pinched the bridge of my nose. *I just didn't know how or why.*

"Why would Ivans want her dead?" Harm folded his arms, watching as I started to pace, my mind churning through possibilities.

"I don't fucking know," I muttered and ran my hand along my chin in frustration. "Athena said they'd only been on a few dates. She didn't want a new relationship...yet."

My brother looked particularly hard at me as the conversation drifted toward silence.

"I'll look into this payout he mentioned," Ty offered. "Even with an offshore account, I might be able to get a lead on where the money came from, and that could give us a better idea of what's really going on."

"Thanks," Harm said. "If it does have to do with Ivans, we're obviously missing something. A part of the relationship we're not seeing."

Not seeing...

I growled, an idea starting to form like the first darkened clouds of a storm. "We knew she was seeing Ivans. Remington knew...what if we weren't the only ones?"

"What do you mean?"

"Our assumption is that Ivans returned to the States to blackmail Belmont and Wenner and GrowTech. He was at GrowTech's fucking fundraiser; they have to know he's here—what he wants from them," I said, rambling as I tried to keep up with the flow of the thought. "What if Belmont is behind this? What if his plan is to kill Athena and pin it on Ivans?"

"Frame him."

Just like they did before.

"Exactly."

A ripple of cold worked down my spine. "Did you find out anything at the gallery?"

"The paintings you described are there. I spoke to the owner, Glenn, but she wasn't there the day of the explosion.

All she could tell me was that those two paintings are there, but there are three others that were there but aren't any more."

"There's three missing?"

"She said to come back later this week to talk to Carol, who was working that morning. She would've let Athena in."

I made a low noise.

"She also mentioned seeing Ivans—Iverson come around a bunch to see Athena and look at her work."

"Right." I exhaled loudly. "I'll...talk to her."

"Dare..."

"What?"

My brother crossed his arms and looked at me. "You can't spare her the truth anymore."

"About Ivans," I clarified, as though there were some chance he was referring to the truth about who I was. "I know."

My breath exhaled in a bitter burst of laughter, thinking of how that conversation had to go. I had to tell Athena that her ex-husband was paid to blow her up to frame her new "boyfriend" for the crime and that her new "boyfriend" was a wanted fugitive.

"I'll do a deeper dive into the payout to Martins and let you know what I find," Ty said.

When our call ended, Harm added, "Since we're here, I'll see if Hadrian can go through the evidence from the bomb one more time. If they were going to frame Ivans, there would need to be more evidence tying him to the bomb or the car or... something."

"Yeah." I nodded, my mind still staked to my own task. "I'll tell Athena and then take her back to her house. See if anything jogs her memory."

"You think she'll be okay with that?"

"She will be if she's with me."

"And what about you?" His stare narrowed like the scope of a sniper. "You going to be okay?"

I didn't answer him and ignored the target the words painted on my back as I walked out of the room and headed for my bike. Normally, as soon as I was on the road, my mind would settle. Not today.

All I thought about the entire drive was the feel of her fingers on my face...and the look I'd bring to hers when I told her the truth.

"Let me talk to her."

"No." My shoulders lifted and tensed. "I said I'd do it."

I turned and faced Rob, who stood with her shoulder propped in the doorway to the rec room. Per usual, she was in her uniform of all black with her hair braided over her shoulder. I remembered one time we'd gone to a local Celtic fair, maybe a year or so after her parents' deaths, and a little girl had walked by us, pointed at Rob, and exclaimed, "*Look, Mom, it's Merida!*" It was funny. Cute, even. But Robyn was no princess, though she was brave.

"I know, but I think I should."

"Why?" I demanded like an idiot—like Rob hadn't been the one spending hours with Athena each day.

"Because I understand." She reached for the chain around her neck, and I turned away.

I jolted and then threw back the remainder of the whiskey in my glass. "And I don't?" I shook my head. "No one understands betrayal more than I do. No one understands what it's like to realize the person you love tried to kill you."

Not just me. My brother. *My brothers.* My feelings for Amira had almost cost all of us our lives that day. All because I'd been too blind to see the truth.

"And do you want to relive that?"

I gritted my teeth, breathing as though flames were sinking into my chest with each breath. "I told her I'd tell her when we knew about Brandon. I promised her the truth."

She paused, and for a second, I thought she was giving in—giving up. *I should've known.* "And what about your truth?"

I froze. "I told you. I'm not telling her who I am. There's no point, only more pain for her."

"Not that truth," she said, and I cocked my head in her direction. "That you care about her."

Brave.

"I care what happens to her. There's a difference." And that difference was a hill I would die on. "She's vulnerable and under our protection."

"You care more than that."

"No, I don't. I can't. *I won't.*" I was a glutton for punishment—for her anger. I wanted her to feel toward me what she should. Resentment.

"Then let me tell her."

Rob was right. I should let her talk to Athena. I should let her break the news. But dammit, I couldn't. I couldn't trust anyone else with her pain. It was mine and mine alone to suffer.

And to comfort her was my punishment. My redemption. To be there for her in the way I wasn't all those years ago.

I shoved away from the bar and strode over to my sister, towering in front of her. "And what do you know about love and betrayal?"

Something flickered in her gaze. She let go of the ring on her necklace and let her arm fall to her side.

"More than you know."

Her answer surprised me. More than I was ready to process right then, which worked out because she didn't give me the chance.

"I'll be in the garage with Ty if you need me." And then she was gone.

Chapter Seven

Athena

I carefully felt for the nightstand, my fingers instinctively finding the familiar barrier of pill bottles, a water bottle, and tissues along the edge.

Everything had to be in the same spot for me to find it—to know where it was. *Necessity bears proficiency.* My mind was used to creating images. Layouts. Design. Structure. *Artwork.* And that skill helped me now. *Or at least, I liked to think it did.*

Using my hand as a guide so I didn't knock anything over, I found the box of crayons I'd set behind the tissues and pulled it to my lap, fumbling to return whichever color I'd chosen back to the box. Rob apologized earlier, saying that the only art supplies she could scrounge together on such short notice were ones that belonged to her nieces.

I didn't mind, I assured her. I wasn't going for a masterpiece —just memory. Of him.

Was I losing my mind? Dare was a stranger to me in the most basic sense of the word. *Except he wasn't.* The shape of his face, the feel of him—it was both foreign and familiar at the same time.

The lines of his face. The ridge of his brow. The curve of his lips. The memory of his skin under my fingertips. The scent of him still lingered in my nose. The rasp of his voice is still buried in my ears. The feel of him, hard and angled and damaged. And the taste—

"Stop licking your lip."

With the rest of my senses in overdrive, I swore I could taste him on my tongue. Rich and heady and masculine. But it was an invisible taste that made me hungry for more. For a man I couldn't see. A man who'd protected me.

That was the funny thing about senses. Just because sight sometimes dominated the others didn't mean that without it, the rest couldn't paint a better picture. And trying to draw Dare was like creating a portrait of a flame. Sure, seeing the shape and color of the fire was part of it, but it was nothing compared to the picture painted by the other senses. From the sound of its power crackling and popping. To the scent of its consuming strength. And finally, to the pulsing, dangerous caress of its heat. Even if I could see Dare, I had a feeling the sight of him would only be a small part of the way he burned in my mind.

I traced my fingers over the paper, searching for the roughness where the wax crayon had marred it. I'd learned very quickly that everything I knew about drawing went out the window when I couldn't rely on my eyes. My first several attempts ended up in crumbled balls to be thrown away. The trick was the crayon couldn't leave the paper. Like peeling an orange by trying to remove the whole skin in a single, intact piece, his portrait was made of a single weaving, turning, curling, and cutting line.

The drawing was still probably terrible, but that didn't

matter. I didn't want it to be seen, I only wanted it to help me remember the handsome, scarred man who'd saved my life.

And the activity made the last several hours pass in what felt like minutes—something that would've instead felt like centuries if I'd instead spent it pacing along the walls of the safe house, wondering where Dare was. What he'd found out. If he'd found Brandon. If Brandon had...

Oh god.

I walked my fingers to the small alarm clock at the farthest end of the nightstand, hitting the first button on the right, and instantly, the clock's drone voice announced, *Eight thirty-seven.*

It was late. Too late. I let out a small whimper and reached for the eye mask, tugging it off my head. The day had passed. Rob had brought me dinner. And now, I needed a new distraction because I obviously wasn't getting any answers tonight.

I closed the notebook over my drawing and pushed it to the side of me. My feet worked their way to the floor, my hand on the nightstand as I stood. There was a method to make it safely to the bathroom.

The edge of the nightstand guided my first two steps. Then there were another two steps in an open abyss. From there, the doorframe of the bathroom was within arm's reach, providing my next support to guide me into the room.

Every time I stepped onto the cool tile floor, I heard Rob's voice in my mind as she'd described the room to me.

"On your right, yup, right there is the vanity. One sink. Okay, and when you get here, hold the corner and turn to your right. Now you're straight in front of the toilet. If you don't turn, another three or four steps this way...will put you right at the shower door." My fingers pressed to the glass, streaking it with my fingerprints, until I reached the handle. *"Don't open the door all the way because it will bang into the side of the tub, which is on your left."*

I paused. A bath sounded good. *Relaxing*. It sounded like something I could use tonight.

I moved even slower to the left, suddenly in uncharted territory. Usually, my travels ended at the shower. It couldn't be more than a—

"Oww—" I swallowed down my cry as my leg banged into the edge of the tub. "Crap." My exhale rushed from my chest, taking some of the instantaneous pain with it. *I was getting better at getting injured.*

Moving with a kind of painful slow motion, my hands mapped the oval shape of the tub and the anchor on the faucet on the right side, turning the handles one at a time until I determined which tap was hot and which was cold.

As the water filled, I undressed and tried to remember the last time I'd treated myself to a bath—Brandon always complained about how expensive it was to draw one in our house in Sacramento. *Very expensive apparently when he was gambling our life away.*

How could I not have seen it? Could I have been that—

"Because you don't pay attention, Athena. It's like you don't give a shit—"

"I do care, Brandon!"

"Right. Which means you've got nothing more than a pretty face."

I flinched, able to recall that particular insult with the same clarity as if he'd physically slapped me. Reaching for the waist of my pants, I shimmied them down my legs, lifting one foot out first, and when it came back down, it was into a pool of water.

"*No!*" I cried out. One more thing I didn't think of—monitoring the water level as it filled.

I scrambled for the faucet just as a loud bang echoed from somewhere else in the house.

"Athena!"

I spun at the sound. *Dare.* And mid-turn, my foot caught on my pants that were still attached to one ankle, slipped on the wet floor, and pitched me forward.

This time, even Dare wasn't fast enough to stop my fall.

"Ahh!" Pain erupted in my hip as it smashed into the tile an instant before my palm miraculously found purchase and stopped my face from becoming the next casualty.

"*Athena!*"

Those familiar hands grabbed my shoulders—*my bare shoulders.* Of all the thoughts I'd had in the last three seconds—the water on the floor, the impending injury from a fall, the sound of Dare rushing to save me—the recollection that I was practically naked wasn't one of them.

But now, it was my only thought.

Not the water under my palms. Not the pain in my hip. Not the rush of the faucet I hadn't managed to completely turn off. Nothing except that I was naked and alone with a man I hardly knew.

I should be afraid. Embarrassed. I should be scrambling for cover. But if I felt any of those things, they were burned away by the heat of him. Charred by the warmth of his touch. Scorched by the sudden ache that made my nipples pebble and the center of me clench with want.

"Are you alright?"

My chin jerked down.

"Okay. Don't move," he husked, and his hold disappeared for an instant. I heard his steps splash through the water before his heat was in front of me again.

"Here." The soft terry of a towel pressed to my chest, and as soon as I held it, he said low, "I'm right here. Just going to stop the water."

A task that would put his back to me. For privacy.

My throat went tight. *Of course.* For a second, I cared less about him seeing my naked breasts than I did about him seeing my blush—*the color of a fool who wanted him to look.*

I wanted him to look in the same way I wanted to know the taste of his lips on mine and the feel of his tongue in my mouth. I wanted him to look in a way I'd never be blind enough to ignore.

And that was ridiculous as well as unprofessional.

He'd saved me—was protecting me. Of course, he wouldn't take advantage of that.

I hissed as I pushed up on my knees. Unfolding the towel, I pressed it to my chest, listening to the flow of water stop and the gurgle of the drain open up.

"I'm sorry," I offered, gingerly feeling for my hip bone until a shot of pain made me wince. *That bruise was going to be one for the books.* "I shouldn't have—I didn't realize it would fill so fast. I'm such an idiot—"

The sound that came from him was absolutely lethal and very, very close. "Don't," he warned, his hands taking my shoulders from behind. A shiver barreled through me, feeling the way he loomed behind me like an angry shadow. "Don't ever call yourself that."

"Dare..."

"Take my arm." He took one of my wrists and moved my hand to his forearm. Thick. The ridges of muscle cut sharp edges into his skin. *His hot, bare skin.* "Hold on to me and get in the tub."

"But—"

"No buts."

I bit into my tongue, the urge to cry almost overwhelming me. I'd been prepared to give up on the bath after the mess I'd made—one more habit I'd learned with Brandon: *if I didn't get something right the first time, there wasn't a second chance.*

I shifted my weight, and the layer of water under my toes almost made me protest again; *I should be the one cleaning all this up.* But then the sharp pain in my leg and hip from my fall coincided with Dare's deep command.

"Get in the water, Athena."

"Okay."

I held his arm as he turned as far away from me as he could. For the first time since meeting him, I wondered if he had a girlfriend. Not a wife; there was no ring on the hands that touched me. Or if he was just truly a gentleman.

Just get in the water, Athena.

My other arm released the towel I'd been holding tight. When it landed on the wet floor with a soft slap, Dare tensed.

My heart pounded into the front of my chest. A drumbeat that marched me forward down this heady, uncertain path. I reached down and untangled my soaked pants from my ankles, deciding to wait until I was in the water to remove my underwear. At this point, it seemed like the safest option.

Feeling for the edge of the tub, I lifted my leg over the side and stepped into the hot water. I shivered, the sensation so incredible I couldn't move fast enough until I was sinking down into the heat. *Dissolving was more like it.* A deep, satisfying moan bubbled through my lips as the warm water seemed to erode away all my aches but one.

"You alright?"

"Yes," I breathed out, noting the rasp of pain in his voice. I wanted to ask the same of him, but instead could only manage, "Thank you."

He responded with a grunt, and then I heard him move next to the tub. There were slapping and sloshing sounds. *He was cleaning up the water.* Guilt bubbled in my chest.

"I'm so sorry about the mess," I said softly, feeling tears prick back at the corners of my eyes.

"It's fine, Athena. Really." His voice was both gruff and soft. "It's just water."

At that, I felt some of the tension drain from my shoulders. "If you say so."

He made a low noise, and then his wet footsteps moved away from the tub. Biting my bottom lip, I took the opportunity to reach for my underwear and work them over my hips, hoping his focus was where he was—on the other side of the bathroom.

When I heard a cabinet stretch open, I quickly lifted the hand and discarded the soaked string of fabric over the edge of the tub, thinking it would land discreetly on the towel I'd left piled there.

Instead, it landed with an unmistakable, unignorable sharp slap on the floor.

No. My pulse faltered, but I hadn't imagined the sound. *He'd moved my towel—used it to mop up the water.* But the realization came too late. And it was instantly followed by Dare's low, swift grunt as though I'd fired a bullet straight into his chest.

I held my breath, wishing it would slow the loud gallop of my pulse as I waited for what happened next. Maybe he would ignore it—pretend he hadn't heard. Hadn't looked. I could pretend, too. It wasn't as though I could actually see him staring at my discarded thong on the ground, his body tense and his jaw pulsing. It wasn't as though I could watch his hot stare start to smoke as it lifted and settled on me, the depths of his gaze churning with hunger.

It wasn't as though I could see if any of this affected him the way it was affecting me.

"I'm going to get Rob."

My exhale fired from my chest. *Of course, he was.* Because I wasn't his guest. I was a victim. His charge.

"Wait," I called, my voice cracking. Instantly, his steps

The Villain

halted like they were under my control, not his. "Why did you come? Did you find something? Did you find Brandon?"

I didn't want him to leave. Out of all the things I wanted about this man, the thing I wanted most was for him to stay.

The catch of his breath betrayed his answer.

"What did he say?" I sat forward and pulled my knees to my chest, hating to beg. "Please, Dare. I need the truth."

"Sacramento PD picked him up this morning. We questioned him, and he confessed to the gambling debts and to taking out the insurance policy." His voice came closer. Lower. He had to be crouching near the tub.

"And the bomb?"

"Athena..."

Next to. He was next to the tub.

"The truth," I whispered, knowing he was close enough to touch—to reach out and hold on to. A flame in my darkness.

"He planted the bomb on your car."

The confirmation was like another bomb. Different. Silent. But no less harmful.

"Athena..."

Heat exploded from my fingers and ricocheted through my body. I blinked and registered the source—his hand on top of mine, where it rested on my knee.

"There's more," he said, his voice drawn tight. *More?*

"Brandon claims the bomb wasn't his. He said...someone paid him to put it there."

Someone...paid him...

"I don't..." I closed my lips and tried to swallow, but it felt impossible. Reality was too big and bitter a pill to swallow. "I don't understand. Someone *else* wants me dead?" My head started to sway, and the water started to feel even hotter than when I'd first gotten in it. "Who wants me dead? Does he know? Do you know?"

"No—"

"And why?" I interrupted him, my voice pitching higher. "I was nothing, Dare," I protested, half on a sob. "Brandon turned me into nothing for years. Until I went to divorce him. Then I became something—someone again, but not someone that anyone would want dead. I can't—"

"Athena." The sound of his growl and the tightening of his grip reeled me back. Anchored me. "We have an idea."

An idea.

Of who wanted me dead.

Of who paid my ex to blow me up.

"Have you heard of a man named Bernard Belmont?"

Belmont.

"The CEO of GrowTech?" My jaw went slack.

"So, you've heard of him."

"Heard? Yes. But I—" I released my breath and gave my head a small shake. *This couldn't be real.*

"What is it?" he demanded.

"I met him. Briefly," I admitted. "Three of my paintings were featured at a fundraiser of theirs a few months ago. Not GrowTech, but—"

"GrowGood."

"You know..." I trailed off, listening to the steady stream of his breath blow tightly through his lips. "Glenn—the owner of the Tableau—arranged the connection. I guess she'd sold several pieces of art to Mr. Wenner, who is—"

"The COO of GrowTech. Belmont's right-hand man." His thumb started to stroke mine, brushes of electric heat back and forth on my skin.

"Yes." My voice hitched, trying to focus on the conversation and not the forbidden feel of his touch. "I was introduced to both of them at the fundraiser, but nothing more than a few words. Actually, that was where I met Rick for the first time."

"Athena," he rasped, his voice sounding as though it were being flayed from his vocal cords. "We believe a former employee of Belmont's is trying to blackmail him."

"Okay..." *But what did that have to do with me?*

"That employee's name is Dr. Ray Ivans."

"I don't know that name." Which was why it made no sense to feel a chill along my spine. *Ray.* No, there was no familiarity there. Was there?

"You don't know it because he doesn't use it anymore," Dare said, the sound of his voice becoming nothing more than a rumble of syllables as he spoke aloud the fear in my mind. "He now goes by Richard Iverson."

"Rick." I couldn't stop the shiver that went through me.

"It's why we haven't been able to locate him. He has several aliases that he's been using, and none of the ones we are aware of are linked to any properties or rentals. He's been MIA since the explosion."

"Aliases?"

His slight pause gutted me. *It was going to get worse.*

"He's...a fugitive. An international criminal. Wanted for theft, assault, fraud"—his voice cracked—"and murder."

*No...*I wanted to sink beneath the water. Even without my sight, suddenly everything was too much. The sound of my unsteady breaths. The hammer of my heart.

"A mur..." I couldn't even say the entire word.

"Athena—"

"Where do I fit in?" I forced the question out. It was either that or tears would overthrow me.

I heard the way his teeth ground together before he answered, "We think Belmont realized you two were seeing each other and thought, by killing you, he'd have leverage over Ivans to stop the blackmail. A warning that he could be next."

"Collateral damage."

He didn't have to say anything for me to know it was the truth.

"That's why you were at my house that morning—because of him." It had occurred to me more than once how fate had put this man in the right place at the right time to save me. But it wasn't fate. It was facts. Evidence.

"We had a source provide a photograph of the two of you at dinner. I was coming to question you about him...to warn you."

My chin bobbed slowly. *Maybe a little bit of fate, then.* I inhaled deeply and then exhaled. The darkness felt like a small blessing right now, letting me drift away into it.

"I don't know what's worse...that my ex-husband tried to kill me, that the man I was seeing is a criminal, or that it's now his enemies who want me dead," I said, and as soon as the words were out, a sound followed them. A rolling, tenuous, bubbling sound. Maybe some would call it a laugh, but it seemed wrong for laughter to come from the pain in my chest.

"I'm sorry."

I shivered at the bone-deep pain buried in those words. It was so real—so raw—that for a second, I thought I saw him. Not clearly. Not anything more than a shift in the shadows. But that was the only reason why, when I stretched my hand out, it landed with perfect precision on the rough plane of Dare's cheek.

"It's not your fault."

Chapter Eight

Dare

> *Three weeks. It's been three weeks since we said goodbye. Since you've said anything to me...*
> *Mom's cancer is back, but she won't let me come home. Says she's going to beat it again, but I can hear it in her voice she doesn't believe it.*
> *Why tell me something she feels deep down isn't the truth? Don't I have the right to prepare for the worst, too? —Athena*

It's not your fault.

I couldn't breathe—I couldn't exhale without the oxygen taking the whole truth with it. *This was all my fault.* I'd left her all those years ago, and if I hadn't, she wouldn't be here.

"All you've done is try to protect me," she said and punctured the inflating truth in my chest.

Protect her...it was the only prerogative strong enough to suppress the truth.

I shuddered, the words like the tip of a knife poised under the tip of my chin. A threat. A promise. *A reminder.* Telling her who I was would make her wary of the only man willing to do anything to keep her safe: *me.*

From Ivans. From Belmont. From her ex. They were criminal pieces of shit who didn't deserve to breathe in the same universe she lived in. But so help me, neither did I.

And not even for how I'd hurt her all those years ago, but for who I was in this moment—a man who still wanted her beyond all reason. I kept my distance not because I worried she might figure out the damn truth, but because the way I wanted her was irrational. Uncontrollable. *Unreasonable.*

"Athena..."

My thumb stroked the back of her hand one last time, her skin like rays of sunshine straight to my cells, and then I drew my hand away. I had to. If I didn't...that warmth would melt my restraint. It would loosen the long-tightened knots from their moorings and set a need free that hadn't been fed in years.

My eyes slipped from their hold, sliding from her wrist along her arm until it disappeared beneath the soapy water where the rest of her full, naked curves dwelled.

Fuck. I jerked my head to the side and swallowed down the hiss that threatened to slip through my lips, a hot traitor ready to reveal the secrets of how damn bad I desired her. I shut my eyes for a second to clear my thoughts, and instead I was greeted by the memory of those curves sprawled on the bathroom floor like a wounded siren.

Of course, my first instinct was for her safety. Her comfort. But now that that was handled, instinct gave way to a sea of images that churned around me. Her hands splayed on the ground, hair falling over her shoulders, her chest heaving. Her full breasts hung with their tight berry tips, waiting to be laved and worshipped.

My mouth had pooled with saliva, and my tongue was so thick and starving with want, I could barely speak.

And now they were inches from me. Just below the surface of the water. It would be so easy to lift her up just an inch or two so I could worship them. *Feast.* Sate the beast inside my chest, turning me gaunt with want.

"I really know how to pick them, don't I?"

Fuck. I bit into my cheek and flung my eyes open.

"Don't do that," I rasped and shifted my seat to adjust my hard dick, my piercings digging painfully where they were wedged inside my jeans. "This isn't your fault."

"Then how do I only attract men who want to use me—hurt me? Kill—" She couldn't finish.

"It has nothing to do with you. Nothing. You hear me?" I heard myself. The frustration etching my tone, the anger elevating my voice.

I balled my hand into a fist to stop it from moving. If she only knew how many times I wanted to reach for her—how many times I had to stop myself from touching her. Comforting her. Drawing her to me and never letting go.

"No?"

She rested her chin on her knees, her gaze staring blankly in front of her. She looked so...small. So fucking defeated. And yet, she hadn't broken down. Hadn't cried. Hadn't freaked out. *What the hell kind of woman held her cool after all that?*

"No," I practically growled.

"Then why can't I see how bad they are for me?" Her head tipped to the side so one cheek rested on her knee, and her haunted stare was aimed directly at me.

I couldn't stop myself. I reached out and brushed my

fingers on her cheek, loving the way it made her breath catch and color rise to where my fingers touched.

"Because you don't see the bad, Athena. You only see the beauty." If finding the good in everyone were a moral treasure hunt, she would be as rich as Croesus.

"You think so?" Her tongue slid along her lips, and it took every strength I had not to send my thumb following it.

"I know so."

The blush on her cheeks deepened, and just as she turned into my hand, I managed to pull it away. Before I touched something I shouldn't. *Before I touched something I wouldn't be able to let go.*

"I still can't believe Brandon..."

Dammit, I knew I should've punched the fucker.

"He owes a lot of money to a lot of bad people."

"Not that," she murmured. "I believe that." Her sigh broke off another piece of me. "I just can't believe I never saw it after years together. Never realized he was still gambling—that he had a problem."

"When—" I stopped and cleared my throat. "When did you two meet?"

"In college." A sad smile brushed her cheeks. "I was in this...shell...after my mom died. Not spiraling, just orbiting. Brandon was vibrant. The life of the party. He wouldn't let me stay in my orbit and pulled me into his. And it was good—what I needed."

Because she hadn't had me.

"I'm sorry about your mom." *And I'm sorry I wasn't there.* I'd written the words so many times in those first few months after I'd heard the news, but I never sent them. Not when she wrote to tell me. Not when she wrote about the funeral. Not when she begged me.

"Thank you. She was sick for a long time." Judy Holman

was a saint, and everyone used to say that was why God called her home sooner than the rest. "Part of me used to wish she'd been alive to meet Brandon, but not anymore. Obviously."

Two times, Judy had survived breast cancer, but the third time...the third time was it. And it was quick. They'd found the cancer right after I'd left for basic training, and she was gone by Christmas.

Athena shifted in the water, and a wince creased her face.

"How's your hip? You went down pretty hard."

"Less bruised than my pride." She sighed heavily. "What am I missing? What is it about me that only attracts men who want to use me or hurt me?"

The band around my chest tightened. "That's not true."

"It is true." She couldn't see me, but somehow, her stare felt like she saw right through me. Right through all my lies to the truth. "Every man I've loved has hurt me."

I tensed. "You loved Ray—Rick?" That didn't fit with what she'd said before.

"No." She reared up, sloshing water against the side and dipping the surface low—dangerously low—on her chest. "Not him. Before I met Brandon, I loved someone who...hurt me."

My heart beat heavily, all its sharp, broken pieces puncturing fresh holes inside me. *This was it.* The moment I had to face the man in the mirror and the pain I'd caused her, and I deserved to do it without the opportunity for forgiveness or redemption. Because God help me, I knew she'd give it.

I didn't trust myself to hear my name from her lips or what it would do to me, so I asked instead, "What did he do?"

Her lips peeled apart, her chest rising and falling tempestuously—and temptingly—at the edge of the water. "Why are you going to arrest him, too?"

"Maybe." I gritted my teeth. "Maybe something worse."

"He..." *Left me. Abandoned me. Promised me the world and*

broke his promise. I filled in all the appropriate possibilities, and she went with none of them. "Disappeared."

What? No. Anger bolted through me. *Disappeared* wasn't enough—wasn't bad enough.

"What do you mean?"

"We were high school sweethearts, and after graduation, I left for art college, and he joined the military. I thought we were going to make it work, but I never heard from him again. I wrote to him. Waited to hear from him—for him to come home. Even when my mom died... nothing."

"He sounds like an ass," I ground out, my fist flexing on the edge of the tub. "As bad as the rest of them."

She laughed softly. "I don't think so."

Goddammit, why couldn't she just hate me the way I deserved?

"I think he didn't know how to tell me."

"Tell you what?"

"That I wasn't worth it."

There it was—the exquisite pain I'd been searching for.

"You're wrong," I said, my voice hoarse from stretching through all my sharp barriers.

"How do you know?"

This time, I didn't even try to stop myself from reaching for her because, fuck it. Fuck everything except making it crystal fucking clear to this woman that she was worth everything. Every goddamn thing.

She shivered at the first brush of fingers, and I felt like an ass for surprising her with the touch, but I didn't stop. I brushed damp strands of hair from her cheek and then continued trailing my finger along the side of her face. Her ear. Her jawline.

"Because you're perfect. And any man who can't see that

isn't a man but a fucking fool." *And I was the biggest of them all.*

The catch of her breath was like a jumpstart on my heart, and the way she turned her face into my hand was the kind of thing that would've brought me to my knees if I wasn't already on the ground.

And then, something even worse happened. Something I hadn't expected—something I never should've been close enough to make possible.

Her soft lips pressed to the edge of my rough palm in an unmistakable kiss, and my cock jolted against my jeans.

"Athena..." I couldn't hold back my groan, unable to fucking see straight with how hard I was. It couldn't be normal. It definitely didn't feel survivable. I angled slightly and stretched one leg out, barely able to breathe again as my dick throbbed along the side of my thigh.

Fuck. This couldn't happen. *She* couldn't happen. I turned to pull my hand away, but she grabbed my wrist, stopping me with the trail of her touch up my arm. My shoulder. Finally, to the side of my face.

I was worse than a fool—worse than an asshole. I was a villain for the way I let myself want her...and the way I let her continue to want me without knowing the truth.

"How did you get this scar?" The pad of her thumb carefully traced the newly raised flesh.

I shivered, her touch inflicting a new kind of wound on my skin. Invisible. Immovable. Indefinite.

"Capturing a man who worked for Ivans, who hurt a friend of ours." My voice cracked when she reached the intersection of the scar with my lip. "He liked knives."

"I'm sorry."

Was she sorry his knife found my face? Or was she apologizing because her touch had now migrated onto my lips?

"Don't be," I murmured for either scenario, watching unabashed desire darken her eyes.

It was...breathtaking, the freedom of her expressions when she couldn't see anyone else's reaction—when she couldn't judge herself or worry what others might think. And it was heart-stopping to feel her touch.

I inhaled and closed my eyes, savoring the warm press of her fingers in the way she felt mine.

Later, I could pretend this would feel the same if it were any woman. That I was coming out of my skin for the sole reason that I hadn't let any woman touch me in years. But it was only another layer of lies to hide the truth behind: *no other woman's touch would ever make me feel this way.*

Even Amira. Even with the way I'd wanted her and cared for her—even with the way war and danger had intensified those feelings to the point of folly—it still didn't compare to the heat of Athena's touch. The way it was so hot, it seemed to cauterize wounds I thought would bleed forever.

My eyes went wide, and I grabbed her wrist. "I should go."

She sat forward, moving onto her knees. Her next inhale teased the pink edge of her nipples, and I realized I was being tortured.

"Why?"

My jaw locked so tightly, the tension rippled onto my skull. "It's not...right."

In fact, it was every definition of wrong.

"Right?" Her breathless laugh killed me. "Every *right* man has turned out to be wrong for me. Maybe I need to try a wrong one for once."

"I can't..." *And I needed her to not let me.* "Not with you here. Like this."

Her brow creased, pain lancing her gaze. "Like what? Blind?"

The Villain

I hissed. "Jesus—no, that's not what I meant." Words, reasons, logic—she was twisting them all. "I mean, you're vulnerable—"

"Aren't we all?"

"Athena..."

"I'm blind, not incapacitated. Just because I can't see doesn't mean I can't think or know what I want." Her hold tightened on my face, her thumb positioned right under my lips, and I couldn't tell which one of us she was pulling closer.

No.

This shouldn't happen.

Couldn't.

I needed to stop. Back away. *Run.*

Instead, I remained an inch away from her face—a breath away from her perfect, tempting mouth—and asked, "And what do you want?"

Her full lips parted, and her tongue wet them like an executioner sharpening his blade. My body went taut, and the pulse that pounded in my ears only served to pump blood to my aching cock. This was going to kill me. *She was going to kill me.*

"To kiss a man who wouldn't hurt me."

I let out a soft groan. "Athena..."

Her forehead touched mine, and she breathed, "Are you going to stop me?"

I wish I were that man.

A stronger man.

A better man.

But I wasn't.

I was nothing more than a man who'd lose his mind if she didn't kiss me now.

"I couldn't even if I wanted to."

The first touch of her lips to mine was the second explosion I'd experienced in her presence, and this one I wasn't sure I'd survive.

It had been years…so many years. My body went into shock, stilling completely under the play of her soft mouth. She was sweet and forbidden like alcohol on a recovering alcoholic's tongue—except the desire I felt wasn't one-hundred-proof, it was bulletproof. Unstoppable and deadly.

Her mouth pressed and played over mine, a gentle but determined exploration.

I never thought it would happen like this. In all the years since Amira, I thought, at some point, I'd weaken and cave. That I'd be the one who reached for a woman despite what the last one had cost me. But I hadn't reached for Athena—I hadn't kissed her. *She'd kissed me.*

And instead of the kiss being part of an injury that wouldn't heal, her embrace was like a balm over an open wound.

I held steady until the first swipe of her tongue—the soft pink tip I'd tracked so many times over her lip now made its first pass across mine, and there I crumbled. The shield of my restraint constructed of piecemealed strength, that touch tearing away an integral part of the foundation like the Jenga piece that sent the tower toppling.

A deep sound rumbled through my lips, ushering with it my tongue to tangle with hers. I slid my hand to her hair, fisting the damp mass to angle her head and deepen the kiss. Water sloshed in the tub as she rose up to meet me.

The Villain

"Dare," she panted, nipping at my bottom lip until my mouth claimed hers once more.

Dammit. I needed to stop.

Her tongue stroked mine, wiping every thought from my mind except how that same motion would feel along the length of my cock. Distantly, I registered her fingers curling around mine, pulling my hand from her face, and I prayed she was coming to her senses because God knew, I seemed to have none when it came to her.

But she didn't pull my hand from her skin. She moved it. Down her neck...over her collarbone...

"Athena." I tried to catch my breath—catch the reins of my control again—but I wasn't fast enough.

The gentle shackle of her fingers lowered my hand to her breast, the soft weight filling my palm like a bomb with a dead man's switch. To hold her—touch her—risked my life. But to let go...to let go assured sudden death.

"Fuck," I hissed, black spots striking like mallets in my vision.

"Please," she murmured, holding my hand to her breast for another second before letting it go—before trusting me to give her what she needed. *She shouldn't trust me.* "I dream of you... touching me."

A curse erupted from my lips, and the world started to tilt as I let desire take me under. My hand moved on instinct, kneading and teasing the weight in my palm. Memorizing every inch of its softness and the feel of its firm peak, storing how perfect she was—how perfectly she fit to me—deep in the caverns of my mind where all my fantasies sprung from.

This would be enough—it would have to be. I wouldn't let myself take more.

But then her soft moan reached my ears like a siren's call,

drawing me and my resolutions deeper into the depths of desire.

Growling low, I wrapped my free hand around her neck and took her mouth savagely. My tongue plunged deep into her mouth, sparring against hers, but she wouldn't stop moaning. She'd wanted this. She had no idea who I was or what I was, and still she wanted this. I wouldn't judge her for that, but neither would I pretend to be something I wasn't.

I wouldn't pretend to be sweet and considerate and gentle when the reality was I was a man starved of intimacy for almost a decade. An animal. Feral for her. So, this kiss was nothing like the first. This one was a warning. A threat. It marched straight into the promise of punishment that lacked all remorse.

And in return, her kiss back lacked any hesitation.

She clutched the sides of my face like my mouth was her only source of oxygen.

"You're perfect," I rasped, and then locked my lips to the corner of her neck, sucking hard as I kneaded her breast. "So fucking perfect." I was drunk...drugged...unhinged the way my mouth moved lower, hungry for more.

Her hands slid from my face, her slender fingers coiling in my hair, pulling me harder to where her nipple strained for my touch. I pinched and rolled it in my fingers, doing everything I could to keep my mouth away.

But everything wasn't enough when faced with her breathless, "Please."

A deep groan split from the seam in my chest as I faced the tub from the outside and moved her so she did the same from the inside. Unseeing, she stared at me as she tipped back, the rosy peaks of her breasts sitting like ripe fruit above the water.

For a second, I let myself stare and stare and...suffer. I grabbed the edge of the tub as a wave of desire crashed through me, the intensity of it threatening to make me black out. When it passed, I let out a tight exhale.

I was going to have a permanent imprint of my zipper in the skin of my cock and punctures to the fabric of my jeans where the metal ends of my piercings broke through. But there was nothing I could do. One touch—even to adjust myself—and I knew I'd come. That was what the woman of my dreams naked in front of me did to a man who'd spent the last eight years in celibacy.

"Dare."

I closed my eyes, letting the weight of my name on her lips bear down on my shoulders. Later, I'd realize just how much heavier this would make my guilt. But right now, there wasn't anything in this world or the next that could've stopped me from lowering my head to her chest and capturing one perfect nipple between my teeth.

Water splashed over the edge as her body jerked. "Don't stop."

Never.

Hands tangled in my hair, holding me tight as I licked and sucked the velvety, firm peak. Her moans and whimpers were like a hail of gunfire falling all around me, and the only way to make it stop was to give her what her body craved.

I circled and flicked my tongue over her nipple, memorizing what each movement did to her. The way it made her move. The sounds it drew from her lips. I reached my hand to her other breast, ready to pleasure it the same, but I never got the chance.

She grabbed my wrist and sank it below the water with all her might. And like the perfect anchor, my fingers plummeted straight to the depths between her thighs.

I growled, my teeth biting into the tender skin of her breast as my fingers spread the soft folds of her pussy. *God, I wished the water was gone—drained—so I could feel how wet she was for me.* But it was better it wasn't. The water kept me from her—kept me from mauling her like some rabid beast.

"Yes," she moaned, squeezing my forearm when I pushed two fingers inside her.

"Is this what you dream of?" I dared to ask, lifting my gaze up her body and taking one breath. And then another.

"More."

My cock pulsed hard and began to leak. *Fuck.*

"As you wish." I captured her other nipple in my lips and set my tongue to the same rhythm as my thumb over the swollen bud of her clit.

She was a siren, and her song of pleasure made me want to drown in her depths. It no longer felt like years since I'd touched a woman, but a lifetime. A lifetime because it was her. Because this wasn't just mindless pleasure like I thought it would be. Because it meant something—because she had meant something to me once.

She rocked into me, her body asking for what her lips could no longer form.

"I dream of this," I muttered, her tight heat around my fingers threatening to shred all of my sanity. "Of you needing me. Begging me. Completely vulnerable to my touch."

After what I'd done to her, the way I still fantasized about her was an unforgivable sin. But her body mocked my guilt, her sex rippling around my fingers as they found the sensitive spot along her front wall.

"Yes," she moaned, arching into my touch. The soft word sent my own body rocking forward, my groin bumping into the side of the tub.

I hissed in pain, in pleasure, and in insanity. And in that insanity, I reached for my cock without thinking…without remembering it would only make it worse.

As soon as my palm pressed to the strained front of my jeans, a violent need for release snapped through me like a whip. *No.* I squeezed my eyes shut, trying to focus only on the sweet pebble of her nipple between my lips or the tight grip of her pussy around my fingers, but I couldn't.

My stomach tightened. Air stopped entering my lungs. Some part of me decided it would be better to pass out than to touch myself with her like this...until her hand settled on my shoulder.

Maybe it was support. Maybe it was simply another plea for more. But my body—my own need—took it as permission.

My eyes flung open, need dilating all my senses into a single purpose: pleasure. A feral noise rumbled from my chest as I tore open the front of my pants and fisted my throbbing length.

And then it was everything all at once. The drag of my lips on her nipple. The press of my fingertips on her G-spot. And my firm grip yanking long, punishing strokes on my cock.

She had to know—had to feel my shoulder jerking under her hand—but I could pretend like her own pleasure erased it from her senses.

My tongue and hands all moved to the same rhythm, sending pleasure rocketing through us both until she couldn't take it any longer. *Thank God, because neither could I.*

"*Yes!*" She came with the sweetest cry, her body arching all her softness into me like the most beautiful offering...and one I didn't deserve. From there, it was only my name on her lips as she rode out her release, and the sound of it was my undoing.

"*Fuck,*" I groaned under my breath, feeling the pressure in my spine an instant before my own orgasm erupted. My cock jerked wildly in my grasp, shooting my release in thick streams against the tub and onto the floor.

She panted, her chest rising to my lips, and in return, my

teeth sank into her skin, heaving in a breath like I took the oxygen directly from her lungs. There, in the riotous, blinding pleasure, it felt like we were the only two people in the world. No present. No danger. No past. No betrayal. Just Athena and me.

"Dare..."

Her voice found me in the darkness—it pulled me from the fantasy and back to the moment when I saw her beautiful, flushed face. Her eyes glistened with pleasure, similar to the way they'd glistened with tears the day I'd left her.

Fuck.

"Let me get a towel," I said hoarsely, drawing myself away from her. "There's water everywhere." *And my cum streaking the side of the tub.*

I straightened and wiped the evidence of my failure from my pierced tip, carefully tucking myself back into my jeans and using my footsteps to mask the sound of the zipper.

The first towel I placed on the floor, wiping up the water, and then quickly over the side of the tub before tossing it to the side.

"You can stand up; I have a towel for you."

I wanted to look—wanted one last look. But the guilt I'd expected—the guilt I'd hoped would give me a moment of reprieve—hit me with its full force, and I turned my head under the weight.

The sound of the water rushing down her body mocked my restraint as my mind just imagined all her curves anyway. As soon as she was upright, I wrapped the towel around her middle with almost robotic-like efficiency and guided her back to the bedroom, where I deposited her on the bed and pushed fresh clothes onto her lap.

"I'm just going to finish cleaning up the bathroom," I said

quickly, and I made sure to shut the door behind me so she knew I meant for her to get changed without me watching.

For five painful minutes, I stared at the damn tub that had been my undoing. The water. The woman. The want. I threw the towels in the hamper with a curse and returned to the bedroom. Thankfully, she was not only changed, but she was underneath the covers.

"We'll talk tomorrow," I said, as though that would give me enough time to figure out what the hell to say.

"Dare—"

"Goodnight, Athena." I strode toward the exit. *Fled, more like it.*

"I'm sorry."

Her words stopped me like a gun to my back, and I turned. For the first time, I wished she could see me—see the way I looked at her. "Don't ever apologize for that."

She licked her lips, and my damn cock stiffened again. "But you're upset."

"I'm not upset with you."

"Then what is it? Why do you feel like what we did was wrong?" Her question gutted right to the center of it.

So I gave her as much of the truth as I could and prayed it was enough to stop this from ever happening again.

"Because if you knew me, you'd know I don't deserve you."

Chapter Nine

Athena

"*You're perfect.*"

The words were too sweet to seem real—so sweet that with every passing minute of the morning, it got easier and easier to believe they were a dream.

But while his deep voice and the pleasure erupting from my body were things I could—and had—dreamed about, there was one piece of last night that promised reality. *Okay, two.* The pain in my hip where I'd fallen on it.

And the sound and feel of him pleasuring himself. His low grunts tucked between my moans. The undeniable sound of a fist tugging on hard flesh. The fevered bounce of his shoulder under my hand.

To have seen it would be one thing...but to have the memory built from every other sense, that was what made it indestructible.

And the memory was just as perfect as it was painful at the

end. The way he'd left. My throat tightened when I tried to swallow.

I should apologize again. Dare wasn't in his right mind to refuse it last night, and I'd been in the wrong. To beg him when he was trying to keep things professional and not take advantage of the situation.

I was sorry for begging him, but I wasn't sorry for wanting him.

I adjusted the eye mask on my face, finding one more reason to wish I was healing faster. *Because when this was all over, there wouldn't be any reason to regret the way he wanted me, too.*

I turned, hearing the handle of the door.

"Dare?" My heart leaped into my throat.

"Athena?" Rob's calm voice oozed through the room.

Not Dare. Even though he said we'd talk in the morning.

"Hey." I smiled like I wasn't wishing she was someone else.

"I brought you a strawberry smoothie for breakfast. How does that sound?" Her footsteps got louder, her voice closer.

"Great." I moved the sketch paper back to the nightstand, following the same path I always did, to make sure I could find it easily next time.

"Here you go." She put her hand on my shoulder first, revealing her position, before that same hand took my wrist so she could hand me the smoothie.

"Thank you." I felt up the cup to the thick straw, holding it steady to my lips.

"How are you doing?" she asked after I'd taken a good couple of sips, and I swore I heard the slight rustle of paper next to me as though she were looking at my sketch.

"Fine." I swallowed and licked my lips, adjusting the mask on my face. "I mean, no change."

No sight. No memory. If I asked to see Dr. Nilsen again,

they'd bring him here, but it wasn't fair to him or me. He'd already given me an answer about my condition—that these things would return in time when my brain healed. To ask again was a pointless sprinkle of salt in the wound.

"I meant after last night," she said as I took another sip.

Last—I choked on the smoothie, coughing and sputtering as Rob took the cup from my hand. "Sorry," I croaked, catching my breath.

"It's okay. I just wanted to see how you were doing after Dare last night."

No...she couldn't be talking about that. I swallowed over the ball in my throat and wished she'd given me back the smoothie so I could hold the cup to my cheeks and try to cool down my face.

"After Dare..."

"After he told you about Brandon. And Richard." She paused. "What did you think I was talking about?"

What else would she be talking about, Athena? My jaw snapped shut. Of course, he hadn't told her about...*the bath.* What was I thinking?

"I'm okay," I said slowly, unsure truthfully of how I felt. "I think I'm still in shock. I don't know." I started to shake my head when she set the smoothie back in my hands. I clutched the cup like it was a nice, cold lifeline. "I stopped loving Brandon a long time ago, but to think he'd agree to try and...for money..."

"Sometimes, I think it's harder to lose the idea you have about someone to reality than it would be to just simply lose them."

"Yeah." She was exactly right. I had this idea in my head of who Brandon was—even in spite of our issues. And losing him —divorcing him—wasn't as hard as learning he was never the man I thought he was. I took another sip and then added, "And

The Villain

to learn Rich...Ray...whatever his name is..." I shivered. "I'm surprised, but I didn't really know him that well." A sad laugh bubbled up. "I'd say lucky me, except Dare said you think it's his enemies that paid Brandon."

"It's a possibility. We showed him several photos of those men, but he didn't recognize any of them. We didn't expect him to, though; they're the kind of men who don't get directly involved."

I made a soft sound and continued to drink the last of my breakfast.

"I'm sorry, Athena." Her concern was genuine.

A sad smile tugged at one corner of my lips. "Like I told Dare, I really have a knack for picking winners."

"You told him that?"

"Not exactly. I asked what it was about me that only attracted men who wanted to hurt me."

"I'm sure that...did a number on him."

"What do you mean?" I asked, feeling the edge of the bed dip under her weight.

"Never—"

"Please." There were many of Rob's characteristics that I'd probably never know, but how smart she was wasn't one of them. She had to see there was something between me and Dare, even if she had no idea what happened last night.

"Dare carries a lot of...weight...that doesn't belong to him," she finally said quietly, as though she were revealing something she shouldn't. She took the empty cup from my hands. "Especially for those he feels...protective of."

I could feel that. It vibrated through his entire being when he was around me—when he was trying to keep himself away from me.

I don't deserve you.

"Do you think he'll be by today?" My voice trembled. I

didn't want him to feel that way around me, especially after last night.

The way he'd spoken to me...kissed me...touched me...I'd felt more worshipped in that short span of time than in the culmination of minutes of my entire marriage.

"I'm not sure. He went out to the gallery earlier—"

"The gallery?" I interrupted her. "Why?"

"He wanted to speak to the woman who was working the morning of the explosion. She wasn't in yesterday when Ty went to talk to her—oh." The bed shifted, a buzzing sound growing louder. "Speak of the devil," she muttered, and a second later said, "Hey, Dare. Were your ears ringing?"

He'd called her. I held my breath.

"I'm with her right now. I'll put you on speaker—"

"No, don't—"

"You're on speaker. Athena is right here," she interrupted him, but not before I caught the start of his protest. *He didn't want to talk to me.*

Was I now one more weight he carried? Was last night one more guilt piled on his shoulders? Or was it because I'd begged him to kiss me—to touch me? Had I made him feel so guilty for saying no that I'd guilted him into saying yes?

"Hello, Athena."

Instantly, I was back in the water. Those lips of his on my chest. His hand buried between my thighs. Heat bloomed in my cheeks, but I refused to let it bleed into my voice. "Hi."

Rob spoke when the silence became pronounced. "I figured this was easier than you asking me to ask her...I already told her you went back to the Tableau this morning to talk to Carol."

He tried to scrub the rasp from his voice by clearing his throat, but it didn't help. "Carol was working the morning of the explosion. We're trying to retrace your steps and see if it gives us any clues."

The Villain

"I understand." I swallowed. "What did she say? Are my paintings there?" In the mix of gambling-husband-turned-would-be-assassin and rebound-date-turned-hardened-criminal, I'd forgotten about the paintings I'd remembered putting in my car that morning. *Or maybe I'd just assumed I'd lost them along with everything else about my former life in those minutes.*

"They are."

I hadn't realized I'd been holding my breath until my chest deflated with a loud whoosh. "Oh, good." My voice wobbled, and I lifted my hand to my cheek, feeling the foolish spill of a tear. To cry over a painting..."I'm sorry."

"Athena..." His rumble reached me even through the phone. Warm and thick, it wrapped comfort right back around me. And for a second, I believed that even though I didn't have my sight or my safety, I had him.

"I'm okay," I assured them both as Rob silently placed a tissue in my hand as though it had magically appeared there.

"The paintings you told me about are here, but Carol said you didn't just drop them off, you picked up three others from the gallery that morning," he continued on.

"Picked them up?" The mask shifted as my brow creased. "That doesn't make sense. I was bringing pieces over for the show. Why would I take three back?"

"She said you told her someone had already bought them. You didn't say who, but she's confident by the way you spoke that it was Ivans—Richard."

"Oh—ow." I hissed and pressed my hand to the side of my head, where the pain came from.

"Athena—" Rob touched my elbow, letting me know she was there.

"I think that's right." I interrupted her before Dare realized something could be wrong. "I don't...remember...exactly, but that feels right." I didn't know how else to explain it. "We met at the fundraiser because he admired my work, and he kept telling me he was excited for the show because he wanted to purchase some for his house. He insisted on coming to the gallery for a preview of what would be shown."

I remembered walking him through the back room, revealing my hard work piece by piece, and feeling a sense of pride that I was finally doing this—*finally pursuing my dream*—and someone appreciated that. And me.

Too bad he'd turned out to be a criminal.

"There were three he really liked." Seascapes from the California coastline. "He kept asking me to set them aside for him." My head pounded as I dug through the muck for more of my memories. "He asked me at dinner the night before if he could buy them ahead of time. Begged, really."

"What did you say?"

"I told him I'd think about it." I could remember that was how I'd left it at dinner. "I guess I decided to do it the next morning."

"Athena..." Dare's voice lowered like he was about to ask something important. "Do you think you picked them up and took them to him that morning? To his house?"

My lips parted. I wished I could say yes—I wished I could be certain about it, but it was all still a void. "I could have. If they weren't in my car...unless I brought them back to my house to set them aside for him." I bit my bottom lip, the sudden pain in my head now a splitting ache.

"Dare—" Rob tried to break in, and I could tell she saw I was in pain even though I did my best not to let it show.

"Would you have a record if he bought them?"

My spine straightened. "Yes. I should have a copy of the receipt." The pain was getting worse, but it finally felt like I was helping. Finally felt like I was useful.

"At your house?"

"If it wasn't at the gallery, and it wouldn't have been if—since I sold him the paintings before the show—then it should be in my files. On an invoice—"

"Where?" he demanded, and I could hear a motorcycle rumble to life.

"Enough, Dare." Rob's weight lifted off the bed as she snapped, the thread of warning in her voice was thin and as sharp as a garrote to his throat.

"Sorry," he apologized. "I'll go back and look—"

"Take me with you." It was my turn to insist on something. "Everything's kind of a mess since I moved back…I'll know where to look, and maybe going back will trigger…"

"Athena." Rob touched my shoulder.

"It's okay. I'm okay," I assured her through the headache that chugged around my skull like a freight train. "Please, let me help."

No one said anything for a long minute, and then Dare's voice cracked through the silence. "Two days."

"What?"

"I'll go look today, but regardless of what I find, I'll bring you back to the house in two days."

"Why two days?" I asked softly, and my heartbeat slowed with each second that passed. There was only one thing of significance in two days—the end of my divorce.

"Dare…" Rob prompted when he took too long to answer. "What is it?"

"Ty got a call this morning. Apparently, Brandon never made it back to Sacramento PD to be booked and processed."

Never made it…"Oh my god, is he—"

"He escaped custody. Still no details, whether he's in hiding or fled or…anything else. So, until I know more or until the timeline on his insurance policy runs out, I'm not taking you from the safe house."

There was no room for discussion in his voice.

"Okay." I tried to swallow. "Will you let me know if you find anything?"

It wasn't exactly what I wanted to ask; the real questions knotted into a tangle in my throat. *When will you be back? Will you come see me? Will we talk like you said we would?*

Will you let me stop wondering about last night and if you're avoiding me again?

I didn't ask any of the questions I really wanted to, and yet the answer he gave me answered them all.

"Someone will."

Message received.

Chapter Ten

Dare

I write, but you never write back. Has something happened? Did you change your mind about forever? If you did, just tell me.

If you did, I might write anyway. I don't know who else to talk to.

Mom's not going to beat the cancer this time. Her doctor said it spread everywhere, and she doesn't have long. And she won't let me come home. She says doesn't want me to remember her like this...

I'll never understand why she gets to decide that the pain she's sparing me from is worse than this alternative. Don't I get a say in how I want to be hurt? —Athena

. . .

This was the third time I'd pulled up to her mom's house in less than three weeks. The day of the explosion. The day I'd gone and failed to find this invoice. And again today.

Three times, and it should've gotten easier to pull up to the curb out front and not remember the way the front door would swing open, Athena's face beaming when I'd come to pick her up for a movie. Easier to not think about how close we'd cut it to her curfew, making it back just in time only to spend twenty minutes kissing in the car. How her mom would flicker the outside lights to bring us back to earth, and Athena would smile at me like I hung the moon and then hurry inside; meanwhile, I'd sit in the car another twenty minutes thinking about how all I wanted was to kiss that girl forever.

It should've been easier to be here. And maybe if I hadn't kissed her again—*touched her again*—it would've been.

Instead, driving here was like going back in time. Back to the days we spent at the beach, her painting and me in awe... and nights we spent on a blanket in her backyard picking out constellations from the sky.

I put Rob's Mercedes in park. I'd borrowed her car because I wasn't putting Athena on my bike. My motorcycle was my haven—the one place where the guilt and regret couldn't catch me. Sherwood had been that place, too, until I brought her there. Now, my bike was the only spot untouched by her. By her memory. By the way I still wanted her. It also rained all morning, and they were calling for showers the rest of the day, which made asking Rob require less explanation.

I reached for the engine button and froze, the sunlight glittering off the leftover raindrops on the grass catching my attention. It looked just like the dew on the lawn had that morning.

Fuck. I forced my eyes shut. *The good memories were painful; the bad ones were worse.*

But there was no escaping this one because, when I closed my eyes, all I saw was Athena's face from the other night. There were a million new memories from that night. A hundred other expressions I could've envisioned. The relief when she'd lowered into the tub.

Instead, I kept going back to the last look she gave me—the one where she tried to hide the pain she was feeling inside when I told her I was leaving.

It was the same hidden hurt that had been in her eyes the last time I'd told her I was leaving almost two decades ago. The day I'd left for basic training, she'd smiled with hope as though I couldn't see how she wanted to cry.

I hadn't known how I'd hurt her then—I hadn't known that the forever I'd promised would be a lie—but what difference did it make now?

"Dare..."

A whip of self-loathing snapped through me.

"Yeah, we're here." I punched the button, shutting the engine off, and got out of the car.

Being around her now made my body react like I was at war. Every muscle tensed. Adrenaline thumping. Prepared for danger and attack at any moment. Except the danger was desire, and the attack was self-inflicted each time I touched her.

"I've got you." My teeth ground tightly together as I took her hand and helped her out of the car. "Curb," I warned.

She lifted her foot higher, leaning closer—harder on me for an instant—until she was on the lawn. And then I heard her inhale, her breath like a key in a lock, before she gently pushed away from me, wanting to move forward on her own.

"Athena..." She should let me guide her.

She turned her head, and the way the sunlight bathed her

was almost too painful to bear. Her blond hair moved gently with the breeze. Her white summer dress—also borrowed from Rob—hugged each and every curve, which was now memory rather than fantasy. The soft part of her full lips and my sunglasses resting on the bridge of her nose—the aviators looked better on her than they did on me. Like they belonged to her.

Just like everything else of mine.
My cabin. My bed. My bathtub.
My hands. My mouth. My—

I let out a groan and stepped my feet apart, feeling my cock start to thicken.

"Even blind, I know when I'm home," she said firmly, thinking my groan was directed at her. And I didn't correct her.

Touching her the other night was a mistake of the first order. But touching myself while I did it...that should've been a fucking felony.

But I couldn't control myself. I couldn't control the need raging through me when she pulled my mouth to hers. It was like a dam burst inside me. Mind, body, and every bit of my broken soul were flooded with wanting her.

And I couldn't let it happen again—I wasn't even going to let myself get close. And part of that plan involved not discussing the other night at all even though I'd told her we would.

What was one more broken promise except a good reason for this woman to stop wanting a man she never should've wanted in the first place?

I hoped she'd come to a similar realization, and that was what kept her quiet. Regret rather than unrequited want. Like we'd created our very own bomb, and we were now too ashamed to get close to it for fear of what destruction it would cause.

The Villain

"Dare—" Athena stopped suddenly when she reached the door.

"What is it?" I was by her side in an instant, barely managing to hold myself back from reaching for her arm. "Do you remember something?"

She turned her head. This close, I could see her wide gaze through the dark filter of my glasses. "How did you get inside the other day?"

Shit. I tensed, cleared my throat, and then lied straight through my teeth. "Picked the lock."

"Oh, I'm sorry. I should've told you there's a spare key underneath that planter." She pointed with surprising accuracy at the small container I was already reaching under—*the key exactly where I'd found it—and then returned it the other day.*

"Got it." I went to let us inside, but I wasn't fast enough.

"My senior year, I snuck out to watch a meteor shower with my boyfriend." She started to reminisce, her soft voice catching the memory inside me like bait on a hook, reeling a fresh burst of heat through my veins. "We watched the sky fall for what felt like hours, and when we got back, my mom had locked the door."

"So, you climbed in through a window?" I asked like I didn't already know the answer, shoving the spare key into the door against the protest of the old, rusted lock. *I was going to replace the whole damn thing before I let her go home for good; this deadbolt was garbage.*

"No." I heard her smile. I hated when she smiled and it was because of me, the boy who'd left her. "My boyfriend insisted he could pick the lock."

"Yeah?" The door gave way, and my relief blew through my lips. "Door's open."

But she didn't budge. Instead, she finished the story, not

realizing it was my memory, too. "We were out here for forty-five minutes until he got it open."

"Sounds like picking locks isn't in his skill set."

"I didn't have the heart to tell him there was a spare key hidden under the flowerpot." The left side of her lip curled into the same smile she'd had that night, and my gut tightened. She was so damn beautiful. Then. Now. *Always.*

And the words were out of my mouth before I could stop them—before I could think. "Maybe he knew and didn't have the courage to tell you he didn't want the night to end."

Her breath caught, and my body snapped taut. That was my problem around Athena. I acted before I thought. *I acted on what I felt—what I didn't deserve to feel.*

"Let's go in," I muttered, and because my brain still hadn't caught up to my racing heart, my hand didn't land on her shoulder to guide her inside but on her lower back. And once it was there, the only thing worse would've been to yank it away.

She shivered at my touch but, thankfully, didn't say anything as we stepped over the threshold.

"I'm sorry for the mess," she apologized instantly like she could see. "Everything has just been in chaos since I moved back, and I'm trying to get on my feet..."

The house was an obstacle course of furniture and boxes. Maybe some would've called the place a disaster, but all I saw was the disorder that came when someone started their entire life over.

Like the start of a puzzle when all the pieces are strewn over the table. They all belonged. They all had a place. They would all fit together as she figured out how her new life was going to look.

When I'd been here the other day, the first thing that struck me was how little the home had changed. All her mother's furniture and decorations and photographs...it was all still

The Villain

there. A time capsule from the year I'd left...but then there was also all the evidence of the years that had gone by since. The boxes and boxes of the life I'd left her to—a life with a man who'd tried to kill her.

"You don't need to explain," I said, the house feeling different from being inside it with her.

My eyes roamed the familiar landscape. The yellow floral couches were tucked against blue wallpapered walls. Vibrant and vintage and homey all at the same time.

"Was this all your mom's?" I fed into my persona like I didn't know.

"Mm-hmm."

Pictures of the two of them were interspersed with some of Athena's artwork from high school. Sketches. And some of those watercolor paintings of the beach.

I jerked my head away, practically propelling her into the living room, where I'd found a box labeled *Invoices* the other day, but it hadn't contained anything for Iverson.

"You have a box here for receipts, but I didn't see anything for Iverson." I thumbed through the handwritten papers again like I'd find something different; I didn't put it past myself to have been so distracted by the memories that I missed what I was looking for.

When she didn't respond, I looked up and found her standing in the center of the room, her fingers pressed to her mouth.

I was in front of her in a blink. "Are you alright?"

"There's something..." She trailed off, lifting her hand and pulling my sunglasses off of her face.

"It's okay—"

"No, it's not." She huffed. "I'm trying to be patient with myself, but I feel like it's right there—like the answer is right in front of me." Her head tipped up, and I couldn't help but stare

145

into her eyes. Like those twin blue pools were clear enough to wash all my sins clean. "It feels like there's something right in front of me. Something I know—something I've known..." My jaw worked tighter with her every word. "Something familiar." Her voice went quieter. "The truth."

Me. I was in front of her. Cloaked in all my lies.

"Athena..." I rasped, lust punching me in the gut when her tongue slid over her lips.

She stilled, and it was like we both realized how close we were at the exact same moment. My hands on the sides of her arms. Her head upturned. Our breaths colliding in the narrow passage between us.

Color rose in her cheeks—a bright, beautiful warning for what came out of her mouth next. "Dare...about the other night."

Fuck.

"Don't," I begged. "Please."

Pleasuring her—and myself—had been a double-edged sword. On the one hand, it swiftly severed the idea that I'd ever be able to want any other woman—a boon for someone who'd sworn himself to celibacy. But on the other hand, it cut me deeper every moment I had to be around her and keep my distance.

"No, I need to apologize."

"Apologize?" I gaped, stunned, and blurted out. "For what?"

"For guilting you into touching me."

I reeled. *Was she—she couldn't be fucking serious.* I'd never heard something so...*wrong*...in my whole goddamn life.

"You wanted to walk away—to be a gentleman because of my condition," she went on, forcing me to realize she was serious. "And I used that to beg you to touch me—"

"*Absolutely fucking not.*" I knocked over a box as I spun her back to the wall, my mouth claiming hers in an all-too-familiar yet downright dangerous way.

Her soft sound of shock was gone by the time my tongue delved between her lips, meeting hers with hungry strokes. She opened underneath me, like a taste of heaven in the midst of my own personal hell. I could take anything—bear anything—except her believing I didn't want her.

Anything except that.

I licked and tasted every corner of her sweet mouth. For all she'd given me the other night, I still felt the same as I did those past-curfew nights all those years ago: that I'd happily agree to live a life on her kisses alone.

She pressed against me, her soft curves fitting too perfectly along all my hard edges.

"Dare..." Her soft moans were my small mercies. Her little pants, my penance. If only I could pay her in pleasure for the cost of my cruelty. My lies.

Dammit.

I tore my mouth from hers and dragged in a deep breath. "Just because you begged doesn't mean I didn't want to."

"Then why are you avoiding me?"

"Because wanting to doesn't mean I should have—and not because of you," I added quickly before she went back down that path. "There are things...about me..." I went silent and exhaled my frustration.

She slid her hand up my neck to cup my cheek, her thumb finding purchase on the seam of my scar. "You can trust me."

I jerked like she'd pulled the pin out of a grenade. *Trust her.* It wasn't warning bells that went off but more like an air-raid siren that rang through my skull.

Trust.

I turned my head away—out of her hold. I couldn't trust

anyone. Not anymore. Not after Amira, and especially not Athena. She could promise it now and mean it, but not once she learned the truth.

"We need to keep looking. It has to be here somewhere." I backed away from her and the temptation, returning to our task. "When I got here the morning of the explosion...you were rushing out. You had a gym bag—"

"Wait." She spun in the direction of the hallway but only made it one step before her knee banged into the corner of another box, and she cried out.

"Dammit," I muttered and took her arm, needing to help her. Hating to have to be close to her. Hating to want to be close to her. "Where do you want to go?"

"The bedroom."

I moved before she could feel me tense, guiding her through the stacks of boxes and down the hall to the master bedroom. I'd already looked there, but maybe I hadn't been fully focused on my task because I'd been trying to avoid my past.

"Wait, sorry. I meant my old bedroom," she said as soon as I angled her to the left, so I immediately course-corrected to the right, and she stopped, forcing me to stop behind her. "How do you know which room it is?"

I stilled as my heart slammed to the front of my chest. "I checked every room the other day." I brushed off the question easily enough.

Another lie.

I hadn't gone into her old bedroom. Stupid, I knew, since it could've held the answer. But I couldn't. Maybe I was afraid of what I'd find. *Maybe I wanted some justification for needing to be here with her today.*

"Oh." Her cheeks colored.

I moved in front of her to open the door, ignoring the

dangerous contact of my body against hers as though it wasn't as dangerous as sparks to dry kindling.

Thank God, she couldn't see me. Because walking into that room was like having a bullet dug straight out of my heart—one that had been embedded there for almost two decades.

The same floral bedspread. The yellow sunflower lamp. And the Polaroid photo of us from her eighteenth birthday at the Hibachi restaurant. They'd given her a massive hat and me a ridiculous gong to hold for the picture.

I didn't remember much about the meal, but I did remember dessert; that night was the first time I tasted between her thighs.

A deep sound slipped through my defenses and escaped from my chest.

"What is it?" She searched for me, worried.

"Just some dust in my eye," I said quickly.

"Oh, I'm sorry. There should be tissues on the dresser."

Nothing was in my eye, but I needed space, so I used the excuse to move to the other side of the room, keeping a careful watch on her as I did so.

"Why do you keep apologizing for things—things that aren't your fault?" I wondered and grabbed two tissues from the box.

"Habit." Her tone was sad as she walked her fingers along the edge of the bed. "I never seemed to be able to do the right thing for Brandon. Even little things—too much mayo on his lunch sandwich, but if I added more, it was too much—so apologies became a habit. I didn't realize how bad it was—how bad it had gotten—until after I left him."

I wished we'd never let that fucker go. Jail would've been a welcome consequence for being able to return the weight of those unwarranted apologies to him in the form of my fist.

"He didn't deserve you."

"Well, you know what they say, hindsight is twenty-twenty." A half smile tugged the corner of her full lips. "Ironically, it's the only sight I have right now..."

I looked away for a second and noticed the top drawer of the dresser was partially open. But it was what was inside that caught my eye: a stack of envelopes banded together, my name printed on the front. *They looked the same as what she'd sent to me.*

I glanced at Athena before carefully sliding my hand inside and pulling out the pile. There were at least two dozen here.

"What did you say I had that morning?"

My attention snapped to her. "Your gym bag."

"A duffel bag?" she corrected.

"Yeah." I'd assumed it was for the gym. "Navy-blue one."

Her head swiveled to the closet, her hand on the bed keeping her oriented to the space. "I kept that bag in there, but I wouldn't have used it for the gym."

I could see her frustration all over her face, her brain trying to recall the details of that morning.

"But if I came in here to get it...with all the boxes..." Her head angled to the left. "Can you check the nightstand? Or maybe I can—"

"Let me—" I had a split second to decide—and in that split second, my bad intentions got the better of me. Instead of returning the envelopes to the drawer, I tucked them into my back pocket to read later. *They had my name on them, after all.*

"Here," she exclaimed, finding a folded piece of paper on the nightstand just as I made it to her. "Is this it?" The desperate hope in her voice was gut wrenching. "I must've set the invoice down in a rush..." She trailed off, trying to jumpstart her memory that refused to cooperate.

I took the paper from her and opened it, my exhale rushing through my lips.

The Villain

"Dare—"

"Richard Iverson. 224 Cliffside Court." I read off the information at the top. "You found it." I pulled out my phone and snapped a photo of the address, sending it immediately to Ty.

Her brows pulled together. "I think...I think I took the paintings to him that morning."

"We'll figure it out—"

Her hand flung out, colliding directly with my chest—directly over my heart. "Wait..."

Wait? I couldn't fucking move. Her small palm stopped me in my tracks like an arrow through my breast.

"What do you mean?" I rasped.

"There's more...I can almost remember more." Her chin dipped, and she bit into her bottom lip. Hard. *Too hard.*

"Athena." I tried to caution her, but not in time. She cried out, and I caught her as she started to crumple forward.

"Enough." I pulled her to me and steadied her. Her deep, gasping breaths of pain cut right through me. "Don't force it. You don't need to force it," I begged, but the damage was already done.

I slid my hands to the side of her head, slowly massaging her scalp. The tension released from her shoulders after a minute, her breathing more even as she lifted her head.

"Shit," I murmured. She'd broken the skin on her bottom lip, blood pooling on the surface.

"What—"

"Don't move," I ordered, the blood already smearing from that one word.

Fuck. I tried to focus on the injury, but what the hell was a little blood compared to the feel of her soft lip under my thumb.

"Your lip is bleeding." There was no hiding the sudden roughness of my voice. Not when my thumb pressed to the fullness of that bottom swell, the edge of it just inches from the sweet haven of her mouth.

A little closer, and the tip would be between her lips. And if she sucked on it, my fantasy could easily exchange my finger for the head of my cock.

Motherfucking fuck—I was going insane.

"I need a tissue," I ground out and started to pull away, but she clutched my wrist. "Athena—"

"It's okay."

Too late, I saw the tip of her head. Too late to avoid being at the mercy of her tongue as it darted out and licked my finger.

I wasn't going insane...I was going straight to hell.

I couldn't move as the velvet tip of her tongue stroked over my skin, warm and soft and absolutely fucking sinful. I wanted to feel that tongue everywhere. In my mouth. Along my chest. Around my cock. *Fuck*...my heart rammed against the front of my chest. It wasn't her blood that stained the pink of her tongue red, but the blood of my breath as she licked the very life from me. *Again and again and again.*

"*Athena...*" Her name came from some part of me that acted on its own—that begged with my very last breath to release me.

My finger was clean almost from the very first swipe, but she didn't stop—and it wasn't her fault. She couldn't see the blood was gone, so only I was to blame.

I should've stopped her. *I should be stopping her.*

But I wasn't.

The sight was too mesmerizing. The fantasies it inspired were too fucking addictive. And my cock was so fucking desperate for her, I swore I felt every lick along its throbbing length.

My eyes started to drift closed. *This was it.* I was too fucking weak to resist her. Too fucking deprived to have the strength to withstand this torture. I was going to give in to what we both wanted and fuck her on her childhood bed and make a twenty-year-long fantasy come true.

And then a crack of thunder boomed so loudly outside, the windows shook, and Athena jumped back.

Air hissed through my lips like a punctured balloon.

"Did I get it?" she murmured and slid her pink instrument of torture along her lips.

You got me. Straight to the chest. Center mass. One lick and I was a dead man walking.

"You shouldn't have done that," I managed to grind out in response, hating that it sounded like I was scolding her, but all of my strength was currently channeled much lower in my body to keep my dick from fucking exploding in my pants.

"It was my wound to lick." The softness of her voice let me imagine for a second that she was talking about me—like I was the injured, broken piece of her she had the power to heal.

"We found what we came for. We should head back before it starts to storm."

She nodded gingerly and let me lead her out of the room. Now that we had the invoice—the information we needed—being in the house felt like being held underwater with no oxygen—with nothing else to focus on except the past and the truth I'd hidden from her.

"If you find him..."

"This'll all be over," I promised.

And I'd have to find a way to walk away from her all over again.

Chapter Eleven

Dare

> *She's gone.*
> *The funeral is next week, and I don't know how...I just don't know how I'm going to do this.*
> *She's gone, Darius...and I'm afraid you are, too.*

"Dare."

Ty's voice reached out from behind me, but I stood rooted to the ground until the elevator doors closed. Rob met Athena and me right as we returned from her house, and I quickly suggested my sister take Athena back to the cabin so I could touch base with Harm and see what Ty found on the address.

I needed to cool my fucking jets from...whatever the hell that was back at her house. *Her torture by tongue.* It was time to distract myself with purpose rather than the promise I'd have to keep when all this was over: *to walk away from Athena once and for all.*

I turned to Ty. "What is it?"

He was waiting, half in the hall and half in his office, his expression creased. As I reached him and followed him into the room, my head jerked to the side as though to snap the invisible string that wanted to pull my gaze back to the last place it had seen her. Golden hair. Trembling chest. And eyes that brimmed with questions I didn't have answers—good answers—to.

"You alright?"

No, I'm a fucking fool.

I'd needed to stay away from Athena. After the night in the bath, I needed to get control of myself and treat this situation like I swore I would—like every goddamn case we'd tackled. Without emotion. Without attachment. *Without want.*

And at the first instance to prove I could do that, I'd gone and kissed her again.

"Fine," I answered because ignoring his question would've given away the truth; I was as far from *fine* as fucked got. "Is that address owned by Ivans's alias?"

"It's a stack of shell companies holding the property; it'll take a few days minimum to tunnel through them all."

I didn't have a few days. I wouldn't survive a few more days around her.

"Alright"—I drove a hand through my hair—"I'm going to head over there and check it out—"

"Wait." His word hit me like a gavel, sentencing me to stillness.

His jaw muscle clenched hard, vibrating all the way onto his skull, and my eyes narrowed. His expression was pinched.

His heavy pulse was knocking on both sides of his neck. Something wasn't right.

"What's going on?"

He hesitated, moving from where he stood back behind his desk. *Avoiding the question.* Jesus, when had Ty ever avoided... anything? He was more resolute than Harm. Older than all of us. Perpetually resigned to handle whatever life threw at him with the same emotionless expression. Except this—whatever the hell it was.

"Ty..."

"It's about Athena's ex."

"Brandon? Did they find him?" I folded my arms, feeling the stack of envelopes crinkle in the pocket of my jacket, and I stilled. "Is he dead?"

There was no small chance that whoever helped Brandon escape custody did so with the intention of making sure he didn't talk.

"No. No sign of him yet. But you know I've been looking into who paid him..." He clicked around, and then an image appeared on the larger screen. Bank account registers. "The cash I obviously can't trace. But the second deposit he said he received when the bomb went off...I found that." He highlighted a line on the register. "It wasn't a US account, so I called Carina to see if she could...do what she does."

Carina Damiani was a forensic accountant for the CIA and the wife of one of the Covington Security team. Any time we were dealing with money transfers or offshore money handling or hidden accounts and transactions, she lent us a hand.

"Was it a GrowTech account?"

"She traced it through three separate banks and it led to an offshore account in the Caymans—"

"Shit." That was pretty much a dead end.

"We won't be able to find out who owns the account, but

she was able to tell me that the balance in that account is massive. Hundreds of millions."

"Has to be GrowTech," I muttered and shook my head. "I need to go to that house. There has to be something—"

"Dammit, Dare, let me finish." Hard, almost angry emotion cracked through his voice. "Carina found one other transfer the account made. Six weeks ago. Fifty-thousand dollars to another US account."

Six weeks. That was before the mystery financer contacted Brandon. It could've been to anyone—for anything—but if it wasn't something, Ty wouldn't be telling me about it. *If it wasn't something bad, he wouldn't look the way he did.*

"Whose?" I asked low, feeling the thump of my pulse hard against my throat.

He hesitated, and in his hesitation, there was a flicker of concern. Of fear. Of pain, but not his own. *Mine.*

"Athena's."

My jaw went slack. I would've rather the ground open up beneath me or lightning strike straight to my chest. Hell, I would've rather a grenade launched into my ribs than feel this pain. *Again.*

Thump.

They'd paid Athena. *Why would they pay her?*

Thump. Thump. My heart protested every beat as though it were a hammer beating a stake into the center of my back.

I forced myself to speak the same way adrenaline forces you to act—to move—after you've been gravely wounded.

"So, the same account that paid Brandon to plant a bomb on Athena's car and kill her *also* paid Athena fifty thousand dollars?" Each word was slow and methodical as my tongue stitched them together, piercing one hole after another into the way I'd looked at her—thought of her.

"Yes."

"You're sure?" *Sure that I was a fool? Sure that I'd let my emotions blind me once more? Sure that I'd let my own guilt about Athena cloud her own?*

"Yes." His nostrils flared. "We don't know who the offshore account belongs to—"

"It has to be GrowTech," I snapped, my frown so sharp, it was a miracle I wasn't bleeding from the way it cut across my face. "Who else would be involved in this with that much money? But why pay Athena only to pay Brandon to kill her a few weeks later?"

"I don't know—"

"If they were going to kill her to frame Ivans, then paying her must've had to do with Ivans, too." The anger inside me was sharp and savage as it cut a story into my mind like it carved it straight from stone.

"Dare—"

"She was close to him—or getting close to him. They must've been paying her for information—to find out what he knew or what he was doing or where he was..." It was the only scenario that made sense. Why else would the same account pay both of them? *"They paid her for the information and then paid to eliminate her."* Thump. "Or they paid her and she started to fall for Ivans, and they realized she'd become a liability."

"Those are all theories. We need more information—"

"And I'm going to get it." I spun and yanked the door open; it would've swung into the wall if Ty hadn't been there to catch it.

"Dammit, Dare." He grabbed my shoulder. "We don't know. Just don't talk to her like this right now."

Me? All that, and the person he had a fucking problem with was me?

I yanked my arm away and stepped in front of him. Got in

his fucking face. He didn't control me or my anger—*or my right for answers.*

"Talk to her like what? Like she's a suspect? Like she hasn't been associated with a criminal and could've been involved this whole time?"

Brandon was taking everything in the divorce—she told me he'd taken everything. Why wouldn't she jump at the chance for an easy $50K to spy on Ivans for GrowTech? And why would she admit to it, especially when she was wounded and her life was in jeopardy?

"Don't talk to her like she's Amira."

I froze. I hated when they said her name—when they reminded me that they remembered my failure, too. When any of them reminded me that I was the one responsible for Ryan's death.

Instantly, the anger I'd aimed at him returned to its rightful target. *Me.* I stepped back, self-loathing sitting like acid on my tongue, and headed for the elevator.

Ty's growl of disapproval chased my retreating steps, but he didn't try to stop me again. I punched in my code, and the elevator doors opened, but before I stepped inside, I looked at him and said, "I won't be made a fool of again."

He didn't respond except with a pointed stare. Not pointed—barbed. A barbed stare that stuck to my mind, so later I could remember he knew I was about to make a mistake.

Rage pulsed like electricity under the edge of my skin, charging each of my furious steps faster toward my cabin and simultaneously bombarding me with memories that fell like rockets from the tragedy of my past.

"Are you sure her intel is good? That they're moving tonight?" Harm had demanded confirmation.

"When has her intel not been good?" I'd felt offended for her. Angry at his question.

"Never."

"Then what's your point?" I'd gotten in his face.

"My point is that while what she's given us has been accurate, right now, moving up our infiltration, goes against all of the other intel we've received."

"You think she's lying?" I was furious in an instant. Harm was the rational one, while anger had always been my strong suit. "She's risking everything to help us—everything to help me."

"You're sure?"

"Yes." I hadn't hesitated.

Me. He'd trusted me. Not Amira. His brother. And my stupid fucking heart had led us to our deaths.

Never again.

Rob and Athena were talking as I threw open the door. Athena jumped, gripping the blanket on either side of her, where she sat at the edge of the bed.

Rob fired an angry glare at me. "What the hell—"

"Who—"

"Were they paying you to spy on Ivans?" I demanded, stalking right past Rob and lowering until my face was inches from Athena's.

I wiped every memory of her beauty and her kindness and her grace from my mind, leaving nothing but a blank slate to scrutinize her.

"What?" Athena choked, her brows pulling together. "What are you—"

The Villain

"Did GrowTech pay you to get close to Ivans?" I growled, searching every grimace and flicker in her expression for a crack that would lead me to the truth. "Did they pay you for information on him?"

"Me? Pay me? I don't understand."

"Yes. You," I snarled, my brain short-circuiting at her heart-breaking tone. The sight of her face morphed into another's. Her blond hair turning black. Blue eyes deepening to brown. My mind spliced present with the past—Athena with Amira.

"No! Why would you think they paid me?"

"Don't fucking lie to me, Athena—"

"That's enough, Dare." Rob grabbed the arm of my jacket and pulled; she might have a certain kind of might, but she didn't have enough strength to move me. Not like she wanted to.

I shook her off and planted my fists on the bed on either side of Athena, lowering my voice. "Fifty-thousand dollars was deposited into your account a month and a half ago. Explain."

Her eyes went wide. *Surprise*—no, it wasn't that. I wouldn't believe it.

"No—" Her head started to shake.

"A month and a half ago was when you started to see Ivans. Were they paying you to spy on him? Why? For what?" I pushed.

"No, they didn't—"

"And either they got what they needed or they thought you were compromised." And pushed.

"No, you're wrong—"

"So, they paid Brandon to plant the bomb." *And pushed.*

"*Enough.*" Rob didn't pull me this time, she shoved me. Rammed me, more like it, and hard enough that I stumbled to the side, catching myself before I collided with the wall. "What the hell is wrong with you?"

"Me?" I charged, jamming my finger into my chest and then leveling it at Athena. "They paid her, and I want to know why. What did they want? What did she learn—"

"Nothing!" Athena stood, her shout cutting through our argument. Suddenly, she appeared wild, wisdom and fury shaping every inch of her. Chin lifted, she looked straight ahead rather than at either of us, though our voices would've given her some idea of where we were.

And the subtle magnitude of that was enough to shake me to my core. She couldn't see, and yet she couldn't bear to look in either of our directions. Like once more, she was left to face the unimaginable on her own.

"No one paid me anything because I don't have access to my account." As she spoke, I realized the pit in my stomach that had been there from the second I barged through the door. Anger had camouflaged it, but no longer.

"It's okay," Rob said gently and went to her, *thank God*. But when she put a hand on her shoulder, Athena flinched. "Tell me what happened."

Her. *Not me.* Because I was a fucking asshole. Broken by betrayal. Consumed by anger. *Fuck.*

Fuck me.

Ty was right; I shouldn't have come. Hell, I shouldn't have involved myself in this from the start. From that damn photograph. I should've given it to Harm or Rob and let them handle it.

For everyone else, the garage was a haven from the outside world. Not for me. For me, the garage was a cage. Not to keep them out, but to keep me in. Me and all my anger.

"Six weeks ago, the bank called me about suspicious activity in my account. They told me about the deposit, and I panicked. I thought it was Brandon—I thought he was trying to sabotage one more thing before the divorce was finalized, trying to do something to stall or prevent it from going through," she said, barreling through every hitch of her voice like her own pain and vulnerability didn't matter. *I certainly hadn't acted like it mattered to me.* "So, I asked them to freeze the account. There wasn't much money in it before that anyway. I figured it was better to open a new account once the divorce was final—one that Brandon wouldn't have any information on."

The pause she took...the long breath that brought another stab of pain to her head, making her wince...the anger I'd felt coming here now paled to the depths of my self-loathing.

Fuck. Me.

"You can check with the bank," she added, biting her bottom lip when it started to quiver. "I haven't had access to the account..."

I was going to check because it had to do with Ivans—with this case—but I knew we'd only find proof of her honesty.

And of my villainy.

I stared at her. Her eyes were so glassy and blue, it was like staring at the surface of the sea—but not even the sea was big enough to hold the tears I'd make her cry.

"Athena—"

Rob blocked her from my view. "I think you should leave, Dare."

"It's okay. I-I'm sorry," Athena murmured, the words so wounded and habitual, I couldn't stop the groan of pain they pulled from my chest.

"Don't apologize, Athena." My sister's stare pinned mine, unforgiving. "This has nothing to do with you." *And everything to do with me.*

Her apology was worse than her tears. Worse than the pain on her face or the hurt in her eyes. Her apology wasn't her own guilt, it was mine. It was my guilty verdict, proclaiming me as one more person who'd promised to care for her and instead made her the victim of my weakness.

"She's right," I rasped and dragged my hands through my hair, forcing myself to breathe against the weight that threatened to cave in my entire chest. "This had nothing to do with you."

I left for the same reason I had twenty years ago: *so I wouldn't hurt her any worse.*

Chapter Twelve

Dare

It should've been a celebration, not a funeral.
A celebration of her life. Her strength. Her trials and triumphs. Not a funeral.
How do I say goodbye to her? To you?

The door to the gym banged against the wall. I didn't care. My vision saw nothing but red. Nothing but the tears in her eyes until my bare fist connected with the punching bag suspended from the ceiling.

I punched the bag over and over again. Each hit—*each thud*—resonated with the too-familiar sound of Athena's apology on her lips.

I'm sorry.

I was the asshole. The angry, blind asshole. *And she was the one apologizing.*

Again and again, I hit the bag, sending the weight wobbling

and spinning as unsteadily as I was. I didn't feel it when my knuckles broke open, but I saw it. The blood slashing the fabric. *Finally.* Every strike after that meant I was hitting myself—the real villain.

After everything...to assume the account belonged to GrowTech...to assume she'd been paid by them and then lied to us about it...I hadn't just made an ass of myself. I'd proven why, after all this time—all these years—I didn't deserve any more from life than the bare minimum. *And definitely not something as good as her.*

I continued to swing, blind to anything and everything except the torture of my own mind, until my foot slid on something, throwing me to the side and almost taking me to the ground.

"What the..." I stilled, staring at the mess on the floor.

Her letters.

I'd completely forgotten they were in my pocket. The way I was beating on the bag had sent them onto the floor. Dirt and blood now scuffing the envelopes.

"Shit." I grabbed a towel from the rack, and the rest of the room with its racks of weights, wall of mirrors, and handful of other lifting equipment came into focus.

I blotted my knuckles, staring at the mess I'd made. I hadn't thought I could make this any worse, but the dirtied, torn letters proved me wrong.

Crouching, I started to gather them up. Some were bent. Others ripped. I shouldn't look—I had no right to. I shouldn't have even taken them. And now...I sat back on the floor, staring at the gentle curve of my name as it stretched over the front of one envelope.

But she'd written them to me.

Something clawed inside my chest like a beast against a cage. Something that fought for freedom, ripping my breaths

The Villain

into a ragged rhythm and tearing down the speed of my pulse.

Carefully, I organized the stack back in order by date like I'd found them. But when I reached the last one—which was the first one—my fingers fumbled and then acted in spite of my restraint. I slid one letter out and unfolded it, my gaze greedy for the contents—for more punishment.

I don't know why I'm still writing to you. I know I'm not going to send this, but I can't stop myself. Writing to you is the only thing...the only thing that can stay the same as before, and I'm just not ready for everything to change.

I just need to hold on to you—onto this for a little longer.

Air started to burn inside my lungs, and I pinched the bridge of my nose, feeling it overwhelm me. She'd kept writing as though it were a diary—her diary that she'd still wanted to share with me.

I folded it back up and returned it to the envelope. Every few days, it looked like she'd written, a few dozen before the time between them grew longer. That was where I pulled out another one and slid out the letter from inside.

I met someone. He's funny and outgoing. He gets me out of this...tomb of grief it feels like I've been living in. He's a little wild, but I think I need it. Like adrenaline to bring me back to life.

He's there for me. He's...there.

Brandon. *Fuck.* I reached for the last one. I wanted to read what made her stop writing. I wanted to read the point where she realized I never deserved this treatment—this grace—and finally gave me her anger instead.

I still think of you when I look at the stars. Like my very own constellation of wishes and hopes and dreams for a long, long time. But now, I have to see them—and you—as you are.

A distant illusion. A memory. A ghost.

We see the light of a star long after the star itself has died. For too long now, I've looked for you; I've held onto your light. And now, it's time to accept you're not really there—here. I need to live my life, Darius. Not continue to wish on a world that's nothing more than a galaxy of ghosts.

The letter fell from my fingers, the pain of her words making the whole of me ache. Like there was too much hurt to be contained in my bones.

I had to apologize.

Not for what happened then, but for how I acted today. She deserved the truth about how I'd failed. Why I was broken. Why I lashed out.

It was the least she deserved.

Unfortunately, it was the most I could give...*it was all I had to give.*

"Athena?" I rapped my knuckles on the door.

No response.

I waited another second and then tipped my ear closer. "Athena, it's Dare." *Who the fuck else would it be?* "Can we talk?"

Still no response.

Even angry, she'd at least answer me. My eyes shut as I knocked again, and the memory of her crumbling on the bathroom floor flashed in my mind.

"I'm coming in." Within seconds, I pushed through the door and barreled into the bedroom. "Athena?" She wasn't there. Not in the bathroom either. "Athena!"

The Villain

Where the hell—I stopped short, a flicker of white catching my eye outside.

She couldn't be outside. *Shouldn't be.* It wasn't safe.

I pushed open the door. "Athena." Her name rode out on my exhale of relief, seeing her standing only a few feet in front of the cabin; her head had been tipped back until she heard me.

"Dare." The shadows weren't enough to hide the way her cheeks colored. She wrapped her arms over her front, cinching the long T-shirt at her middle and riding it higher on her bare thighs.

Dammit.

My cock hardened, the ends of my piercings snagging on my clothes, and I had to adjust myself immediately. *Something she mercifully couldn't see.*

"What are you doing out here?" I grunted and took a step toward her, approaching like she was a wounded animal and I was the predator who'd mistaken her for prey.

Her lips parted and then shut again. *She wasn't sure.*

"I just wanted some fresh air."

"You shouldn't be outside without..." *Me,* I wanted to say, but instead went with, "Anyone."

I hated how her face fell, but it was the truth.

"Nine heel-toes," she said quietly.

"What?"

"Nine heel-toes," she repeated and then began to count, "One. Two." With each number, she positioned her steps heel to toe, and I understood what she meant. "Three. Four."

She'd counted the exact number of steps from the door to where she stood, so she knew how to get back.

"Five. Six—"

I grabbed her shoulders before she crashed into me, and the way she tensed was like a knife to my chest and no less than what I deserved.

She retreated from my hold and then turned away from me. And the knife in my chest twisted.

I balled my fists at my side, doing my best to stop the urge to reach for her again. I needed her forgiveness, but I had no right to want anything more.

"Athena—"

Her head tipped toward the night sky. "I was imagining a meteor shower."

"No meteors tonight."

"Stars?"

I let myself glance upward, my eyes adjusting to the darkness and the sky that was salted with sparkling stars—constellations she couldn't see. *A galaxy of ghosts.*

"Yeah, they're out."

Her shoulders rose with a deep inhale, but when she exhaled, they trembled. "Did you know we still see the light of a star even after it's died?" Her voice softened. "I like to think that's how it is with people we've lost. That by remembering them, we still see their light."

Jesus. The air let out of my chest with a whoosh. It had been two decades for her, too. Two decades since she'd described those constellations as something that needed to be buried.

"And what if they're just here to haunt us?" I rumbled, not sure why. Avoiding the apology and the truth that came along with it.

"Maybe," she murmured and then shook her head. "I'm sorry," she had the audacity to apologize again—like I wasn't the one about to get on my knees. "The darkness..." She pressed her fingers to her cheeks. "It gets overwhelming sometimes. Like it's impossible to find the light."

Before I could stop myself or consider just doing what I

came here to do, I moved behind her and set a hand on the side of her arm, her skin so warm under mine.

"It's going to be okay."

"How do you know?" she whispered back brokenly. "What if I never see them again?"

I gritted my teeth. *Dammit.* I didn't know what I was doing, but I knew it was wrong. From the moment I lifted my other hand to when my fingertip landed on the flat of her shoulder blade, I knew what I was doing went against every goddamn thing I'd come here for.

To apologize. To create distance.

I pressed my finger into her back, creating a path of dots in its wake.

"Dare..."

"The Big Dipper is in front of us," I said, mapping out the stars of the constellation. "The handle and then the spoon."

She realized what I was doing and started to relax, the tension in her muscles melting as I traced through all the dots I'd just marked.

"And then the little dipper." I outlined the similar but smaller image on her left shoulder blade, ignoring the goose bumps that rose on her arm.

The woods shrouded us in a kind of bubble, leaving nothing but the rustles of leaves, the buzz of fireflies, and the electric crackle of attraction threading through the air around us.

"And straight above us..." I slid my finger to the center of her back, along her spine, feeling her shiver. I wished I could blame a chill in the air, but there was nothing but warmth around us...and fire inside us. "Is Orion's belt."

Slowly, I plotted the warrior in the center of her back, hearing the slight catch of her breath each time my finger moved lower, dotting his infamous belt right where the strap of her bra would be...if she were wearing one.

"How do you know it's going to be okay?"

My finger moved with infinite slowness, connecting the dots, because I didn't want to stop touching her.

"Because I'm going to make it okay."

"You're going to bring my sight back?" She let out a shaky laugh, and I used it as an excuse to pause, letting my finger wade up and down along a single inch of her spine.

"I'm going to make it so you can see."

I couldn't promise a medical miracle, but I could promise this: to give her stars in the darkest of nights. And an apology—and the truth—for dragging her into the shadows that haunted me.

I finished the last leg of Orion and let my hand fall to my side. "Athena."

She turned, her hand landing flat in the center of my chest, her fingers curling and crawling up my shirt, higher to my neck.

My jaw locked when she cupped it. I never should've let her touch my face, but the feel of her soft hand on me...damn, I was a strong man. Brave. Courageous. Whatever the hell other words they used to describe a man riddled with the scars of a soldier and haunted by heroism. But so help me, God, just her hand on my face was enough to bring me to my knees.

"We need to talk—I need to talk to you about earlier." If I didn't say it now, I never would.

"I understand how it looked—why you were angry."

"Dammit. Don't do that." That same anger surged.

"Do what? Be understanding? You saved my life, protected me, cared for me, and to think I betrayed you—"

"Stop," I hissed and pulled her hand off me. I couldn't stand her touch. Not now. Not after how I'd treated her earlier. *Not knowing the truth I had to tell her.* I couldn't bear the reminder of her unfailing tenderness in the face of my cruelty. "Don't make this okay—don't make how I treated you okay because it's not. There was no excuse for how I acted."

Her chin notched up. "I disagree."

Of course, she did. Of course, this bold, beautiful, and merciful woman had the forgiveness of a saint.

"You thought I lied to you—betrayed you."

"No, Athena...it had nothing to do with you," I rasped and heaved in a breath, my lungs feeling like all the air in the world wasn't enough to keep me from drowning in guilt.

"I don't understand." She crossed her arms again, and the dim light that oozed out from the cabin captured the hard peaks of her nipples against the fabric. I swore I could even see their dusty pink color through the white shirt, but maybe that was my memory overlaying reality.

"My anger...it wasn't at you. Or because of you." The tension built in my bones, every word turning them more brittle, ready to crack under the weight of the truth.

"Then who was it for?" Her brows drew together.

"Me."

"Why?"

My chest constricted, and it felt like I was trying to speak for the very first time. And maybe, after all this time, I was. Avoiding physical contact wasn't the only kind of abstinence I'd engaged in since we'd come home; I'd also abstained from this story. This memory.

Like sex, I thought if I never spoke about what happened, it would suffocate out the guilt. It hadn't. Instead, it packed it tight inside me, like C-4 into a stick of dynamite. Harmless until lit. Until now. *Until Athena.*

"Because the last time a woman betrayed me, it cost the life of one of my best friends."

Chapter Thirteen

Athena

I knew there was something weighing on him. Like a buoy in the midst of the sea, rising and falling with the waves like he were free, but tethered underneath the surface by an anchor that wouldn't release him from its hold.

I imagined it was something—something more than a bank deposit—when he'd whipped into the safe house earlier with the fury of a firestorm. But I never imagined it was this.

I didn't need to see his face to know his expression. Pain. Torture. It was in the ragged rhythm of his breaths and the way the ground bent under the shifting of his weight.

"My team and I...and Dr. Nilsen...we were Special Forces. Our mission was to infiltrate an insurgent camp. There was intel that one of the major rebel leaders in the region was hiding there, and we were tasked to take him out."

I bit into my bottom lip. Meanwhile, the darkness in front of me twisted and shifted into shapes. Images fabricated from imagination to the tune of his tale.

The Villain

"For weeks, we'd been working the area—in the local village—to collect information on where the camp was, how to best access it, and when."

The trees rustled with a slight breeze, but I didn't turn my head from the direction of his voice.

"It was a slow process. Grueling. Everyone was afraid to trust us. Afraid of what would happen to them. One day, there was an attack on the home of one of the local village leaders who supported us. A bomb. It destroyed most of the structure. I was closest when the attack occurred—I got there first to find him dead, his daughter wounded and weeping over him."

My arms pulled tighter around my stomach, trying hard to hide how the pit there seemed to grow.

"I pulled her away. Stayed with her. Comforted her." He paused as though telling this story involving the creation of a new language in order to speak it. "I saw her regularly after that. First, to check on her. Then, because she wanted to help us..."

"Because of her father."

"Yeah," he rasped and then cleared his throat. "She started bringing me information. Good intel. The best we'd gotten. And we...became close."

Something new coiled in my chest at those words. Something sharp and possessive that tinted all the darkness around me green. Something I definitely had no right to feel.

"For a few more weeks, we pooled all our data. Analyzed it. Tested it. Came up with a plan." His voice grew tighter, like a rubber band being stretched closer to the brink of its elasticity. "And then she told me the camp was moving. Imminently. Our plan had been to hit them when they were going to move, but we thought it would be another week at least. Now, we had one night, or we'd lose our best shot."

My lips peeled apart, my breaths growing shallow.

"We argued. My—our team leader and I went back and forth for hours, but I swore up and down that I was right; that my source could be trusted."

"The woman you loved." I couldn't stop myself from speaking, hating the heartbreak in my voice. Not just for him, but for some insane reason, my own heart hurt, wondering what it would be like to be loved by a man like Dare.

He ignored my words and pressed on like a recording that couldn't be paused. "We moved up our timeline. And I was so sure. So damn sure that come morning, I'd be collecting apologies from all of them for their doubts."

"Dare..." I pressed my hand to my mouth, willing myself to stop. I wanted to comfort him. To touch him and hold him and, in some way, make it easier to wade through this pain like he'd done for me. But he didn't want that; I could feel it. He wanted the pain. He wanted to walk through this memory like it were a bed of hot coals, each step scorching his flesh and burning the guilt in his soul.

"It was an ambush. There were dozens of them waiting for us, and by the time we realized what was happening, it was too late."

I knew the end of this story before it began, but only now, when his voice sounded like it was losing its grip, did the hot drip of tears leak down my cheeks. I had no idea if he could see them or not—if he was even looking—but I didn't wipe them away just in case; I didn't want to draw attention—I didn't want him to know. I hoped the darkness hid them.

"Thank God, Ty managed to get us a single fighter on air support, otherwise, we all would've died. Instead...instead, it was only my friend Ryan who was wounded badly. We got out of there, but he...he didn't make it."

"I'm so sorry." The words didn't feel big enough. They never did. I thought back to when Mom had passed, all the

The Villain

apologies felt like a single drop in the sea of sorrow, evaporating too quickly before they even had a chance to soak in.

"Why? Why did she betray you?" As deep as the hurt I felt for his loss, I also felt a sharp surge of anger. *How could she have forsaken a love like yours?* "After her father—"

"She killed her father."

I sucked in a breath, another gust of wind blowing around us, even nature shaken by the depth of his pain.

"She'd been working with the insurgents the entire time—brainwashed by them first to spy on him, but when we showed up asking questions, they decided on a bigger plan."

"She killed her own father..."

"To gain my sympathy. My trust." *And his blind affection.*

"Dare..."

"Don't feel sorry for me," he ordered harshly, his words sounding like a kind of self-flagellation. "Feel sorry for Ryan who lost his life because of my mistake. For the rest of my team who almost died that day. Feel sorry for them, but not for me."

I wanted to protest. I wanted to protest so badly, it made me nauseous to swallow the words down. And then it made me start to shake. My stomach. My chest. My shoulders. I squeezed my eyes shut, but it wasn't enough to stop more tears from falling.

"Athena..." His groan tore from the center of his chest, and then the warm pad of his thumb brushed my cheek. "Don't cry for me. I don't deserve your tears."

I lifted my chin. "Then what do you deserve?"

"Pain. Penance." His suffering was raw and bleeding from his voice.

Death was what I heard in his tone. He believed he deserved to die, too.

I reached out again, finding the hard base of his chest, the muscles underneath rippling with tiny detonations of desire.

"Athena..." he pleaded as my hands slid higher, up the thick column of his neck, the pound of his pulse greeting my fingertips until I reached his face.

"And what if I want to give you peace?"

I didn't know a man as big as him could quake the way he did. A massive shudder that seemed to loosen his muscles from his bones and shake every ounce of oxygen not only from his lungs but from each cell of his blood.

"You can't," he said flatly. "A man died because of me."

How had he carried this weight for so long? I knew loss. I knew how the pain of losing a loved one scarred the heart so it never beat the same again. But this...to have every good memory knotted to guilt, and to have that guilt then tied to the idea of love...

"And I'm alive because of you," I countered, feeling how he tensed, surprised by my claim.

He took a deep breath and released it with a low curse. "It's not enough."

He was so...good. So heroic and protective, tender and loyal. When I thought of him, those were the only things that came to mind. It was strange to describe someone in those words, but what other ones did I have? I didn't know if his eyes were blue or brown. If his skin was as pale as snow or dark as coffee. If his hair was black or blond. I was an artist. All my life, I've relied on sight to describe a person in my mind and translate that onto a page.

But I didn't have that with Dare. All I had were words that made me feel like I saw him better—saw the real him. All the parts a person didn't need eyes to see.

Even the feel of his face hadn't painted a picture of him quite as clearly as his actions did. The way he took care of me. The softness of his touch. The utter devotion of his protection.

The Villain

And the pain he caused himself as penance for a guilt that didn't belong to him.

He didn't deserve the way he treated himself. Even if he wasn't mine, I had to be the one to make him see that.

"What would be enough?" I probed, inching myself closer to him. "Their everlasting hatred? Your own death?"

"It should've been me. I was the one who trusted her. I'm responsible for Ryan's death. I should've been the one who died that day." He tried to pull away, but I wouldn't let him.

"Instead, you've been the one who's died every day since."

He stilled. "What?"

"You gave them information—the best you had and to the best of your ability—like Prometheus gave fire to the humans. You gave them something you thought had potential. For good or for bad. You didn't force them to use it—"

"No, but I fought like hell for them to listen to me, to act—"

"You made a decision. They made a decision. It ended tragically. But that doesn't make you responsible for his death." Another tear made its way down my cheek. I couldn't see, but I could see him. I could see the layers of man and muscle ripped open by his own hands. By the sharp claws of guilt sinking into the depths of his vulnerability and shredding it until there was nothing left but a tortured soul. "How many days have you ripped yourself apart because of this?" I whispered.

"Too many." His jaw flexed. "Not enough."

"What will be enough?"

"Athena..." He couldn't wipe my tears away fast enough. "Please, you can't fix this. I'm not worth it."

Once again, I felt *more* because of the darkness that engulfed me. I felt his desolation. His isolation. And I felt my heart break.

"But you are," I murmured, my fingers finding their way

over his cheekbones to the bridge of his nose, and from there, down until I felt the softness of his lips. "You are worthy."

His groan rumbled against my fingertips. "No, Athena, you don't know me—"

"You're wrong. I might not know what you look like or all about your past, but I know the scent of you like my lungs know oxygen. I know how your voice changes when you're worried or when you're calm. I know the gentleness of your touch. The bravery of your heart—"

"Enough." He tried to pull away, but I wouldn't let go.

"Is it me? Am I not worth it?"

Suddenly, I was against him, his arm barricading my back from all escape. "Never say that," he rasped, his forehead pressing to mine.

"Then what is it?"

"You deserve better." His lips were close, the rush of warm air that carried each word caressed my own.

My head swayed a little. He didn't understand. Not at all.

I might be blind, but Dare was the one who couldn't see.

"Better?" I murmured, tipping my head and moving my hands to frame his mouth. "There is no one better than you."

His lips were parted in protest when mine pressed to them. He wanted to keep fighting for his own guilt—his own villainy—but I wouldn't let him.

He stood so still, like a stone tomb resting above the ground, housing the soul of a man who deserved to live rather than bury himself alive.

I whimpered and slanted my mouth, pulling closer to him.

The Villain

How could someone have used him that way? To take the trust of a man who was so willing to give everything and then use it against him?

There wasn't any room for jealousy of the woman who'd captured Dare's heart so strongly, only disbelief and pity. She'd forsaken one of the very best of men, and in doing so, had wounded him in a way he wouldn't let heal.

"Athena..." Dare murmured, the whole of him rippling with restraint.

I wished in that moment not for my own sight but for his. For him to see that I wanted him...and that he was deserving.

And so I dragged my tongue along his lips and murmured, "All of your broken pieces, I see them. I see them, and it doesn't change the way I want you."

The groan he made was the sound of stone cracking. Shattering and then crumbling. His tomb breaking open and setting him free.

His arms snaked around me, holding me as the kiss deepened. Now, it was tongues sparring and twisting, the bold strokes painting desire in vibrant shades of red all through my body.

"Dare." I shivered when his hand cupped the back of my neck, letting my head fall back so his mouth could settle on my throat and the thump of my pulse.

I angled toward him, needing to be closer, and shivered when his other hand found my ass and held me tight to the hard length at his waist. My hips rocked forward, and he tensed like I'd just brought him to the edge of a cliff.

His heavy breaths rushed against my neck as he drew back with the painful precision of a man who was defusing a bomb.

"Athena, I can't," he croaked. "I shouldn't—"

"I'm not asking you to," I murmured. "I'm asking you to let me." I reached between us and felt for his cock.

"Let you—" He broke off with a hoarse groan that melted into a hiss, pain and pleasure coming together in the most exquisite way, like rain and sunshine into a rainbow. "Jesus..."

The long ridge filling my hand swelled even thicker, and his arms released me. "You shouldn't—"

He meant to let me go—to push me away and punish himself. But I wouldn't let him. At least, I was going to do everything I could to prevent it.

He'd saved my life, and now I wanted to show him there was no guilt for him to live his. *Or to want me.*

So, I lowered to my knees, the grass cool beneath me.

"What are you doing?" He took my wrists, imprisoning them at his waist, but he couldn't bring himself to move them away.

I tipped my head, staring into darkness as I slid my tongue over my lips. "I want to taste you." I'd never been so bold. Never used words to paint a picture of exactly what I wanted. But there was a comfort in being around him...and a kind of freedom in this cognitive blindfold.

"No, you don't." He ground out, but he still didn't move my hands.

"Why not?"

I could easily distinguish his forced exhale from the soft rush of the breeze.

"Because you don't know what you're in for."

"I don't care. I want you."

He took both my wrists in his one hand, the movement sending both a rush of heat from my core and a knot of panic in my chest. *Was this it? The only thing worse than a fool was one on her knees.*

And then a sound caught my ear—one that sparked hope—and then ignited into a full-blown flame when the subtle peel of a zipper reached my ears.

The Villain

Instantly, every inch of my body came to life. My nipples tightened into my shirt. The ache in my core intensified. And my mouth parted, anticipation making it impossible to swallow.

I couldn't see a single thing, but I felt the moment he pulled his cock free. A wave of relief went through him, reaching all the way to the fingers that imprisoned my hands. The air around me turned thicker. Hotter. Filled with something big and foreign.

"You say you don't care..." He fed one of my hands to his other one, my palm instantly opening like a brazen beggar.

And then thick, soft steel filled my fingers.

His hips jerked the instant I tried to grip him, and he let out a rough curse.

He was big—so big that the adage "seeing is believing" wouldn't have been enough. This was the only way I could know—*could believe*—by trying to hold all of him in my grasp.

"You have no idea." He sounded like I was torturing him—like I was killing him with a single touch.

And then he dragged my hand along his length. Inch after inch after inch, until I started to wonder how much more there could be, my body sensing how close my hand drew to my mouth. But then my hand hit something unexpected. Something hard and protruding and...metal.

I gasped, my fingers frantic in their exploration to understand. "What...is this?" The huskiness in my voice betrayed my desire as I fingered each end of the piercings.

Four metal balls protruded from his tip, the cool metal nestled against his straining heat. I'd never...I mean, I knew of genital piercings. Things like a Prince Albert or a Jacob's ladder. But this...

"A magic cross." His voice was stretched to its breathing point, with more roughness than tone.

Magic cross.

My mouth watered over the image my hand painted. His massive length pierced straight through by two bars, leaving four round ends adorning the head of his cock.

"You've tortured yourself long enough," I murmured. "Tonight, let me torture you."

"Athena..." His groan was so deep, I swore it rooted him to the forest floor as I closed my lips over his head.

He felt incredible in my mouth. Soft and hot, my tongue swirled around him before finally licking over his tip, tasting the salty bead of moisture on my tongue.

"*Fuck.*" His control snapped. One hand anchored the back of my head, the other grabbed my chin, forcing it wide to accommodate his piercings.

They felt foreign against my tongue and the roof of my mouth—immovable steel that seemed to make the rest of him feel even larger between my lips than he had in my fingers. But the power they gave me over him was electrifying.

His shivers and grunts became my very favorite compliments as my tongue explored his cock and its hardware. Swirling and licking. Sucking and stroking. The rough curses charging through his lips spurred me just as his hand on my head coaxed—begged me to take more of him.

But I didn't want more. I wanted it all. I wanted all his broken pieces. All the rough edges and sharp corners. All the emotion he bottled up and all the wants he thought he didn't deserve. I wanted every inch of him—*unrestrained*. And I still didn't have that yet.

He still kept the well of his desire in check, and I didn't want that. I wanted his vulnerability. Needed it. So, I drew him deeper—sucked harder. All those inches deep into my mouth, headed for my throat as saliva dripped down my chin.

"Torture me? You're going to kill me, Angel."

Angel. I stilled—a memory hitting me that had no place in

this moment. A memory of another time. Another man. And then it was gone. Replaced by the very large, very real savior in front of me.

I slid my hand to cup his balls, and he lost it. His hand braced my head as he thrust deep, the tip of him knocking against the back of my throat, making me choke.

"Is this what you had in mind?" he growled, angry at himself as he tried to pull back.

But I wouldn't let him. My hands found anchor on the sides of his thighs, holding tight as I did my best to nod, *Yes*.

"My broken pieces weren't enough, you wanted my pierced cock, too," he said, fisting my hair and angling me so he could push deep again. "You deserve better than this." But the strain in his voice confessed he couldn't stop himself now.

And I didn't want him to.

I flicked my tongue along his length, enjoying the soft curses it ripped from his lips.

"But you look so beautiful. God, I've never seen anything this beautiful." He spoke like he knew I needed to hear him. "The way your lips are stretched around me. You're drooling like such a good girl."

I held tight while he used my mouth like a man undone. I took and took and took everything he was willing to give, feeling my own pleasure swell like a wave of fire between my legs.

"Fuck," he rasped, the husk of his voice reaching between my thighs. "This is going to end me. Is that what you wanted? To kill me with your lips?"

I moaned, and the sound tightened my throat around him.

"Fuck." He jerked free.

I gasped in a breath, searching the darkness for him as I murmured, "Isn't that what you want?"

"Not even close," he swore, his fingers framing my chin, his thumb running back and forth over my swollen, tingly bottom lip. "I want to have my fingers buried inside you. My tongue. My cock. I want to put every piece of me inside you like you can make me whole again."

I shivered. "Yes."

"But you can't," he warned. "You think I'm a good man. I'm not. I've dreamed about your breasts since the other night. The way they hung heavy in front of you when you fell. How red the hot water made your nipples." He let out a harsh laugh. "The water and soap didn't hide them from me, did you know that? I looked my fucking fill as I fingered you—"

"I didn't know," I interrupted boldly. "But I hoped."

"Dammit, Athena..."

"I won't hate you," I pressed. "I know you want me to. I know you want everyone to so you feel justified in hating yourself, but I won't. I refuse."

"I could make you hate me," he rumbled, and then he pressed his tip back to my lips.

My tongue darted out to catch a taste before he was gone. "You could try."

"Touch yourself," he ordered. "Touch yourself like I did the other night. Make that sweet little pussy of yours come like a good girl."

I didn't need more encouragement for my hand to reach between my legs and find the aching bud of my clit.

Stars exploded as I rubbed myself. I was so turned on by the way he ravaged my mouth that I could come without any touch. But I wanted to please him. God, I wanted to please him.

"Please, Dare," I begged, my body spiraling higher.

"Such a good girl, my angel." His thumb pressed on my bottom lip, forcing my teeth to release it. "So good...too good... the second I'm back in your mouth, I'm going to come."

Between his words, I heard the steady drag of his hand along his length, simultaneously giving himself some relief while holding himself at bay.

"Yes," I murmured, my toes curling against the dirt.

"That's it...get there so I can fuck your beautiful face."

I gasped as my orgasm ripped through me like I'd stepped on a landmine. My body tightened and exploded in violent pleasure, but the scream that welled in the center of my chest never made it free.

His cock pushed through my rounded lips all the way to the back of my throat, spearing my scream with the point of his promise.

My moans, my gasps for air, they all crumbled around the invasion of his cock. Thrust after thrust after thrust, his piercings marked their very own path to the back of my throat. And then, above the sparkling pleasure of my release and the feral feel of him in my mouth, I heard him—the roar of a man slain.

Or perhaps the roar of a man rising from the dead.

The sound barreled out around us as he came deep in my throat, my tongue trying to swallow down the thick heat of his release. There was too much of it—or too much of him in my mouth—that everything overflowed, leaking from the corners of my lips and running down my chin.

"Fuck." He let off the pressure, air instantly filling deep into my lungs. I'd forgotten the essential nature of breathing until he'd slid his length from my mouth, and I sputtered for breath.

Resting back on my heels, my body fought to stabilize itself, but my mind only searched for him. The taste of him on my tongue. The scent of him was still pinned to my nostrils. And the sound of him—his rough breaths and the slick sound of flesh on flesh.

"Dare..." My voice hardly existed after the way he'd claimed my throat.

His only response was another low groan, followed by a soft patter, almost like raindrops on leaves. I inhaled sharply. *He was still coming...but onto the grass next to us.*

"Shit, I'm sorry." He huffed, and I heard the rustle of his pants and zipper as he tucked himself away. "That was—I was—"

"Incredible."

The air bent and warmed as he crouched in front of me. "You're incredible." His palm framed my cheek, and I let my eyes flutter closed as he wiped my lips and chin clean with his shirtsleeve. "Let's go inside."

Strong hands didn't just help me up, they reached under my knees and around my back, lifting me entirely off earth and into his arms.

"Dare..."

"Shh."

I settled against his shoulder, listening to the steady beat of his heart as he brought us back inside. I didn't speak, afraid to break the tenderness of the moment as he carefully set me on the bed.

"Don't move."

Heavy footsteps. The rush of the faucet. The sound he made when he cleaned himself. And then heat of his return. The warmth of his palm on my knee.

"Spread your legs."

I did...but far wider than he needed.

"Goddamn." His hand tightened.

He hauled me to the edge of the bed and covered me with his mouth.

"Dare," I gasped, clutching his head as his tongue fluttered over my sensitive clit.

The Villain

Instantly, I was spiraling again. Toward the cloudless sky. Toward the constellations. Toward release. I clawed his head as he ate me like a man starved.

"So fucking good," he growled. "Couldn't help myself, Angel."

I shivered. There was still something about the way he called me Angel.

I started to tip and tilt, surely a trick of my mind on my body. The world shouldn't be shifting. Tipping. Except it was.

I let out a cry as he moved backward and took me with him. My arms shot out, though it was his hold that kept me from landing anywhere but on his face.

"Are you okay?" I tried to move off of him, but he wouldn't let me.

"I'll be okay when you stop worrying about me," he groused.

I knew the words were meant to be superficial—a careless order—but there was a depth to them I couldn't help but hear: the depths of a broken man who didn't want to take anyone down with his self-inflicted misery.

"Dare..." I moaned when his tongue slid through my folds, the firm velvet marking a path from my entrance to my clit.

"Stop talking, Athena. Stop worrying," he ordered, dipping his tongue inside me. "Now, be a good girl and fuck my face."

My back bowed with pleasure, my body obeying his command. I ground into his hungry mouth, rocking against the torture of his tongue.

"Good girl," he cooed, using his teeth to scrape along my clit.

"Dare," I panted, rocking faster. Harder.

Could I break his face? Was it possible? I didn't know—couldn't see—*couldn't care.* And then his grip tightened on my ass as though he knew what I was thinking, and he urged me on—begged me to use his mouth like he'd used mine.

"God, yes," I hummed, my head tipping back.

His tongue swirled and flicked with the expertise of a painter's brush, creating a masterpiece of pleasure. I twisted my fingers in his hair, whimpering as I barreled toward another climax. And then his lips closed around my clit and sucked, and it was like a lightning bolt straight to my chest.

Thousands of volts of pleasure right to my core.

And then he did it again.

I came again, but this time, my cry blistered around us. It was too much—too intense. My heart galloped out of my chest. My lungs refused all oxygen. And for a second—a single split second—I swore I saw the shadowed outline of a man between my legs, the vague shadows of his scarred face hungrily devouring my pussy. And then the split second was gone, leaving nothing but the drowning sensation of his tongue milking my clit.

By the time any semblance of reality started to come back, I was convinced I'd imagined the image of him—an image that was both reality and fantasy at the same time.

"Good girl," he rumbled against my sex, dragging his tongue in one more firm lick over me.

Darkness sparkled around me, my orgasm glittering the pitch black with a myriad of colored flecks. I hardly realized when he was lifting me and laying me back on the bed. Now, my limbs felt like stranded stars, waiting for gravity to pull them back into a familiar shape.

The warm fog of my orgasm eventually shifted into the cozy comfort of the sheets as he pulled them over me.

Just me.

I felt the small puncture into my blissful bubble. "Dare..." I felt his pause. "Will you stay?"

The Villain

The second pause was even more painful in length.

"You should rest."

That was a no.

His steps were quieter over to the door, almost like he didn't want me to hear him go.

"You won't even go one night without punishing yourself?"

His rough exhale was the brittle skeleton of a laugh. "To only have one night with you would be a punishment for every night for the rest of my life," he said with such painstaking sincerity that my heart was still floating in the words when the door clicked shut behind him.

Chapter Fourteen

Dare

I jolted awake when my foot fell off the edge of the couch. Not fell—I *was pushed*. Ty stood at the end, his arms crossed and a frown stretching over his face.

"Yeah," I croaked and rubbed my face. "What's up?"

His head cocked. "Why are you torturing yourself?"

I grimaced, burying down a groan as I sat up on the couch. I'd slept on the leather sofa in the rec room every night since Athena had taken over my cabin. One more dumb thing to add to my list of idiocies; there was a guest cabin with a perfectly good bed, but I couldn't bring myself to sleep there. Not when I felt like I needed to be here—guarding the hallway and the elevator like there'd ever been a time or a possibility for someone to break into the compound.

I rubbed my face. "Not you, too."

"Someone has to. You're almost handling this badly in an impressive way at this point."

I stilled, looked at him, and then laughed. "Fuck you."

The Villain

"I'm serious, Dare. Enough is enough." He took a tone I hadn't heard before—at least around me. It was almost... parental.

"I'm handling it—handling myself." Lies tasted like acid on my tongue—the image of Athena, a fallen angel on her knees, her mouth stuffed full of my cock, and begging for more—more of all my broken pieces that would inevitably tear her apart. "Fuck," I hissed and ran a hand roughly through my hair.

"Yeah, seems that way." His sarcasm was unmistakable.

Tension pulsed through me. "Is that what you woke me for? To give me shit?"

"No, I came to tell you that I confirmed Athena's story." His jaw pulsed. "Her account hasn't been accessed since the deposit; I have the recorded call where she asked the bank to freeze it because of suspicious activity and worried it was her almost ex-husband trying to stall the divorce."

I tried to swallow but self-loathing swelled in my throat. Of course, Rob had told Ty to confirm the information. Like we all needed more proof that I was the fucking villain here.

"Yeah." I stood. "Is that it? Because we have a lead I should be exploring."

It was early-fucking-o'clock in the morning, but what the hell. Crime didn't sleep. At least if I went to Ivans's house this early, I wouldn't be tempted to go back to my cabin and sit there and wait for her to wake up.

I grabbed my jacket off the back of the couch where I'd thrown it last night, my brain too scrambled to think about anything but her. The feel of her. The taste of her. *God, I was so fucked.* Like Lucifer imprisoned by Persephone in his own hell.

"No, it's not." He grabbed my arm, meeting my surprised stare. "I'm worried about you."

My jaw locked. "Don't be."

Harm was the leader of our unit—the president of our Vigilante club—but there was something about Ty that was like a father to the rest of us. Maybe because he was a little bit older than the rest of us, or maybe it was this—the way he stepped in when the rest of us took something too far. Like his duty extended beyond justice, but to take care of the rest of us, too.

"Like I said, you're failing at hiding your feelings for Athena in an impressive way at this point," he rumbled and then lowered his voice. "You need to stop punishing yourself for Amira."

"Dammit." I pinched the bridge of my nose like I could cut off the memories. "How I feel about Athena has nothing to do with Amira—Athena knows about Amira. She knows..." Too late, I realized what I'd revealed.

"You told her?" He gaped at me.

Last night was the first time I'd spoken that story out loud since...since it happened. The guys—the unit knew what happened, and Rob knew because Harm had told her, but that was it. I'd never told anyone about Amira who hadn't been there—been a part of the fallout—until Athena.

"I had to." I brushed him off. "After the way I treated her, she needed to know why."

"Bullshit."

I fought to remain unfazed. "Why else would I tell her?"

"Because you care about her," he said simply like it was just one more of his unbreakable facts.

"Of course, I do—"

"Because you want her to care about you."

"No." I shook my head. "I'm trying to keep her away from me."

"And you're doing that by staying with her in your cabin into the middle of the night?"

The Villain

Shit. I hissed out a breath. Of course, he saw. He saw everything.

"What do you want from me?" I said, my voice thick.

"For you to stop punishing yourself. Ryan would want it, too."

"I'll stop when you do the same. Just because you're better at hiding it doesn't mean I don't see that we carry the same weight." The words were out before I could stop them, but there was nothing I could do to take them back, no matter how the sudden wounded expression on his face made me want to.

Ty hadn't only lost Ryan. After we came home, he'd signed on for one more mission with his oldest friend and mentor, and that mission had claimed his life, too.

Ty stepped in front of me. We were similarly built and matched in size, but there was an invisible weight to him—something that was both a shield and a weapon the way it protected him and wounded me.

"If I had someone who cared to fight for me—who gave me peace—I would," he said, his voice low.

"She doesn't—" I exhaled deeply and protested once more. "She doesn't give me peace; she doesn't even know who I am."

His head lowered. "She might not know your full name, but you just told me she knows more about you than any of us."

"No, she knows what you know."

"Wrong," he countered. "We know what happened. She knows what happened to you. There's a huge fucking difference."

I gritted my teeth, fighting against his statement. There couldn't be a difference. *She couldn't be different.*

"I'm going to check out the address," I declared, moving away from the conversation like it was a tightly packed explosive. I reached the door before I turned and asked, "Are you coming or am I going alone?"

"I'll meet you out there."

We pulled into the development right at the time when half a dozen soccer moms were out for their morning runs, all of them staring at us, leathered up on our Harleys like we were death eaters from another realm rather than bikers.

We were out of place, there was no doubt about it. Even at a slow speed, the rumble of our bikes gnawed straight through the perfectly crafted middle-class background noise. Lawn mowers. Pool splashes.

Ty followed me down the dead-end street. The houses were straight out of the American dream storybook. Two-story monstrosities landscaped to perfection. The one we were looking for was just before the cul-de-sac and obscured by two massive trees in the front lawn.

"We should make this quick," I said after we parked at the curb. Nothing like getting the cops called on us while we were hunting a criminal they couldn't manage to catch.

The house we wanted had a white brick exterior with all the windows drawn shut. Compared to the neighboring homes, the lawn was less kept up on. The house a little dirtier. From a distance, it fit in, but up close, it wasn't cared for—a good indication that it wasn't somewhere to live but somewhere to hide.

"Yeah." Ty agreed, his stare calmly tracking every detail of our surroundings like he was preparing for another ambush. "I'll take the front."

"Got it." We strode up the driveway, at the end, he veered for the path to the front door, and I ducked around back.

The upkeep was practically nonexistent behind the house.

Weeds were overgrown everywhere. The grass wasn't cut. *What the hell was this place?* I moved onto the concrete patio, positioning myself closer to the house and resting my hand on my weapon. I peered through the window.

Kitchen to my right. Dining table to my left. A doorway into the living room—*Athena's paintings*. I tensed, seeing the stack of three propped against the couch. And then on the floor —*blood*.

"Dammit," I swore and reached for the handle, the bad feeling in my gut growing when I found the door unlocked.

The smell of death was the first thing to hit me when it opened. It was the kind of smell you couldn't forget, not when I'd breathed my fill of it overseas. I cleared the space in swift, silent movements, making my way around the island and then the table and chairs over to where blood streaked on the floor, leading me to—

"Dare."

I spun and instantly lowered my weapon, seeing Ty in the doorway to the living room.

"Front door was open."

"So was the back." I holstered my gun and stared at the two dead bodies on the floor, a gun in each of their hands. The one closest to me was face-up, blood covering the front of his shirt from three bullet holes. "It's Brandon." I held my breath as I bent forward and took a closer look to confirm; meanwhile, Ty crouched by the other body that was farther away.

Well, now we knew where Brandon had gone—and why we couldn't find him. I'd have to tell Athena—

"Dare..." Ty turned and looked at me, his expression unreadable. "It's Ivans."

I stilled and then straightened. *No.* "No," I echoed my thoughts, moving to stand beside him. *It couldn't be...*"Shit."

It was.

Ray Ivans was dead. Shot by Athena's ex-husband, from the looks of it.

"Shit." I repeated the curse on a deep exhale, staring at the still body of a man we weren't even sure was alive for almost two decades, and when we did realize he was, we weren't sure we'd ever track him down.

I crouched and scanned the still lines of his face. The facial reconstruction he'd gone through made him appear nothing like the doctor who'd told Rob's parents not to worry. He looked younger than he was, though gray peeked at the edge of his hairline. And from this angle, up close, the scars of his surgeries framed his face like the seal between past and present.

"I'll call Rorik," Ty muttered, rising and reaching for his phone.

Someone needed to break down the scene and do an autopsy on the bodies, and it was probably better that it wasn't the police.

It seemed too easy—too unreal for the man we'd been hunting for years—to wind up dead in our laps. I should be thrilled. Fucking elated. Ivans was dead, and that meant Athena was safe. Instead, I thought about last night. I thought about the way she gave me her mouth and then her body, the taste of her sweet pussy like oxygen on my lips.

I remembered the way she'd responded to the truth about my past—the truth of what had broken me. Christ. And when Athena begged to touch me, I almost revealed the rest of my sordid trauma: that I hadn't let a woman touch me since. But no matter how much I revealed, it changed nothing, certainly not the truth. I wasn't her savior; I was simply the first man to break her heart.

"How many days have you ripped yourself apart over this?"

I wondered how many times I would remember her words before I forgot the sound of them from her lips or the unspoken plea to forgive myself. She couldn't fix me. And if she knew the truth, she wouldn't want to.

Yet, I opened up to her. I gave her part of my past and let her feel her fill. I suffered every painstaking touch, barely breathed when she found the heads of my piercings—the cross I'd nailed my celibacy to—and then died under the heat of her mouth. What kind of man was I to fuck her mouth like I had? So rough and savage. To unload so much cum I had to pull out and empty the last of it onto the grass. Sure, my cock hadn't felt a woman's touch in a decade, but this was more than that. This was her.

My undoing was all her.

And she'd wanted me to stay, even after all my broken pieces had cut and scraped her in order to get close.

And now, I had the proof it was safe to let her go. The thing I'd wanted from the start. Her safety. *Her distance.* And I should be relieved. She deserved better than me. Better than my apology. Better than all my broken shards. I was nothing more than a means to her safety, and now, my purpose was fulfilled. *Finished.*

So why couldn't I stop wondering what would happen if I gave in? If I stopped walking away from her and stayed instead?

"Does this scene make sense?"

"What?" I shook off my thoughts and refocused on Ty; he was snapping photos of the crime scene with his phone, documenting all of the details so he could examine it all later.

"Does the position of their bodies seem strange to you?" He looked between the bodies. "If they shot each other, wouldn't they both be facing up?"

My head cocked. Brandon was on his back with the three gunshot wounds to his chest, but Ivans was on his stomach.

"He was hit in his shoulder." I point to the wound. "It

could've made him turn as he was going down." *Possible, but was it plausible?*

"I guess we'll see what Rorik has to say," he said, finishing up his photos. "I wonder how long they've been dead."

"Brandon escaped four days ago." I wrinkled my nose. "I'd bet around then."

"So, Ivans busted him out of police custody and then killed him?"

"He was a loose end." *And a piece of shit.* "At some point, he would've tied the bomb back to Ivans."

Ty made a rumbling noise, and I couldn't tell if it was agreement or uncertainty.

"You'll wait for Rorik?" I said, stepping over Ivans toward the front door. "I'm going to head back."

"To tell her?"

My lip twitched. "To take her home."

He stilled. "You think that's wise?"

"Brandon and Ivans are dead," I said tightly. "She's not in danger anymore."

"You should wait for Rorik to confirm—"

"Why?" I didn't let him finish. "Even if someone else was here—if someone else did this—the only reason Athena was targeted was because of Ivans, and now he's dead."

"That may be—"

"So, then what's your concern?" I demanded.

"That you're not thinking," he said low.

My fist balled at my side. "This is the first clear thought I've had since I brought her back to Sherwood."

She was safe. Yes, she still couldn't see, but that didn't require her to stay in my cabin. In my bed. She could go home. Be comfortable. Be in a place that was familiar to her. Try to get back to some semblance of her life. And then she could forget about me.

"Is it? Or are you just afraid of what will happen when she realizes who you are?"

I stilled with my hand on the doorknob. "I'm not afraid of what will happen—I know what will happen, and I'm trying to spare her any more pain."

The past should be left in the past, and I was her past.

I turned, stalking through the door. As I closed it, I noticed a dark sedan parked across the street start its engine and slowly pull away. *Goddammit, Ty.* Now, instead of seeing nosy neighbors, I was seeing danger where there was none.

"Is it true?" Rob stood in the hallway, blocking my path.

My chin lowered. "Ivans is dead."

I caught the way she shuddered, relief and rage rippling through her small form. She was happy, but she wished it had been her to face him—to end him.

"Are you okay?"

"Ty thinks there was a third shooter." She changed topics, and her tone had me thinking she had her own ideas of who the third shooter could be.

"Ty can think what he wants," I said and approached. "Even if there was, Ivans was the crux—the keystone of this whole damn thing. Finding him. Framing him. Whatever the hell the plan was, it ended with his life. Along with the danger to Athena's."

Her eyes widened. "Are you going to tell her?"

I nodded. "And then I'm going to take her home." I walked around her, hoping to make that the end of our conversation.

"Dare..."

I let out a breath and called the elevator, preparing myself for one more criticism—one more clear critique of my innumerable failures.

"She's starting to see shadows."

My head snapped to the side, the truth written all over her face: I was on borrowed time.

If I didn't get Athena out of my life now, I'd have to tell her that one more man she'd trusted was a liar.

Chapter Fifteen

Athena

"You're back."

His scent. His steps. They were all familiar at first. But now, there was a shadow to him. A kind of phantom darkness that took over the foggy screen of my sight.

I couldn't believe it when I woke up earlier and saw...light. It was fuzzy. Like cotton or wool pulled over the sun, but the total darkness was gone, replaced by a cloudy reality of light and shadow.

And Dare's shadow was big—big and suddenly still as my head followed his movements.

"You can see."

"Shadows." But it was something. *Hope.* And then he was in front of me, the whole of him still invading the rest of my senses like they'd never get enough. "Dare..."

His hand pressed to my cheek, holding it like I was something fragile—a flower to be crushed if he wasn't careful. And there was something about his touch that was familiar in a way it hadn't been before. Something that went deeper than this moment, all the way down to the depths of a memory. *But of what?*

I was going crazy. Foolishly burying the seeds of his tenderness and hoping he'd let them grow into something more.

"We just got back from Ivans's house." *Straight to business.*

The first thing Rob told me this morning when she'd come was that Dare and Ty had gone to the address on the invoice. I wanted whatever answers they'd uncovered, but for some reason, not as much as I wanted answers about last night.

Had he left because of what he told me? Because he thought I would see him differently now, knowing what kind of betrayal he suffered? Or was it me that kept him away—was it what happened afterward that brought his barbed-wire walls back up?

Whatever the answer, it would have to wait until he said what he came here to say—something I should be more concerned about considering it was my life in jeopardy.

"Was he there? Do you know why he wants me dead?" My heart thudded, as I was able to discern how he lowered his head. "What is it?"

"We found him," he said slowly. "Brandon, too."

My jaw slackened. The idea that my ex-husband had been so easily swayed to try and kill me was still a hard pill to swallow.

"They're both dead, Athena."

Dead. For as prone to earthquakes as California was, none of the numerous times the ground had shaken were felt by anyone but me—because the quake belonged inside my mind. A boom that rippled through the thick shadows. *Brandon was dead.* My heart leaped into my throat.

Dare's hands bracketed my arms, and that was when I knew I'd started to sway. "Athena."

"He...I never..." A hot tear sped over my cheek. "I never... would've wanted this."

Even after everything, I never would've wished him dead.

"I would," Dare declared without missing a beat, his hand leaving my arm to brush off the droplet from my cheek. "For hurting you. For trying to kill you." He exhaled forcefully, continuing to guard my cheeks from the second charge of tears.

It was hard to believe this was the same man who had the willpower to walk away last night when I'd asked him to stay.

I tipped my head, the shadow of his face so close. The dark dips and lighter swells. *I could almost...*

He moved away, taking his hold with him.

"What happened?"

"They were both at the house."

"So, it was Rich—Ray—who helped Brandon escape, and then he killed him?" I shook my head, trying to unscramble my thoughts. "Why?"

"To tie up loose ends."

My nod turned into a steady bob as thoughts tipped my head back and forth like a buoy caught on the tide.

"Athena..."

"They're both gone...the men who wanted me dead," I said weakly.

"Ivans was the root of all of this—the bomb, the money—" Dare huffed. "You're safe."

"Safe," I repeated slowly. Funny how one four-letter word could change so many things.

I was safe from the men who wanted me dead...but ironically, I was also now safe from needing Dare's protection. The one thing I no longer needed but wanted.

"So, what happens now?"

His shadow turned to stone, and we stood there, letting the

seconds stretch into silence as though the weaver of time needed a head start before we could move forward again.

"You don't need to stay a prisoner here any longer."

Prisoner. What a word to use when the only thing he'd ever made me feel, truly, was precious.

"I see," I muttered and winced, realizing too late how tongue-in-cheek my reply was.

"You're safe. Free..."

Free from everything but wanting him.

"I know..."

"Don't you want to go home?" he asked low, the question driving the wedge deep he wanted to use to separate himself from me.

He knew I couldn't say no...because to say I wanted to stay meant I'd have to ignore all the signs he wanted me gone.

"Of course," I answered, feigning a small smile as though *home* was the only thought on my mind for the last four weeks and not *him*.

I wouldn't ask about last night—not after the things he'd shared with me. The man who'd saved my life was tortured and wounded. And since when did any wounded creature let someone close because they demanded it or because they were backed into a corner? Never.

I wanted him to trust me again with his vulnerability, not to have to beg him for it. And if that wasn't possible, then I'd learn to live with it. I'd learn to live without my sight for weeks, and if I could do that, I could certainly learn to live without the desire he ignited.

"Rorik—Dr. Nilsen said being home might help your brain heal faster. Something about being in a safe space."

"That's good." *Where was all my hope? All my optimism? Why couldn't I seem to care about anything I'd just gained when it came with the price of losing him?*

The Villain

"I'll help you get your things."

My mouth felt like a funnel piled high with emotions, but my tongue wouldn't let anything except a *thank you* pass. The shuffle of clothes and belongings set the shadows in my sight to music. A crescendo of connection that would quickly fade into the soft silence of separation.

"Oh." His footsteps came closer. "We found your paintings at the house."

"Oh, good." My art. My show. *The future I'd started to create.* For some reason, it didn't seem real. Like a painting with a tear in the canvas. No matter how I tried to paint around it, there was something unalterably changed by what had happened. Something I couldn't gloss over. *Because I'd met him.*

"When they finish with the scene, I can take them to your house or the gallery." He could return all the pieces of me back to the way he'd found them.

"The house is fine. Thank you."

He grunted. "I think I have everything."

"There wasn't much," I said, unable to keep the sadness from my voice. It felt like I'd lived a whole other life here in this safe house, but in reality, it was nothing more than borrowed time with a broken brain.

His shadow loomed closer, and his arm reached out and then dropped. He struggled to reach for me, and he either forgot or didn't realize that I could see enough now to make that out.

"Are you ready?"

When I nodded, he reached for my hand and guided me from the cabin like before—a steady touch to let me know he was there, murmuring instructions or warnings when we approached any stairs or steps. He made it easy to rely on him—

too easy to trust him to take care of me even in my most vulnerable moments.

And all I wanted was to make it that easy for him.

The concrete echoed our concerted steps, but this time, he led me in a different direction through the garage.

"Put this on." He released my hand, only to slide something heavy and thick over my shoulders. *A leather jacket.* My fingertips crept over the firm fabric, the worn creases, and the emblems stitched into the sleeves.

"What is this for?" I slid my arms into the sleeves.

"We're taking my bike."

I'd never been on a motorcycle before. For all the risks and gambles Brandon liked to take, motorcycles had never been one of them.

But sitting on the back of the massive bike, holding onto its equally massive driver, I never felt safer. Maybe safe was a relative term. My life was no longer in danger; my heart, though, remained in the greatest peril.

I closed my eyes behind the helmet, my body moving and swaying with the meandering shape of the roads, the bike like a rubber-coated paintbrush, bleeding a soot-streaked path back to my house.

I could tell when we got closer. The familiar pattern of turns off the highway. The slower speed. The heartbeat-like reel of shadows blurring through my broken brain. It wasn't only the jacket he'd given me—there were also the large aviators underneath the visor of the helmet. Now that I had a vague distinction between light and shadow, the temptation to look—to stare—was even greater.

My body pressed to the back of his as we slowed, and I knew we were at my house. I felt it—that coming home feeling like a warm quilt over my shoulders.

Once he'd parked, his hand found my waist and guided me off the bike first, following himself a second later. I prayed he didn't feel the flutter of my pulse as he undid my helmet.

"Thank you," I murmured, his shadow blurring across my vision. "For everything."

"Please..." *Don't thank me* went unspoken.

It hit me when he guided me through the front door how glad I was to be home. It was the same feeling when I'd walked through the door after leaving Brandon and Sacramento.

"Athena?" He stepped in front of where I'd stopped. "What is it?"

"I'm sorry. I'm just...happy to be here—to be back." *There was no place like home.*

"I'll set your things in your room," he muttered and carefully placed my hand on the wall to guide me.

His shadow disappeared, and I took a deep breath, cinnamon and must filling my nostrils. Blindfolded or just blind, I'd never not know this place, *and it was the same way I felt about him.*

Gingerly, I moved toward the kitchen. The pulse in my head warned I was straining my eyes—my brain—too much; the shifting shadows I'd clung to all day were now less distinguishable.

I heard him make a noise down the hall, and when my head turned, my foot caught on a stack of boxes, and I cried out.

"Careful—" He was there, steadying me in an instant.

"Sorry, I should've unpacked these long ago," I chided myself.

"It's hard to go back to a place you know when you're no longer the person you used to be," he replied so easily, as though the thought came from his own experience and not just an interpretation of mine.

"Yeah," I murmured, scrambling to say more when my stomach let out a growl.

"Shit." He led me to the kitchen table and tucked me into a seat. Seconds later, I heard him rummaging through the kitchen.

"It's okay. I'm—"

"Hungry," he finished. "I'm going to run to the store down the road. I'll be right back."

"Oh—" I broke off when his hands cupped my face.

"Please, don't move."

My jaw slackened, but the nearness of him made it impossible to do anything but nod. And then he was gone, the sound of the door locking almost as loud as the beat of my heart.

"Oh, Mom." I sighed with a sad smile. "If you only knew."

Carefully, I stood and used my hands to guide me around the table and chairs to the kitchen. At least, I'd managed to unpack all of the kitchen before the accident, so there were no boxes to worry about.

The boxes...

Since I'd moved home, I'd had plenty of time to unpack everything I'd brought back from Sacramento and everything I'd never taken with me—"*We don't need your mom's old things, Athena. We'll buy new.*" Brandon's voice echoed in my head. God, I couldn't believe he was gone; I hadn't even truly gotten through believing he'd tried to kill me, and now he was gone.

Like Mom.

Everything here reminded me of Mom, and I thought it was guilt that kept me from unpacking and settling in. As though I were taking over her space—*her memory*. But coming back like this—*blind*—made it clear that Dare was right.

I wasn't afraid of losing her memory because I didn't need sight to hold on to it. I was afraid of facing the person I was now...because she certainly wasn't the same Athena who'd left here all those years ago.

Was I smarter now? Stronger? Or was I broken, too, for putting my love and trust in someone who'd betrayed me?

Would I ever be able to trust and love someone again?

Had it already happened?

I gripped the edge of the counter, my head lowering, just as I heard a noise outside. I stilled. *Was that footsteps out back?*

My heart instantly vaulted into overdrive. *Oh god.* What if I wasn't safe? What if there was something else—someone else?

I sank down onto the floor, banging my back against the handle of the cabinet. I bit into my lip hard enough to prevent a sound but not enough to stop my tears of pain. Of fear.

What if this was it?

What if, after all that—everything we'd been through—I never got the chance to tell Dare how I felt?

The patio door handle jiggled. I swore it did. *Or was it the front?* Because a second later, the front door opened.

"I'm back," Dare called.

"Dare!" I cried out—choked out. I couldn't even tell.

Heavy footsteps brought him to me in an instant, and the grocery bag landed with a thud beside me.

"Athena—*Jesus.*" Dare lifted me up and pulled me against him.

"I'm sorry. I'm sorry—"

"What is it? What happened?"

"I thought..." I inhaled a big breath. "I'm sorry. I thought I heard someone at the back door, and I panicked." *For no reason, because everyone who'd tried to kill me was dead.* "I'm sorry. I don't know what's wrong—"

"Don't," he warned. "Stay here. I'm going to make sure everything is okay."

I nodded, listening to the mixed sounds of footsteps and metal and the sliding door opening and then closing. For however long it took him, time had a sound. A pulse. It beat like a living drum until I heard the door again.

"Just me."

My exhale whooshed from my lungs. "I'm sorry," I murmured, shaking my head. "I don't know what came over me. My mind got carried away."

"Don't apologize." His low voice was close, and then his hand was on my shoulder. Fear brought the darkness back, but his touch felt like light trying to break in. "Hang on."

"Why—oof." I hardly processed what he said before strong hands lifted me by my waist and hoisted me onto the counter.

He paused, holding me there for extra seconds like there was something that rooted him in place.

"You're safe," he rumbled low, the warmth of his breath close enough to reach my cheeks. And then it was the warmth of his hands that I felt framing my face and the press of his forehead to my own. "I promise you're safe."

There was no room for fear when he held me like this—imprisoned between wanting to push me away and needing to pull me closer. But there was something...something nagging my mind like a loose string begging to be pulled. A string in which my mind tangled.

Memories from high school bombarded this moment in an attack I hadn't expected. Memories of how Darius would hold my face. How he'd smile and promise me his love and then kiss me until up was down and down was up and we were kissing on clouds.

"What is it?" Dare rumbled, breaking me from my thoughts.

I reached for his wrists, anchoring myself to the present, and let out the last of the tension from my lungs, along with the memory trying to hold me in its net.

"I had my first kiss on this counter, like this."

He shuddered, and I knew I'd lost him. "I'm going to make some food." And then he pulled away.

My eyes drifted shut, letting the sounds he made paint a picture in my mind of his big frame moving through the small kitchen. I heard the ding and clatter of the toaster oven being set. The sound of plastic unwrapping. The steady in and out of his breaths.

"What are you making?"

"Grilled cheese."

I shivered, feeling the urge to protest tie a knot in my chest. Grilled cheese was a gateway to more fond memories of my high school boyfriend, who'd make us grilled cheese on the nights when Mom worked her second job.

Why was I thinking about Darius so much?

Was it being back at Mom's house? *But I'd been here for months.* Was it because of Brandon? Losing another man who promised to love me...but didn't?

Or was it because I was afraid of losing this man? *Dare.* A man I hadn't seen but knew his scarred face better than I knew my own. Was it because I was afraid of losing one more person I cared for without understanding why?

I swallowed down those thoughts, and instead, shared a different memory.

"I used to sit on the counter while my mom cleaned the kitchen floors every week. She'd band towels around her feet, step in a bucket of soapy water, and then shuffle them over the floor.

"And then you'd do the same to dry."

My breath caught as my heart faltered. "How did you know?"

He hesitated. "Lucky guess."

The toaster dinged. A few seconds later, I bit back a smile at his low curse of pain. *He'd tried to grab the molten sandwich with his bare hands.*

"Tell me a story about your friend," I murmured as he moved in front of me, his chest brushing my knees.

A deep noise groused from his chest, and I could practically hear the muscle of his jaw locking as he reached for my hand. But he had no choice; it was the only way to give me my food.

"Eat," he instructed as he stepped back as I brought the sandwich to my mouth.

I shivered as I inhaled a deep breath of the warm, cheesy goodness. Scent and taste went into overdrive as I took the first bite, the taste so familiar it was like my tongue was set on a memory.

"Dammit." His angry curse brought me back to the moment.

I swallowed the bite and asked, "Are you okay?" *Had I been moaning?*

"Yeah."

I took my second bite more carefully, opting for a straightforward compliment this time. "This is amazing. Thank you."

He grunted, "You're welcome."

Another few seconds passed, and I found myself returning to the question he'd left unanswered—wanting him to trust me with a little more of the good now that he'd laid out the whole of the bad.

"My mom had cancer—died of cancer. I knew it was coming; we both did. I thought knowing...would make me ready for it." I sighed. "It didn't."

The Villain

"I'm sorry, Athena."

I took another bite, and when I finished, I said, "When it got close to the end, I was...a mess, but my mom, she had this way of making painful things bearable. Even little things like..."

"Cleaning the kitchen floors?"

A laugh bubbled through my lips. "Yeah, like that. I swear she could turn anything for good." My inhale was cut short by the brush of his thumb on my cheek; I didn't realize I was crying.

"That sounds like...quite a superpower."

"She was quite a superhero," I returned softly, taking another bite as I fought the urge to cry. "At the end, I begged her not to leave me, and she told me that everyone dies twice."

"Twice?" He drew his hand back.

"The first time is when our life ends, and the second...is when people stop sharing our stories."

His chest inflated sharply, loading oxygen into its chambers and waiting to fire. *But would the sound be of defense or of surrender?*

"Ryan loved karaoke. Our buddy, Rhys, would strike up a tune, and he'd sing at the top of his lungs even though his voice was terrible," he said, his low chuckle accompanying my own laugh. "And motorcycles. Anything fast and dangerous, really. It was all he talked about while we were away—coming home to buy a damn bike."

"Did he convince you to get one?"

"His death did."

"Dare..."

"He convinced us to get other things." He cleared his throat and then rumbled, "Like piercings."

My mouth formed an "o."

"You have something..."

I licked my lips and heard his approaching groan. "No.

Here." The pad of his thumb brushed right at the corner of my lips. "Athena..."

"I don't want this to end," I murmured. "Us." As though I could be talking about anything else.

Air hissed through his lips, betraying the mounting pressure in his chest. "I can't...he's gone...because of me."

"So, you died along with him?" I murmured, feeling him tense. "Because it seems like that's when you stopped telling your story."

"I should have. I deserved to," he rumbled, the heat of his breath fanning my cheeks.

"No, you don't." I lifted my hand. My fingertips bumped the hard edge of his jaw, but he didn't pull away, so I moved them higher. "How mad would he be to see you like this?"

He shuddered against me. "Athena..."

"He's gone, but without you, who will tell his story?" I cupped his cheek. "If you want to punish yourself, then do it for the good. You owe him his story."

"I owe him my life."

"Exactly." I pulled my face to his. "So, stop giving him your death."

I would've wished to savor his sharp inhale of breath for longer—the sound of my pleas finally piercing to the core of him. But I wished for his kiss more.

His mouth crushed mine with the kind of harsh hunger that gnawed at the inside of my chest. Within seconds, the thrust of his tongue pushed through my lips, punishing me and praising me for daring him to take what he wanted. I clutched his head, holding on like I held him above water. Above grief. Above guilt. And with every stroke and lick, he came to life against me.

His arms banded around me like the roots of a tree, pulling me right to the edge of the counter, where the hard length of him wedged between my thighs. I shivered, recalling the feel of him in my mouth. Long and thick. My core clenched, aching to feel him there. Every hard inch all the way to the metal knobs of his piercings.

With a growl, his fist curled in my hair, tipping my head so his next kiss could go deeper. Deeper and longer and harder.

He kissed me until my body was on fire and my mind was spinning like a top out of control.

"Dare," I panted, locking my legs around his waist as I tried to grind on him, needing more. *Needing everything.*

"Athena..." He broke away with a groan, his chest heaving. "I can't."

"Why?" The heat coursing through me melted all of my resolve, leaving nothing but Jell-O-ed desperation in its place. "I want this—I want you, Dare. And if it's not me, and it's not Ryan, explain to me what it is—"

"It's me," he said roughly and then groaned. "It's me."

"Tell me," I begged. "Please."

My heart pounded into the front of his chest, or maybe it was his hammering into mine. Either way, neither of us moved, our bodies riveted to one another in an unbreakable moment. His silence was the torture he imposed on himself, and it was more painful than his words.

"I haven't...been with a woman since..."

My lips peeled open in shock, setting them apart in slow motion. "Dare..."

"I haven't fucked a woman since her. Hell, I haven't let a woman touch..."

Electric heat warmed over my skin. "Until me."

Another pound. Another heavy breath. All stepping stones through the flurry of facts. Once more, I saw so much in the darkness. So much pain. So much loyalty. So much tenderness. And it broke my heart.

"All I want is to protect you," he rasped.

"From you?"

"From everything. Including me," he rasped. "You deserve better—you deserve everything, Athena."

"Then stay and treat me like I deserve, or walk away and don't look back like the first man who kissed me on this counter." I didn't know where the strength of my charge had come from—where any of it had come from—but I couldn't take it back. The gauntlet was on the ground in front of it, everything I had—everything I wanted—spilling from its rim.

Dare's inhale was as sharp as a knife. His hand tightened its hold, pinning me in front of his hot stare as though he believed some part of me could see him right now.

"He wasn't a man," he growled low, the edge of murder in his voice. "He was a boy. A stupid fucking boy."

His lips were right in front of mine. I could feel them even though I couldn't see them. We traded breaths, like what was left in our lungs was the only oxygen left on the planet.

"And what about you?" I gave him one more of my breaths, hoping he'd let me breathe him in one more time. "Are you the man who stays?"

He stilled, his breath clutched tight like stolen treasure in his chest. And then he exhaled softly and warned, "No, I'm the villain who can't leave."

Chapter Sixteen

Dare

A villain acted without restraint. A villain took what didn't belong to him. A villain pretended he was better than he was.

A villain committed a sin and told himself it was for salvation. And in kissing her again, that was what I'd done.

But God help me, she was my undoing.

"You're so good...too good," I growled and kissed her harder. *My angel.*

Her mouth was heaven under mine. Soft and warm and welcoming. But also bold. She met my tongue stroke for stroke, both demanding to be conquered and then letting it happen—*a voracious victim to my claim.*

Fire bled into my veins as I pulled her closer, her curves fitting me in a way that was the same and different as those decades ago—*when I'd first kissed her here.*

Those memories should've been a warning. A piercing siren. A bright flare. *Retreat.*

But I couldn't anymore. I couldn't run from life—from living. *From loving.* Not anymore.

Groaning, I wrapped my arms around her, my hands finding purchase under her ass as I lifted her off the counter and carried her to the bedroom.

There, I sat on the edge of the bed, positioning her on my lap.

How many times had I imagined having sex with her? When I was a teen, it had been the running soundtrack in my mind every time we were alone, but I always held back. I guess I'd always had this kind of restraint warring inside me—*or maybe I'd always known that Athena deserved more than I could give her.*

But this was nothing like I'd imagined. Fantasy had given my younger self a level of patience that my older self didn't possess.

I didn't take my time undressing her. I pulled off her shirt and bra in seconds, not caring what ripped or tore in the process.

I didn't slowly explore the perfect shape of her body with plenty of time for her to stop or protest. Instead, I sank my teeth into her neck and filled my hands with her breasts, weighing and shaping their soft fullness. And the way she responded was far from a protest.

Athena bowed into my hands, murmuring, pleading for more.

"Fuck, you're perfect," I rasped, bringing my mouth down her chest until I reached her nipple, drawing the soft peak between my lips.

Her gasp was like music to my ears as she clutched me tight, but the way she tasted was pure heaven.

I was gentle—as gentle as I could be. Until I wasn't. Until I closed my teeth on her nipple, and Athena jerked against me, her core bumping my throbbing cock.

I released her on a hiss, pleasure exploding like dynamite in my gut.

"Again," she ordered—or maybe begged.

Either way, I complied, locking the tight bud between my teeth and flicking my tongue over her.

Fuck...

She ground against me, her hips rocking along my angry cock with weight and friction that made me an addict. I bit and licked and sucked until the pleasure—the pain—threatened to kill me.

And then I flipped us—flipped her.

She let out a cry of surprise, her back landing on the soft bed as I rose above her with only a single thought—a single mission on my mind.

"I have to taste you."

I removed her leggings and underwear in one swipe and then settled between her thighs.

Her legs found their way over my shoulders as I kissed the inside of her thigh.

"Dare..." she breathed when I got closer—when I could smell the sweet musk of her desire.

"Keep them wide for me, Angel," I begged, tugging her legs a little farther apart. "This is only my second meal in a decade."

I torpedoed her swift inhale with the slide of my tongue along her seam. From her entrance to her clit, I claimed the whole of her pussy as mine.

Athena cried out, her body rising to meet my mouth as her hands clutched the back of my head.

"Hold on," I warned, and then flicked my tongue over her clit.

For minutes, the wet heaven between her thighs became a

battlefield, and my mouth would settle for nothing less than complete surrender. Her moans became whimpers, whimpers became cries, and cries became pleas for mercy.

"Show me how good you are," I rumbled. "How wet and perfect you are for my cock."

"Dare..." She could hardly get out my name. Her body was arched so tight—so taut—that one more suck on her clit would send her spiraling.

I teased two fingers at her entrance and then steadily pushed them inside. "That's it," I groaned, feeling her muscles tighten.

My breaths labored, need making my head feel light.

"You have no idea how bad I want to be inside you." I spoke because if I didn't, I was afraid I'd black out. I felt every pulse of my dick like it was the beat of my heart. Pure, unfiltered need raged through my veins. "How hard I am right now..." I hissed and reached for my throbbing cock, pulling it free from my jeans. "God, you feel like I might not fit."

I wrapped my free hand around my length, stroking just as I stroked the inside of her hot cunt.

"Dare, wait—ahh!" She whimpered and clutched my head as I brought her right to the edge of her orgasm again. I let her pull my head back, finding her hazy and heavy-lidded eyes. "I want you," she said in a rush, her body breaking apart at the seams. "I need you inside me."

"I know, Angel, but I need you to be a good girl and come for me first. Once I'm inside you, I don't know..." I trailed off, the words alone were enough to make my cock start to leak. "Just need to give you one first." My voice cracked at the end, betraying how on edge—how uncontrolled I really was. "Can you let me do that?"

"Yes," she murmured, and I felt her body become like putty in my hands.

The Villain

I might be a villain for this—for pretending she could be mine—but I definitely was for wanting to give her pleasure like this. I wanted to make her come in a way that would ruin her for any other man. Past. Present. Future. This would be her standard—I would be her standard. For the most pleasure and pain one person could make her feel.

I set my tongue on her again, knowing this was it. Knowing after this, it will be my cock and not my fingers spreading her wide. *Knowing after this, there's no going back.*

I alternated between swirls and flicks, changed speeds and the pressure against her clit until she gushed on my fingers and her strained cries became a single sound.

"That's it, Angel. Drench me. Drown me. Be a good girl and give me everything." Her body trembled and jerked uncontrollably as I curled my fingers inside her pussy and sucked hard on her clit.

And she gave.

Gave in.

Gave up.

Gave it all.

Her release barreled through her like a hurricane, shaking her muscles from her bones and drenching my tongue with her release.

It was so damn good. So sweet and warm and so fucking precious. But I was too fucking feral to enjoy it.

As soon as she was remotely stable, I moved up her body, my mouth branding a path from her stomach to her sternum to her neck. There, my teeth found purchase in the soft corner of her shoulder.

"Hold on," I grit out, waiting until her limp arms linked around my shoulders before I reached for my cock.

I angled myself toward her heat, my tip dripping onto her clit before it was notched at her entrance.

I hissed, sharp pleasure staked to the center of my chest. I couldn't stop. The wet heat of her pressed to me...another few seconds, and I would come right there. I couldn't stop. Couldn't prepare her...couldn't prepare myself.

All that was left of me was the need to be inside her.

I pushed into her pussy. Her hot, wet, tight...I groaned, "So fucking tight. Holy shit..." I couldn't breathe. The hold she had on my cock was also around my throat. Too fucking tight even for air to fit through.

But I couldn't stop.

I heard her gasp when my piercings moved inside her. Metal and man stretched her clenching muscles, forcing their surrender. And the metal inside me...

"Fuck, I've never...I had no idea..." I couldn't form words for what I was trying to say.

I'd gotten the magic cross right before Amira, but Amira and I...we'd never...I'd never been inside a woman after getting pierced.

"Tell me," she whimpered as I pushed forward, every inch spreading her wider.

"You're so beautiful, the way you're taking my cock."

I wanted her to see this. Just like the constellations, I wanted her to see the way I burned for her in the darkness.

"You're so swollen and pink and wet. Taking me deeper even though it looks like I'm too big for you." I had to stop—to groan and push farther. *Can't stop.* "I've fucked my hand so many times to the fantasy of this. Your kiss. Your touch. Your smell. Your taste." I shoved deeper, hearing her breath catch, but I couldn't stop. Wouldn't until she had all of me. "And it was all nothing...nothing compared to this."

I thrust my hips all the way, feeling her body surrender and take the last inch of my cock, so my tip kissed her womb.

"Fuck, you feel incredible, Angel," I rasped, ragged, as I

began to move. Sliding out and then shoving back inside, my piercings stroking her inner muscles as I moved.

"Dare!" She quaked, but I was lost.

Out and in. Harder. Faster. "Relax for me. Relax for my cock," I begged, my chest heaving. "I need you to relax for me like a good girl."

Whether she did or I didn't give her a choice, I had no fucking clue. All I knew was that I moved over her like a beast, driving into her tight heat with feral force.

"Fuck, Athena," I garbled, my body like a beast breaking free of its chains. Her heat. Her tightness. The way it pulled and teased my cross. "I can't stop...I can't..."

"It feels so good, Dare. Please, I want all of you. Please..." she begged, the husk of her voice—the plea. She wasn't just talking about all of my cock or all of my orgasm...she wanted everything.

The sound that came out of my lips was savage. I reached for the headboard, somehow knowing if I didn't hold on, I'd fuck her right through the damn thing.

And then I fucked her like the villain I was. I slammed into her sweet pussy like it was all mine. Mine to fill. Mine to break. Her muscles stretched and clenched around me, her womb met the depths of every drive.

She latched her arms around my neck, my hips moving too forcefully for her legs to hold her steady.

I didn't know how this could go, but I prepared for it to be fast. To be furious. To be unrestrained and unable to focus on her pleasure while being trampled by my own. It was why I'd made her come first. Before.

But I wasn't prepared for what was happening.

I wasn't prepared for the way her eyes went wide when my cross hit a spot so deep and pleasurable inside her, she looked up at me like I'd given her back her sight.

I wasn't prepared for the way her body instantly responded, her pussy growing wetter, tighter, as chasing my release demanded another of hers. Wasn't prepared for her fingers clawing at my back

"Come for me, Angel," I begged. "Come for me like a good girl."

The pulse of her pussy was too much. I couldn't stop my release—I couldn't stop myself from coming undone. My head tipped back with a roar that rattled the whole goddamn house as I drove as deep as I could get and let my orgasm take me.

And somewhere in there, hers came for her, too.

Athena fractured around me, her body holding me so tight it was impossible for any of my pieces to fall apart.

Air dumped into my lungs, but it was something else—something warmer and thicker and stronger—that filled my chest. That reached for all the dark, cobwebbed cracks left by guilt and loss and sealed them all up. *Filled them with her.*

Carefully, I lowered myself to the side, pulling her with me—on top of me as our breaths fought for steady purchase.

"Are you okay?" I said hoarsely, fear creeping in that I'd been too rough.

"I've never been better," she murmured and turned her head, and then I felt her lips press to the center of my chest. "Are you?"

I stilled. I was more than okay. I was…alive. Because of her.

"Yeah." I kissed the top of her head, letting my eyes close as I held her for one more minute. "Now let me clean you."

I maneuvered her to the bed, biting back my own grunt of pain as my cock slid free. I managed to stand before I dripped onto the bed. I was still hard…still leaking the last bit of cum that seemed never-ending, wanting to fill her.

Shit.

"Athena…are you…"

"I have an IUD." She read my mind.

No. If she read my mind, she'd see it picturing her pregnant with our child. Her stomach filled. Her eyes glowing. If it was a boy, we'd name him Ryan. A girl, Judy, for her mom.

Fucking hell. I was imagining our family, and she still didn't even know the truth about who I was.

Tomorrow. The decision followed me to the bathroom. *Tomorrow, this ended.* There was no hiding the truth from her now.

I warmed a cloth and returned to the bed.

"Dare..." She pulled my face to hers, kissing me as I cleaned gently between her legs. When I was finished and drew back, she asked, "Will you stay?"

My heart cracked. That she thought I could leave her now...after that...there was no more leaving. No more running.

Only the morning and the truth it would bring.

"I'll be right back," I told her, returning the cloth to the bathroom and then moving back to her side. The bed sank under my weight, and I heard her breath of relief before I even answered, "I'm not leaving, Angel." *Never again.*

I pulled her body tight to my own and slid my hand to her thigh, gently moving it over my waist.

"Dare..." She shivered when I slid the tip of my cock along her seam, feeling her grow wet again.

I'd never done this before, but I couldn't resist. Having her...having been inside her...it felt like I couldn't breathe right without my body buried in hers.

"In fact, I'm going to stay right here..." I pushed back inside her. "All night..." I let out a hiss as her sore muscles welcomed my piercings and then tightly clutched my heavy length. "So you know I haven't left," I finished saying as I filled her completely, enjoying the way she gave a small shudder in my arms.

"All night?" she murmured, adjusting her position in a way that made me see stars.

"Angel, I'd stay here all my life if you'd let me." The words were out before I could stop them—temper them. I was getting ahead of myself. Letting myself feel too much for the woman who both knew me better than anyone and yet only knew a lie.

If I wasn't careful, the truth would end up claiming two broken hearts instead of one.

And then, on the edge of sleep, with the woman of my dreams nestled in my arms as securely as her body held mine, I realized that hiding who I was wasn't my worst untruth; believing I ever stopped loving her was the greatest lie I'd ever told.

Chapter Seventeen

Athena

I peeled my eyes open, and instantly, the world was on fire —no, not fire. *Light.*

I gasped and sat up, eager to let the light blind me because it was *light*. And I could see it.

My eyes blinked rapidly to adjust, my surroundings coalescing into shapes and colors and shadows.

I could see.

A happy sob bubbled from my chest, and I scrambled out of bed and searched for the first piece of clothing I could find: Dare's tee at the foot of my bed.

My bed. *My* rug. *My* house. *My—Dare.* My nipples pebbled against the loose fabric that draped down to my thighs, the whole of me awash with memories from last night that were just as bright as the sun.

The heat of his mouth. The orbit of his attention. The size of his body.

I was both sore and empty. Sore from the first...and the

following three times he'd claimed me last, his body already inside me, hard, when he'd begin to move. Sliding in and out, arousing me from sleep.

My aching muscles clenched, recalling the thickness of him and the magical—possibly miraculous—way his piercings stroked that elusive spot inside me, flinging me so quickly, so forcefully over the edge of release I could hardly catch my breath.

Especially the last time, when he'd filled me from behind. That time, he'd thrust into a spot that was too pleasurable to be anything but a fantasy, the way it made me come not once but twice on his cock. My orgasms stacking in a matter of strokes that seemed to turn my bones and body into a melted mess of release.

But still, he'd stayed inside me. Slept inside me. And now, I needed to see the man who'd claimed me in a way I hadn't expected or thought possible.

The man who'd saved my life. *The man who'd changed my life.*

I was going to finally see the scar I'd felt a hundred times with my fingertips. The lips that explored every inch of my skin like it was the finest porcelain. The arms that held me when it felt like I couldn't hold myself. And him—the whole of the man who'd punished himself for years—locked himself away in darkness until he'd found me in mine. And we became each other's light.

The clank of silverware echoed from the kitchen as I opened the bedroom door.

More light burned images into my brain, and my eyes glazed with tears.

Dare.

The thud of my heartbeat overpowered my footsteps; my steady steps belied how my heart raced to reach him. Somehow,

The Villain

this approaching moment felt even more intimate than the whole of last night. The last hidden piece of him would be exposed.

His low hum reached my ears first, my other senses were still heightened while my vision remembered how to work.

I rounded the corner and stopped short.

He filled my small kitchen. The sight of him. The scent of him. The sound of him. My skin broke out in a rush of warm ache. He filled my home the way he'd filled me. Completely. Utterly. *Irrevocably.*

Silently, I watched the muscles of his tanned, bare back move as he sliced a bagel in two. Smaller scars dotted his skin like constellations of courage and sacrifice. My gaze lowered to the waist of his dark jeans and then darted back up to his neck and then the dark waves of his hair, the ends curled like they still held the shape of my fingers in their inky strands.

"Dare." My voice was half whisper, half rasp, and I found myself reaching for the wall for a different kind of support.

His big body stilled, and my breath caught and held like a fish on the end of a line, waiting as he turned slowly and reeled the oxygen out of me.

Thick, strong arms, the tanned skin printed with tattoos of crests and numbers I'd ask about later.

The sharp profile of his nose and cheek.

His scar.

He faced me fully, and the ricochet of my heart exploded into silence.

"Athena."

My jaw dropped. Too many times in the last few weeks, the ground has given way underneath me, but never like this. Never with such a sudden, sharp, deep foreboding. Even oxygen didn't bother to enter my lungs, knowing I was a lost cause.

I didn't stare. I blinked. Over and over again, willing each fresh look to bring me a different sight. *Willing, even, for it to take me back to the darkness once more.*

But it didn't.

In the span of a second, I'd traded in my broken brain for a broken heart.

"Darius." There were so many things I thought I'd feel in this moment, but recognition wasn't one of them. The man who'd given me my last kiss was the same man who'd given me my first. *On the same kitchen counter.*

The light burned my eyes, but it was the truth that brought them to tears.

Darius Keyes stood in my kitchen. The man who'd saved me—cared for me—was the same boy who'd broken my heart.

"Athena." He knew. *He knew that I knew.* He stepped forward, and I instinctively stepped back. Pain creased his face, which had only grown more handsome with the way life and experience had shaped it. "Please," he begged, lifting a hand as though I were a wounded animal about to bolt.

"Why?"

Why hadn't he told me? All this time, everything we'd shared...and he hadn't told me who he was. The way he'd kissed me...touched me...I gripped my stomach, nausea hitting me like a freight train to my stomach. Last night, the way he'd... I gasped, but the invisible band around my chest made it feel impossible to breathe.

"Athena—"

I shook my head wildly, drawing away from him like a cornered, frightened animal.

I needed air. Fresh air. I spun and bolted for the front door, my feet hitting boxes and my shoulder bumping the wall along the way.

I needed a minute. Fresh oxygen and a single minute to

The Villain

process the fact that I'd let the first man I'd ever loved break my heart for the second time.

I stumbled onto the front porch when his hand found my shoulder.

"Please—"

"Don't." I yanked out of his reach, banding my arms over my chest as I backpedaled onto the lawn. "Tell me why."

He stood with that familiar stillness, the one that always made me feel as though he worried his next step would be on a land mine.

And I was the land mine.

"Athena..."

"Why didn't you tell me who you were?" I said, my voice cracking. "Were you trying to see how long you could fool me?"

"No—"

"Was I some sort of unfinished business?"

"Stop."

Stop what? Stop hurting? Stop crumbling? Stop wondering if I'd just fallen in love with a man who was the best at breaking my heart?

"Please, Athena." His voice was the most honest thing about him. Ragged with self-loathing and crackling with remorse. "Please, just let me—" He broke off suddenly, his eyes narrowing over my shoulder.

I turned to follow his line of sight. "What is it—"

"*Get down!*" he shouted right before the weight of him crashed into me with a bang.

No. The bang wasn't from him. It was from a gun.

The thud of my body hitting the ground wasn't as loud as the sound of gunshots firing above my head. Pain bloomed through me, his big body shielding all of mine.

I clung to his chest, wishing I could crawl between his ribs and hide there until this was all over.

"Stay down," he ordered, and then lifted his weight with a grunt just as I heard the squeal of tires pierce the air and then fade.

I turned on the ground, air heaving into my lungs as he sprinted in the direction of the disappearing car.

Someone had just shot at me—*tried to kill me.*

Again.

I pushed myself upright with a gasp, half-afraid my vision was going to disappear again. But it didn't. It wobbled and blurred and took a few seconds to focus. But then it did, and that was when I saw it. The red patch of blood on my shoulder.

Oh my god. First, I'd almost been blown up. Now, I was shot—*Wait, where was the pain?* I hurt, but not gunshot-wound hurt. I shoved the fabric aside, seeing unmarked skin underneath.

No.

My head snapped to Darius and the matching bloom of red on his bare shoulder and the distinct dark circle where the bullet had gone through him.

"Oh my god." I scrambled to my feet as he came back, striding and scanning the surroundings as though he weren't injured at all. "Darius—"

"Get inside and get your things," he snapped. "We're leaving."

"Your shoulder—"

"It's nothing." He barely looked at it as he moved behind me, using his frame like a human shield to protect me.

"Who was that? Why—"

"Athena, please." His grimace of pain scolded me. "We have to go."

I snapped my mouth shut and nodded, walking quickly into the house. While I changed and gathered my things that I hadn't even unpacked from yesterday, Darius stood guard with his weapon by the door. I heard his strained voice speaking low as I got closer, but as soon as he saw me, he ended the call and shoved his phone in his pocket.

"Ready?"

"Darius..." I dropped my bag and rushed to the kitchen for a clean towel. When I returned, he was looking at his shoulder wound, the blood oozing in a thick stream down the ridges of his torso.

I rushed over, wiping the smear of blood and then carefully pressing the towel over the bullet hole until Darius groaned.

"Sorry," I murmured, catching how he locked his teeth as though this pain was the least he deserved from me.

He placed his hand over mine, and my head snapped up to meet his gaze. There was something about looking into his eyes after all this time...after everything. Something I hoped for my sake would go away the more I faced him, because otherwise, I'd have to face a truth I didn't want to see.

"Can you grab that duct tape?"

I nodded, sliding my hand out from under his and fetching the roll of silver tape sitting on top of one of my moving boxes.

"I need you to tape the towel to my shoulder."

Again, I nodded, my throat too thick to say anything. *I gained my sight but lost my voice.* For some reason, it was easier to speak when there wasn't anything to see. *Or anyone to see me.*

Warmth rose in my cheeks as I tore strip after strip of the tape and carefully sealed the towel to his chest, making sure my fingers stayed on the smooth tape and didn't stray onto his equally smooth skin.

"Here." I handed him back his shirt I'd put on earlier. I wish I had a clean shirt for him, but this was it. He hadn't planned on staying the night...or being shot.

He didn't ask for my help to put the tee on, though there was no hiding how painful it was for him.

"We need to go."

My brow creased, and I peered out the window on the door. "Isn't someone coming?" I assumed that was what his phone call had been about.

"We don't have time to wait." He took my arm, ending the discussion as he led us out of the house.

"We're going to take the bike?" My jaw went slack. "But you're—"

"Capable of riding my motorcycle."

"Did you see who it was?" I couldn't stop myself. The questions oozed from me like my own brand of wound.

"No," Darius said with a glance backward. His steps faltered the moment he realized I didn't need his hand on my arm to guide me any longer. I shivered as soon as he let me go.

"You said Ivans..." *Was dead.*

"I know." He stopped at the side of his bike and handed me the helmet.

"Then who..."

He inched closer to me and cupped my cheek. Maybe I should've pulled away, but I couldn't resist the feel of him. The security of his touch. Even knowing *who* he was...and having a million questions about why he'd broken my heart.

"I'm going to find out, Athena. I promise," he swore low.

"Okay."

His hand fell, and he climbed onto the dark silver Harley, the engine awakening with a snarl as I found my seat behind him and carefully wrapped my arms around his middle.

Again, he'd saved my life. Protected me. But this time, the flutter in my chest was weak like a bird whose wings were clipped.

The Villain

It was strange to *see* the garage rise up in front of us. Strange to see a place I'd experienced so differently for the first time. It was large. Impressive, but unassuming. And not at all like what I'd pictured as the front of the safe house.

The hollow in my chest grew larger, realizing there was even more to this I was missing. *More that had been kept from me.*

As we slowed, the bike wobbled for a second, forcing my arms tighter. Instantly, we leveled and came to a stop in front of the open garage bay.

My jaw dropped a little. There were so many bikes perfectly positioned as though this were a museum rather than a garage.

The engine cut off, and Darius held out an arm for me. I tried to put as little weight on the support as possible, but I still heard his groan of pain as I climbed off the bike.

I pulled off my helmet to see him slightly slumped forward on the seat, and my heart jumped into my throat. He needed help. Everything else could wait.

"Rob?" I called into the space.

"Dare!" Another man called from the far end of the garage. His jog slowed when he saw me. "Athena." *He knew me.*

"He's injured—shot," I blurted. "He needs a doctor—"

"Rorik is on his way." *Thank God.* "I'm Tynan—Ty," he introduced himself as we both turned toward Darius.

He stood next to his bike, both hands resting on the helmet on the seat.

"Darius?" *Something wasn't right.* He looked at me silently —*and ashen.* And I started to run.

"I'm sorry," he slurred right before the mountain of his body collapsed to the ground.

"Darius!" I cried out, my knees landing with a thud on the concrete.

I yanked his jacket to the side, the towels underneath soaked with blood. *Oh my god.* This whole time, the whole drive, he risked himself to get me back here safely. My eyes burned as tears instantly collected in the corners, spilling down my cheeks as I grabbed the first piece of clothing from my bag and pressed it over the wound.

Pressure.

It needed pressure.

Shouts and curses echoed around me as Ty and then another man I could now recognize as Dare's older brother, Harmon, appeared.

"Let's get him to his cabin," Ty rumbled. "I don't think Rorik will want to move him again."

"I've got his shoulders," Harm said as Ty moved to his feet.

"Careful. He was shot—" I swallowed the rest of the words, feeling like a fool as I swiped tears from my cheeks. *Of course, they knew he was shot. He was covered in blood. Passed out.*

"Athena." Rob's voice jarred me, and I turned to the woman I'd already relied on for so much these last few weeks...and reached for her support once more.

Our eyes met, and she realized I could see her.

"You know," she said softly.

I nodded, and a fresh round of tears spilled free. I knew who he was. I knew Darius was both the man who'd saved my life and the boy who'd broken my heart. *And I needed to know why.*

"I'm sorry," she murmured as her arms came around me, and though I didn't have siblings, I knew this was what the hug of a sister felt like. Solid and steady as I shook with unshed sobs.

"I'm okay," I insisted, refusing to break down now. Later, once I knew Dare would be okay, I could cry and crumble and do whatever else my body needed. Right now, I needed to be strong for him.

"Let's get some water—"

"No." I shook my head, already following Ty and Harm and forcing Rob to follow me. "I can't leave him. Not until I know he's okay."

We walked behind them, the maze of the compound blurring behind the heavy thump of my pulse. He had to be okay. *He had to.* When we reached the long hallway, time slowed, recognition scratching in the back of my mind. All the doors looked the same, but behind the one they opened, there was a stairwell that had the same number of steps as the one to the safe house.

And at the top, we entered a space my mind had already mapped out—a blueprint of steps marking out the bed and the bathroom and the hall and the kitchen. Seeing the place I'd stayed in for the last several weeks shaded in details, but it couldn't color over the truth.

"His cabin..." I breathed out the words as they carefully laid Darius on the bed.

When I turned to Rob, she held my eyes and then let her chin dip in slow confirmation. *His cabin was my safe house.*

All this time, he'd given me his home. His bed. His protection. And now, I was afraid his life.

"Rorik's here," Harm announced and moved around us to go get the doctor while Ty grabbed towels from the bathroom.

In the commotion, I found a straight path to Darius's side, kneeling on the floor next to the bed and taking his hand in mine. *Like he'd done for me.*

"He'll be okay," Rob assured me, her hand gently finding my shoulder.

My throat was too tight to respond. My chest too tight for my heart to beat. My lungs too tight for me to breathe. Pain and sadness and fear consumed me, but it was anger that held me in a chokehold.

Anger that he'd hurt me again. Anger that he'd lied by omission. Anger that he'd cared for me so fervently and tenderly. Anger that he saved my life without concern for his own. Anger that he'd made me ache and burn for him. For his touch. His kiss. *For more.* And anger that made me want to forgive him for everything if he'd just be okay.

Darius Keyes had to survive this because I wasn't done being furious with him yet.

Chapter Eighteen

Dare

D*amn, that fucking hurt.*
"There he is." The low drone of Rhys's hurdy-gurdy seeped into my ears.

I slowly opened my eyes. "I must be in hell."

Rhys grinned. "Think he's going to pull through, Doc."

Rorik grunted and extended his hand, two massive pills in his palm. "Morphine will probably wear off soon, and you'll want these."

The best I could do was lift a few fingers as I croaked, "No."

"Bullet was a clean shot. Straight through. Nicked a rib. Half an inch more to your right, though, and you wouldn't have made it back here alive." Rorik shook his head. "You should've called someone."

"I couldn't risk it—wouldn't," I said, letting out a hiss as the effort brought a hint of pain to the shores of my consciousness.

Rorik looked at me, his pale blue eyes narrow before they

swung back to Rhys and then my brother. Like a wordless secret passed between them...but it wasn't a secret.

"Someone tried to kill her. Again," I croaked. "I had to protect her." *And it was nothing more than that.* "Where is she?"

"She's resting." Harm moved from where he'd propped his shoulder on the wall. "Rob made her."

My throat burned when I tried to swallow. "How long?"

"Thirty-six hours."

A day and a half I'd been out.

"Athena was here the whole time," Rhys thought it was fitting to add. Like I needed any more guilt added to my plate. *She should hate me. Now that she knows everything, she should hate me.*

"What do you remember?" Ty asked, tapping on his iPad.

My brother stepped forward, a stern frown resting over his features. "You should rest."

"No." I used my good arm to push myself higher against the headboard, ignoring the stab of pain that pierced the bubble of morphine around my brain.

"Darius..."

I tensed. Harm only used that tone and my full name when he stepped into older brother mode. It was a rare mode, usually reserved for our sisters. When you'd gone to war with a sibling...almost died together...it altered the kind of protectiveness he felt he needed for me. Lessened it. Which was why it was strange it came out now.

"I'm fine."

It wasn't like I hadn't been wounded before—like he hadn't seen me injured. I didn't know why this time had set him off.

"If you won't take the pain meds, then you should try and remember now before the morphine wears off. Then, it'll only be pain on your mind."

The Villain

I grunted at the warning. "Not going to change my mind." I didn't want drugs. I didn't want anything else in my system except reality.

"So, what do you remember?" Rhys got us back on track. "Athena said she didn't see anything until she was on the ground and you were chasing the car."

I let out a slow exhale and closed my eyes, but my brain didn't take me to the moment of the shooting. It went further back to when I'd felt her enter the kitchen. Felt her stand there watching me.

And I warred with myself.

Every second was a battle that some part of me was going to lose. She deserved the truth—to know all of it. And she also deserved a man who wouldn't hurt her. The problem was, she wanted me. So, I separated myself from the boy who'd broken her heart; I'd torn myself in two like I'd ripped the very muscles from my bones to give her the kind of man she deserved. And I'd selfishly and greedily relished it—pretending I could be her everything.

But the moment I turned around and saw her, I knew. The look in her eyes had changed. When she couldn't see, her stare had always been searching. For light. For shadow. For objects. For something familiar. Yesterday morning, when she looked at me, she wasn't searching. She'd found me. And the truth.

The hurt and betrayal on her face was worse than the bullet. I'd take a thousand bullets if it could take me back in time and give me the strength to walk away from her rather than stay the night.

I shuddered, and time skipped to us standing on the front lawn. The morning sunlight had tangled in her hair, like it drew its glow from the brightness of the strands. The gentle breeze tugged the fabric of my shirt over her chest, teasing me with her hard nipples and the memory of the feel of them against my tongue. But it was the shadows in her eyes that drew me in—that drowned me.

"Why didn't you tell me?"

I didn't know how to answer her. I didn't know how to tell her that none of my answers were good enough.

"We were in her front yard, and a glare caught my eye. Off a car window across the street, I thought, until I looked..."

"You saw the shooter from there?"

"He was lowering the window, that was what caught the light." I swallowed, hindsight painting a better picture of what had happened. "I thought I saw the gun, but it was the car...I recognized the car and knew something was wrong. It was the only reason I got her down in time."

If I'd just seen the gun, it would've been too late.

"The car?"

"Black Mercedes sedan." My voice cracked, and Rorik handed me an open water bottle. I sighed when the cold water soothed my throat and allowed me to continue. "It was parked outside Ivans's house."

"What?" Ty sat forward. "There wasn't a car there when I finished at the scene."

"It was there when I left. It pulled away when I came outside..." I paused for another breath, wondering if this damn hole in my chest was leaking air from my lungs. "Didn't think much of it because Ivans..." I ended on a groan, the pain Rorik warned about was starting to reach me in waves.

But I deserved that pain—every goddamn ounce of it—for how I'd hurt her.

"Because Ivans was dead."

And I took the explanation at face value because I wanted to get her home—wanted to get her temptation away from me. *Needed to.* Instead, desire got the better of me, and it almost got her killed.

Again.

Again, someone almost died because I hadn't seen the truth.

"Dare." My brother's hard tone jolted me, his stare even more steely. "This isn't your fault."

"She was still in danger, and I..."

"Not you. Us. All of us thought Ivans's death meant she was safe." He moved to the bottom of the bed, looming over the edge like he was God himself.

I didn't respond. I didn't have the strength to argue or the grace to forgive myself.

"Who else? Who else would want to kill her?" It didn't make any fucking sense. She was in danger because of Ivans. Without him, she shouldn't be in danger anymore.

I closed my eyes, searching the memory again like it was a box of puzzle pieces, the one I needed—the one with answers—buried somewhere in its depths.

"It has to do with Ivans." Harm folded his arms as he spoke. "There's no way it doesn't, we just don't know what the connection is yet, but we'll find it. I promise."

"How?" I didn't want promises. I wanted practicalities.

"We go back through everything. There's obviously some part of this we're missing—some other person."

"The house belonged to a shell company—a series of them with no link to Ivans or Iverson. Maybe someone else is involved," Ty suggested. "Someone who owns the house and let Ivans stay there."

"Who?"

"Another enemy of GrowTech? Disgruntled employee?" Rhys chimed in. "I'm sure Ivans wasn't the first person Belmont threw under the bus."

"I'll keep digging." Ty nodded.

It wasn't enough. It wasn't fast enough. "The license plate...

it was C, zero, G..." I trailed off, the details fragmenting like an exploded firework.

"I'll check the nearest traffic cams to both Athena and Ivans's houses and see if I come up with any matching plates," Ty said and excused himself from the cabin.

"You need to rest," Harm said when he was gone and looked to Rorik for confirmation.

"You're going to need to have that arm in a sling for two weeks, so you don't tear anything," Rorik said.

One week, and then what he couldn't see couldn't hurt him.

"I'll leave these if you change your mind." He set the pill bottle on the nightstand, the sight giving me déjà vu for when it had been Athena in this spot and her meds on the table.

"Thanks," I muttered, but I wasn't going to change my mind.

And then there was only Harm and Rhys left.

"You saved her life, Dare."

I grimaced. "I know that."

My brother sighed, the sound of sadness riding out on his breath. "Do you?"

My bitter response dissolved on my tongue. I *did* know, but it didn't change anything.

"I'm going to help Ty," Harm grumbled. "I'll check on you later."

And then there was one.

"I'm fine, Rhys," I said hoarsely. "You don't need to babysit."

"Damn, and here I thought I was getting in some practice."

Practice...my forehead creased and then understanding dawned. "Merritt..." *She was pregnant.*

My friend's face lit up like a lighthouse in the middle of a storm. "Yeah."

"Congratulations." I offered a smile even as the ache in my chest worsened, but the pain wasn't from the wound. At least not the gunshot wound. The wound that ached was deeper. Invisible and scarred over with time. A wound that had once been a wish—a wish for a family with Athena. A wish that had died when I betrayed her. "You don't need to stay, though."

Rhys hummed, his fingers tapping the wooden edge of his instrument where it hung around his neck. "What are you going to do about her?"

My jaw locked. "I don't know what you mean."

"Yeah, you do."

I exhaled forcefully. "I'm going to figure out who's behind the attack and stop them, and then leave her alone."

"Is that what she wants?"

"Yes," I said without hesitation, the recollection of pained betrayal on her face vivid in my mind.

"Then why did she sit with you this whole time? Hold your hand?" he wondered with feigned innocence. "Doesn't seem like the actions of someone who doesn't want anything to do with you."

"She wants to thank me for saving her life, that's all. Guilt and gratitude, nothing more."

"Bullshit." He turned the crank on the hurdy-gurdy and let the instrument's drone ooze into the room. "She wants to see you."

"Don't let her," I warned. I didn't want her here. I didn't want to face having failed her—hurt her again.

"Dare—"

"Don't, Rhys. I fucked up. I keep fucking up when it comes to her—when it comes to this. I keep hurting—" I broke off when he grabbed my shoulder.

I glared at him, watching the easy smile on his face disappear into a hard expression.

"I'm going to say this one time," he began with a low voice. "I know you don't want to talk about it, and honestly, this shouldn't have to be said, but...enough. *Enough*." His grip tightened as he crouched so we were eye level. "Ryan's death wasn't your fault. Amira wasn't your fault—"

"Stop—"

"No one blames you." He talked right over me. "We all dealt with Ryan's loss differently, but had I known your...avoidance wasn't your way of healing but only your way to self-harm, I would've said something sooner. I would've told you..."

I stilled. "Told me what?"

Rhys inhaled deep. "Ryan, he was the one who believed you."

"What?" Suddenly the room felt like it had lost its mooring, everything tilting and swaying.

"Harm and Ty doubted the intel—worried about moving so quickly."

"Yeah." I swallowed through the tightness in my throat. "And then I convinced them it was legit. I convinced Harm we needed to go or we'd lose our chance. I—"

"You didn't," he interrupted me. "Ryan did."

"I don't..." *Understand? Believe you?*

"You were heated when you made your case."

"Yeah..."

"And when you finished, I suggested we go outside for some fresh air." He ticked through the frames of the memory.

I'd been so worked up—so insulted that they dared to question the woman I cared about—that I'd needed a minute to calm down. "And then I told you I didn't want to talk, I just needed to walk."

Rhys nodded. "When I went back inside, Ryan had taken up your fight," he said slowly. "He insisted we trust your intel—

that we act on it. He was the one who convinced Harm and Ty it was the right move."

"And look where it got him," I croaked, but without the bitterness I'd felt before.

I hadn't known that Ryan had argued for me—that he'd argued for the mission that had taken his life. *Did it change anything? Did it change the guilt I felt?* I wasn't sure, but something felt different. Like a sliver of sunlight through years of cloud-covered storms.

"We all made the decision, *including* Ryan, because we are a fucking team. We all risked, and we all lost. You need to stop shouldering all of the blame. If it weren't for Ryan, maybe Harm wouldn't have given the plan a go."

My chest tightened as I thought about what he was saying.

"The point is, we all shoulder some responsibility for his death, including himself. But we all also have to shoulder the responsibility for his memory. His legacy." He straightened and stepped back, the drone of the hurdy-gurdy stretching its melodic fingers through the cabin once more. "And what kind of legacy are you giving him by punishing yourself like this?"

"Like what?"

He arched a brow like I was really daring him to say it. "By staying away from Athena. By denying what you feel."

"That doesn't have to do with Ryan."

"No?" The music grew louder. "It's hard to let someone else forgive you when you can't even forgive yourself."

There was nothing I could do to protect myself from the sharp cut of his words. It went right through the steel of my self-loathing and the chains of my guilt and straight to my heart—to the organ I'd sacrificed on a pyre for my redemption—and resurrected it with a surge of hope and a balm of forgiveness.

"Don't you have somewhere else to be?" I rumbled low.

"Nope." He smiled. "And if I leave, she'll know you're awake. So, just relax and enjoy the music."

My nostrils flared, but I didn't say anything more, letting my eyes shut as I focused on breathing through the pain. Somehow, the long push and pull of the instrument's notes timed with the steady in and out of my breaths.

Maybe I'd remember when the morphine wore off. Maybe the pain would be sharp enough to cut through the fog.

Soon, the random notes pulled together into a familiar tune like moths collecting around a flame. "Bridge Over Troubled Water" played through the room, but it wasn't the slow ballad or Rhys's rich voice that drew me to rest; it was the steadiness of a friend by my side when the storm raged inside me.

The music had stopped, but I wasn't alone. Conscious or not, dead or alive, I'd know the sweet honey scent of her anywhere. *Athena.*

I breathed deep, drawing her in like it was my very last breath, and of her, it might be. *It should be.* When this was all over, she deserved a real fresh start. From Brandon. From Ivans. *From me.*

She deserved more than someone who'd hurt her—betrayed her—twice, even if I'd happily spend the rest of my life giving her everything. She deserved a better man.

Yeah, I pretended for one night like some fucking fairy tale after the trauma I'd survived; I'd pretended like I could be that better man. I'd pretended because she couldn't see me, and if she couldn't see me, maybe I didn't have to face myself. But I was fooling myself to think that could last. She deserved better.

The Villain

Someone who'd give her the truth from the start, for one. *Someone to love her.*

Pain burned in my side like a match struck right in the wound. I didn't want anyone else to love her—it should've only ever been me. But it was too late for that now. Too late to do anything but lay the truth at her feet and hoped she walked far, far away.

One more deep breath of her filled my lungs as I opened my eyes. This time, the pain in my chest came from the squeeze of my heart.

Goddamn, she was so beautiful.

The soft light in the room cast an ethereal glow over her golden hair, which was swept up in a pile on top of her head. She was only in a tee and leggings, but the way the shadows clung to the swells of her breasts and the long lines of her legs— legs that had fit so perfectly around my waist—it was no wonder it pained my heart to beat; I wanted her beyond reason. Beyond rationality.

"Athena."

She looked like an angel, sitting cross-legged on a chair she'd pulled beside the bed. She was an angel, and I'd fucking told Rhys to keep her away.

Her gaze lifted to mine from where she'd been concentrating over the paper in her lap. "Dare." She lowered her pencil. "Are you okay? How are you feeling?"

"Fine." I was in pain, but it was less because of her. Because she was here.

"Here." She came over, took the water bottle from the nightstand, and handed it to me. "Dr. Nilsen—Rorik said you lost a lot of blood."

"I'll be fine," I mumbled and downed several large gulps. "You shouldn't be here."

She shouldn't be anywhere near me. Not after what I'd done.

"So, you can take care of me, but I can't take care of you? The man who saved my life?"

Angry air hissed through my lips. "I lied to you." There was no point in skirting the truth—no point in trying to delay the return of her anger. Her hatred.

"You did." Her chin lowered.

I drained the rest of the water, wishing it were something a hundred times stronger. "You shouldn't want to take care of me."

Pain pulled along her beautiful face, and I hated how even wanting her to hate me caused her pain.

I stilled as she sank onto the edge of the bed, her focus on my torso—on the bandaged wound. And then it strayed elsewhere—to the scars dotting and streaking over my skin.

"So many scars," she murmured, and I breathed out unsteadily when her finger touched down on a scar shaped like a comet on my right shoulder where shrapnel from a blast had caught me.

"I've lived a violent life."

Again, she nodded and then turned, reaching for the paper she'd set on her chair when she'd gotten up to bring me water.

"You're peaceful when you sleep." She set the paper on my lap; it was a portrait of me.

"You drew me." I stared in awe at the soft lines stretching over the paper, coming together to create the image of a man I simultaneously knew but didn't recognize. My features. My body. My scars. It was all me. But the peace on my face...it had to be remnants of the drugs in my system. I hadn't slept good since, well, before the night I'd spent with her...in a long time.

"You sat perfectly still. An excellent subject." A small smile spread across her face.

The Villain

"This is incredible. You're incredible," I rasped and handed her back the drawing, afraid to look too long at a peace I might never find again.

"Well, it's much better than the last time I tried to draw you."

"Last..." I trailed off when another paper landed in my lap. This one was much less refined. It was chaotic. Messy. The whole thing was created from one wild line. "You drew this?"

"When I couldn't see," she confirmed, letting her tongue slide over her lips. "It took me so many tries to figure out how to...make it work. Not that I could see how badly I was failing, but as soon as I lifted the pencil from the paper, that was it. I was lost."

I let my finger trace along the line. For some reason, this drawing meant more to me than the one she'd just done. Maybe because this one was of the man who saved her. The man who cared for her. *The man she wanted.*

This one came before she realized I was the first man to break her heart.

"You should go." I pushed the paper back to her and looked away.

"Go where?" She surprised me by asking.

My mouth opened and shut before I worked out the words, "The guest cabin." *I assumed that was where Rob had taken her.*

"As opposed to this one...which is yours?"

I breathed deep. Of course, she'd realized—or been told. "Yeah."

"But you brought me here before."

"I—yes." It would only make it hurt worse to romanticize my reasons. "It was easier—better for you."

"Like it was better for you to lie to me?"

Another bullet—a thousand bullets—would be less painful than hearing the devastation in her voice.

253

"I thought it would be," I answered with humble honesty. "After what you went through, knowing who I was...am...it wouldn't have helped anything, only hurt."

"So you wanted to protect me..." She paused and tipped forward. "Or were you trying to punish yourself?"

"Athena," I began too forcefully, wincing when my wound reminded me there was nothing I could do forcefully right now.

Her hand splayed across the center of my chest, heat spreading from the firm contact as she moved her touch lower to the edge of my ribs. "Was I one more way for you to let your past eat you alive?"

Her hand was over my liver, connecting her question back to the time when she'd deemed me a modern Prometheus.

"Why do you want to keep me from you?"

I tipped my head back and sighed. "Because you deserve better," I said, sadness eating my tone. "Because if I don't keep you from me, I'm afraid I'll pull you to me and never let you go. And that's not right...not okay."

"Isn't it?"

Heat burned through my veins. Temptation. Desire. Possession. Her words weakened me beyond anything I'd ever felt before, my current gunshot wound included.

"You know it's not," I said brokenly.

"I don't, actually." She met my gaze, hurt and hope shining bright. And then she pulled back and stood. "You should rest."

"Wait." I reached for her, but she wasn't close enough. "I have to tell you..."

She came over then, standing above me like the goddess who'd determine my fate. My breath hitched when she bent forward, time stopping as she came lower—closer to my face. Closer to...I groaned when the warmth of her lips pressed to my forehead, the touch so fucking tender it destroyed me.

"I don't want the truth, Darius," she murmured, the

warmth of her breath caressing my skin. "Not without your trust."

I didn't move—I didn't say a single word as she straightened and walked out of the room. Out of my cabin.

She didn't want my explanation out of guilt; she wanted me to trust her with the last of my secrets. And if it were just my secrets, I could—would trust her easily. But I was afraid it was more than that now. I was afraid that to give her the truth, I'd also have to hand her my heart.

Chapter Nineteen

Athena

"Here."

I turned, a waft of lemon hitting me from the steaming cup of tea.

"Thank you." I took the offered mug, scooting over on the couch as Rob took a seat. "Any news?"

Her pause told me everything I needed to know. *Nothing yet.*

"We're still looking. The car will turn up eventually."

I closed my eyes, frustration filling my chest. I used the pressured emotion to blow a steady stream of air over the cup, venturing in for a sip, even though I knew it wasn't cool enough yet. Sure enough, the hot tea scorched the tip of my tongue, and I winced.

"One step forward and two steps back."

"I know that feeling," she admitted softly, toying with the chain around her neck. She was typically quiet but not soft-spoken. I didn't realize the difference until I met her. Soft-spoken implied shy or unsure or hesitant. Rob was none of those things. She was determined and calculating and reserved, and she was *quiet* because she got more done that way with less interference.

Except right now, there was a softness to her voice that hadn't been there before.

"I can't imagine you ever sacrificing a step back."

She smiled small. "Then I've done a good job."

"At not being in danger?"

Her laugh was short and sad. "At hiding," she confessed, brushing a strand of red hair back over her shoulder. "I've stepped back so far, I couldn't tell you the way forward any longer."

My chest tightened. "I'm sorry." I didn't know what to say —how to help her; I couldn't even help myself.

"Don't be sorry." She patted my hand. "I'm telling you this because I've lived the better part of a decade in hiding; I won't let that happen to you."

"Why are you in hiding?" It didn't make sense; she and Dare and the rest of them hunted down bad guys. No one had said anything about her being in danger.

She took a slow sip of her tea. "I did something stupid to try and catch the men who stole my parents' legacy: Ivans, Sinclair, Wheaton, Wenner, Belmont...all of them."

I winced as pain burst on the side of my head, there and gone in a second.

"You okay?"

I nodded. "Just some pain. Dare's tackle probably wasn't the best thing for my brain, but I guess it's better than a bullet."

She hummed in agreement. "You still don't remember the rest of that morning?"

Slowly, I shook my head. "No."

It was the only piece left. Those few hours...the hour,

really, before the explosion. I still only remembered getting in the car with the paintings, and then nothing until after the explosion. Rorik said it would come back; that if my vision came back, the rest of it would, too, but the secondary trauma of Dare knocking me to the ground set my healing time back.

"It feels like I'm missing something," I said and drank some more of the tea. "Maybe it's just because that's the last...part... of this whole thing I can't get back, but...I don't know. I just have this feeling that there's something important there, and if I could just remember it..."

"You will," she assured me, and then shrugged. "Or you won't, and Dare will figure out who is threatening you regardless."

The mention of his name made me shiver.

"I'm sure he will," I said, my voice quiet. "Then I'll be out of his hair for good."

"You know he doesn't want that." She sounded so sure.

"Doesn't he?" I hadn't seen him since the night I showed him my drawings and demanded his trust. Three days. At first, I chalked it up to his injury and healing. I'd sit here—on the couch in the rec room—and listen to the steady stream of the other guys going down to see him. Rorik to check on his wound. Harm and Rhys and Ty to discuss various parts of the case. But not me.

And it was my own fault.

He'd offered me the truth, and I'd countered with my demand for trust. I was tired of men lying to me—for my better or for my worse. I was tired of their secrets. Tired of their guilt.

What was the point of the truth if it didn't come with his trust? What benefit was an explanation about the past if he wasn't willing to risk opening himself to our future?

I bit my lip and swallowed down a sad laugh. *One night with him was all it took to think about a future...and to turn me into a fool.* It was more than one night, that was why. It was every night—every single moment from the second my car exploded and threw me into his arms. The nights he sat and held my hand. The days he cared for me in every way imaginable. The honesty he'd given me about things he hadn't told anyone else.

Time was just one factor when it came to knowing someone, just like sight was just one sense available to discern your surroundings. Without sight, I'd learned to navigate life. I'd fumbled and fallen, but I'd also adapted, my other senses becoming stronger because of it. And without time, the way I felt about Dare had fumbled and fallen but ultimately had grown.

"Of course he does. Love makes people do stupid things," she said, and for a second, I swore she was talking about herself, but I had to be mistaken.

"How do you forgive someone who doesn't want to be forgiven?"

"He wants to be forgiven, he just needs time. Hard to believe you deserve forgiveness when you've gone so long telling yourself you don't."

We both turned at the commotion in the hallway, Rhys and Harm's voices booming suddenly from the elevator.

"Athena." Harm filled the doorway. "He's asking to see you."

My heart stumbled. *Dare.*

"Go." Rob stood, taking my almost-finished cup of tea from my hands.

"Thank you," I murmured when I reached Harm, staring up at a face that was familiar.

I hadn't known Harm in high school. By the time Mom stopped homeschooling me and I transferred there for junior year, he'd already graduated and had joined the military. There were photos of him, of course, but those tiny images and decades that spanned the war would've made him unrecognizable if I didn't already know who he was.

But I did. And because I did, I saw the resemblance between Dare and his older brother.

"No, thank you." His solemn expression said it all. I'd managed to reach Dare in a way none of them had been able to, and as much as that thought filled me with hope, it stung with equal pain, knowing it might not be enough.

"Dare?" I called, opening the door.

It was strange to enter the cabin this way—as a guest—when I'd been the one living there for weeks. But then again, all the tables had turned. Where I'd been the one injured and vulnerable, now he was. Where I'd needed to take a risk to trust him, now he needed to do the same.

One turn of my head confirmed the cabin was empty. *But Harm had said...*

A flicker of light caught my eye through the front windows. *He was outside.* I went to the door, opening it to a sky that bled the pink and purple of a summer sunset...and to a man who stood tall and beautiful no matter how his life had tried to break him.

"Dare."

He faced me, shoving whatever was in his hands in his back pocket and out of sight. "Athena."

My gaze greedily stole over him. Knowing how it was to not be able to see, I appreciated and hungered even more for every second I could soak in the sight of him.

"How are you feeling?"

His left arm was in a sling, stabilizing his shoulder so he wouldn't overextend and tear open his wound. But other than that, he looked...well. I struggled to explain it, but the shadows under his eyes were less. The pain haunting his expression had started to fade. Something had changed, but he'd been avoiding me, so it couldn't have been me.

"Okay," he rumbled, taking a step closer and then stopping hesitantly.

"Does it still hurt?" I asked, crossing my arms to stop myself from reaching out to touch him. I hated when he looked so solemn and alone like a lost boy who wasn't sure he deserved a home.

"Less than staying away from you does," he rasped, taking another small step toward me, like he was unsure just how close I'd let him come.

I sucked in a breath, shocked by the brutal honesty of his answer. "Dare..."

"I want to give you the truth, Athena, and my trust." *Give me the truth, not tell me.* Hope fluttered in my chest, beating away the shadows of doubt that had crept in like cobwebs to the corners of my heart. "If you'll still take it."

"Of course," I said quickly—maybe too quickly for some.

Maybe anger at him would be righteous, but it would also be wrong. To be angry at a man who'd done the wrong thing for the right reasons, who'd hurt me in order to spare me a deeper pain, and who'd punished himself far longer and far worse than I could've ever done—well, it would be easy, but it would also be weak.

I would be weak to choose anger when forgiveness takes far more strength.

"But first, I want to give you these." He reached in his back pocket and extended his hand, a stack of envelopes in his grasp.

"What..." I recognized them instantly.

"The day we went to search your house. We were in your old room, and I saw them in the dresser. I don't know why—no, I do know why...I took them. Read them." His jaw tightened. "I'm sorry."

My tongue slid over my lips. "Sorry for reading letters that were written to you?"

He frowned. "You never sent them."

"Because if I never sent them, I never had reason to expect a letter in return," I murmured, and when he still looked unconvinced, I added, "I never sent them out of self-preservation, not secrecy."

And knowing he'd read them felt like a weight lifted from my chest that I hadn't even known was there, it had been resting steady for so long.

"I got all your letters, Athena," he rasped. "Every one. And I read them so many times, the ink is too faded to read them anymore."

He hadn't even gotten to the explanation of his silence yet, and already I felt tears prick at the pain on his face.

"The week after I'd left for boot camp, Rob's parents died," he began, his strapped arm clenching and releasing in a fist. "It was such a shock—the whole situation—I didn't know how to write to you about it, and I couldn't come home. My parents were devastated, and Rob...Harm was deployed. Izzy was too young. They asked me to talk to her, to console her. And I just remember sitting in silence on the phone because I didn't know what to say."

I banded my arms tighter over me, imagining the position he'd been put in.

"I was eighteen...you don't experience a lot of death by eighteen." He paused and cleared his throat. "I tried to be there for her. For my parents. But no matter what I said, it didn't feel

The Villain

like enough. And because it wasn't immediate family, I couldn't go home. It was like I was trapped in a room with a door with no knob. I couldn't—" He broke off with a huff. "I couldn't figure out what to say to help them...and I couldn't figure out what to say to you."

"I'd never blame you for that," I said softly. We were both kids.

"I started a letter to you at least a dozen times. I tried to find the right words..." He shifted his weight, shadows haunting his face like ghosts. "But what were the right words to say when your mom was sick again? Back in the hospital? It felt like everyone I cared about was hurting, and there was nothing I could do."

Tears burned in the corners of my eyes, and I fought to keep them from falling.

"You didn't have to do anything, Dare." *Except be there.* "I just needed you."

His mouth pulled into a hard line, his chin nodding like he was signaling the executioner to let the axe fall.

"I was going to call you. I didn't have a lot of phone time, and the time I did have, I kept spending it talking to my family or Rob...but I remember the day I was going to call you," he insisted. "We'd just finished morning drills. I remember the mud on my boots because it rained the night before. I remember I couldn't see the sun through the clouds. But I remember thinking if I just talked to you, it would be okay."

I couldn't hold back the tears any longer, they streaked down my cheeks like my chin was the finish line.

"I don't remember holding my breath, but I do remember the way it rushed out when instead of being released to free time, our drill sergeant told us to head to the chapel on base," he went on, his voice growing hoarse. "My buddies and I thought it was some fresh variation on the...hell of boot camp. And I guess, in the end, it was."

I brought my hand to my throat, needing to feel it bob to convince myself I could still swallow. "What happened? What did they make you do?"

He stared at me, his eyes darkening to a black hollow. "Watch." The single word made my stomach tighten. "There was a soldier—a fallen soldier who'd just been brought back to the base. His body was being delivered to his family."

My pulse hammered underneath my fingertips, imagining him in that moment. Eighteen. Alone. His family suffering through their own tragedy, relying on him to try and pull them through from a distance. Me, needing his support as my mom declined. And then having to face this. The reality of war. *The possibility...*

"One of my buddies asked our drill instructor why we were there. There would be a service where we could pay our respects, but not intrude on a private moment..." He exhaled slowly. "His response was that we all needed to be prepared for our future, should this be it."

"Oh, Dare..."

"It was like you see on TV: the casket draped with an American flag," he forged on. "But they never show you the grief. At least not like this. His mother couldn't stop sobbing. I swear the sound of her cries echoed in the chapel for weeks after that day." He brought his free hand to the bridge of his nose, pinching it as his jaw muscle tightened.

It was then that I couldn't stop myself. I stepped forward until I was in front of him—until I could put my hand on his arm and convince myself that he wouldn't crumble under the pain.

He tensed. I was afraid he'd pull away—that I'd gone too

The Villain

far. But he didn't. He lowered his hand and opened his eyes slowly.

"But it was the sight of his wife I'll never forget." And with those words, my heart broke in its entirety for him. "She couldn't even stand. When she saw the casket, she crumbled. Two of us went to her. Lifted her and held her upright. I fumbled for the same words I'd tried to find for Rob. That she was strong. That she'd survive this."

I bit into my cheek so hard it bled; the metallic taste oozed over my tongue but did nothing to stop the pain in my chest. "Dare..."

"She looked at me and said she didn't want to."

I cried out then, as if my own heart were present in that moment, and felt a thousandth of her pain. I'd been broken when my mom died. Adrift. But if I'd lost Dare that way...I would've drowned. Sank to the very pit of grief with an anchor of my adoration. To lose them both...

"The next day, I got your message that your mom passed, and I couldn't..." He swore low, his big body trembling in the air around us. "I just couldn't, Athena. I thought of how I'd left you...and I thought of that soldier's wife. And I just...I realized I'd rather live with you hating me than risk hurting you. You didn't deserve to lose anyone else in your life."

I couldn't see. Not because of an injury but because of emotion. I'd been drowning in loss, but so had he. And guilt. *And fear.* Tears tumbled down my cheeks unchecked, and my chest couldn't catch a steady breath.

"Dare..."

"I wouldn't do that to you. I couldn't," he rasped. "And after that mission, the day we came home with Ryan's body, yeah, I made a lot of fucking mistakes. I carried all that guilt... but not for this—not for you. I did it all for you because it could've been my body beneath that flag."

I didn't know what happened first—if I reached for him or he pulled for me. All that mattered was that I was cocooned in the warmth of his chest when I started to sob.

"I'm not sorry," he repeated over and over again, and ironically, it was the non-apology that had me forgiving him.

"I don't want you to be," I finally managed to say as I tipped my head back to look at him. "I don't want you to be sorry."

For him to be sorry, he would have to be someone else. Someone who wasn't driven by protectiveness and loyalty and sacrifice. Someone who didn't have those qualities woven into their very DNA that he'd risk my hatred and his own happiness if it meant keeping my heart safe.

"But you have to know," he began again, his voice even thicker than before as he brushed my hair back from where it matted to my cheek. "You have to know that day on the lawn, I never wanted to say goodbye to you. Never planned on it. That day on the lawn, I wanted our forever, and I never stopped."

"Dare..." I tipped my head, aching for him to kiss me, but he pulled back. The stars dotting the rapidly darkening sky were reflected in his eyes, a constellation of hope knitted together by his words.

"You asked for the truth."

"And you gave it to me."

"No, I told you what happened, but this..." He released my face to reach behind him for whatever he'd shoved into his pocket earlier. "This is the truth." It was a rolled leather notebook, worn and wounded with age. And then he handed it to me.

I held it, my fingers hesitant to peel it open.

"It's all for you. Always has been."

Carefully, I peeled open the worn cover, underneath, loose pages started to slide free. I stopped them before they fell, unfolding the top one to a sight that stopped my heart.

The Villain

. . .

Athena,
  I don't know how to deal with death, but I don't have a choice now, really.

My eyes sped over the sentences—a letter written but unsent. With every word, my heart beat faster, reading about what he'd gone through. All the things he wanted to tell me. And when I finished one page, the next opened to more of the same. Letter after letter after letter.

Athena,
  I'm so sorry about your mom. She was such a fighter. Braver than half the guys here. And so are you. Still, I wish I was with you. Holding you. I'm so sorry.

And then the folded papers became pages in his journal. One he'd taken with him overseas. The entries weren't every day, but there weren't more than a handful between entries. And they were all written to me.

Athena,
  He's gone, and it should've been me. It should've been me in that cold, lonely box. At least then I'd feel justified for leaving you.

. . .

"I was so used to writing to you...I just couldn't stop," Dare murmured. "And when we came back, the therapist said I should journal," he breathed out. "I couldn't write to myself—couldn't face myself. So, I kept writing to you."

Years of letters. Some pages of handwriting. Others no more than a sentence. Some scrawled in a hurry, others printed slow, like the sentences on the paper were his only way to escape. I wanted to read them all. I wanted to sit and savor every word that this man had penned so I would know what he'd been through and who he was. Except I'd always known the kind of man he was. It was why, even when I didn't understand it, I hadn't hated him.

"I never stopped loving you, Athena...I just wanted to spare you from pain. I needed to believe I was leaving you to a better life."

I stared at him, my broken knight. "I don't want better, I just want you."

A rough noise groaned from his chest. "Am I worth saving?"

"Yes." I reached for his cheek. "I'll save you if you save me, too."

His head dipped lower. "Tomorrow," he said softly. "Tomorrow, I'll save you," he promised, his mouth inches from mine. "But tonight, I'm going to love the hell out of you."

And then his mouth crushed mine.

Chapter Twenty

Athena

It was a kiss that was decades in the making. One that had faced death and died and was now resurrected.

His mouth consumed mine. Devoured it like he finally had the right to take what had always been his. We'd both lost so much, but sometimes it was only loss that could reveal what we'd always had.

I wrapped my arms around his neck, letting out a whimper of protest as he pulled me to him. "Your shoulder." The last thing I wanted was to hurt his wound.

"It's fine," he growled, biting along my jawline until he reached my neck, settling at the sensitive spot just under my ear, the strokes of his tongue planting a vine of fire in my veins.

"You were shot."

His free hand slid to my ass, gripping it hard so I could feel him. The length of him pressed into my stomach. *"It's fine."*

My fingers curled into the ends of his hair. For a second, I let my eyes drift shut, losing myself to the magic of his mouth.

Tongue and teeth and lips—my skin was a blank canvas for the artistry of his touch. A canvas of dark night tattooed by the start of his kiss.

"Athena," he groaned against me, a thrill of need racing to my bones when I felt how his big body trembled with wanting me.

And then my feet started to leave the ground.

"No!" My eyes went wide, and I backed out of his one-armed hold. "You're not carrying me like this. Injured."

His eyes glittered with lust. "That bullet could still be lodged in there and it wouldn't stop me from taking you back to my bed."

Darius advanced on me like a predator coming for his prey, and I had to stop him. I didn't want him to hurt himself or make his shoulder worse.

"Wait." I pressed my palm to his chest and then slowly slid it up to his cheek, my thumb stroking along his scar. "Do you trust me?"

"With everything I have." His solemn promise would've sent me into a puddle at his feet, melted from the heat of his loyalty, if I wasn't so intent on what I was about to do...and the thrill it gave me.

I met his stare, soaking in the depths of its sweetness, before I murmured, "Close your eyes."

One brow lifted. Surprised. Then intrigued. *Then hungry.* And slowly, his eyes drifted shut.

I bit into my bottom lip, never having done anything like this in my entire life, but the way I needed him—the way I wanted him to have me and trust me—was beyond anything I could deny.

Carefully, I reached for the edge of the wrap used to sling his arm to his chest. Pulling it free, I slowly unraveled the

The Villain

fabric, feeling the heavy thump of his breaths like a bull blindfolded before the charge.

"What happens if I peek?" he rumbled, and I swore he stole a quick glance once I had the bandage wrap in my hands.

"Nothing, because I'm going to make sure you can't," I murmured and stretched the fabric over his eyes.

"Athena..." His tone was hoarse and hesitant as I wound the fabric around his head, blinding him completely.

"I want you to know...to feel what it's like to trust me the way I trusted you," I said softly, securing the blindfold in place.

I caught the flare of his nostrils and the ripple of tension in his body. He wasn't used to being vulnerable. Not with his past. Not with his secrets. And not with his body.

"Then do your worst, Angel."

I hummed, warm pleasure oozing from his words.

My fingers traced a light path from his head, along his cheek and neck, and then down his torso. The ridges of his abdomen rose up against my hand, every muscle pulling taut as I got closer to his waist and the thick length that stretched against his jeans. The way he wanted me to touch him was practically electric in the air. I felt his need buzz in my nose and tingle on the tip of my tongue. But I wasn't going to touch him. Not yet.

I took the edge of his shirt and pulled it up. Wordlessly, he followed my lead, letting me slide the fabric over and off his good side before carefully peeling it down his injured shoulder. Without the sling, his arm rested gingerly at his side.

It wasn't cold, but he shivered.

"Tell me what you feel," I instructed as I took his shirt and went behind him, laying it open on the grass.

"The air," he said, his head following my sound. "Like a million brushstrokes over my skin."

I made a soft noise, removing my own shirt and adding it to the ground next to his.

"And how about what you smell?" Next went my leggings, left in a pile next to our other clothes.

"The sea," he rasped as I moved back in front of him. "And sin."

"Sin?" My head tipped.

"I smell you. Your desire."

I smiled and shook my head. He wasn't being serious now.

"You took off your pants."

"How—" I broke off in disbelief. He was guessing...he had to be.

"I'd know the sweet scent of your pussy anywhere." He shredded my thoughts and sent heat churning in my core. "I dream about it. On my nose. In my mouth. Around my cock."

I couldn't stop the whimper that escaped me, my body quaking with lust.

"I want the scent of you all over me—"

"Darius," I interrupted him, desperation bleeding into my tone. I was going to come just standing here listening to his words, and I wanted this to be for him. "Get on your knees."

Air hissed through his lips. "Gonna need you to undo my jeans for that, Angel."

My cheeks burned, and I felt my mouth go dry. I'd thought about this part, but suddenly, I realized I hadn't thought it all the way through. I was going to see him for the first time. The long, thick part of him that drove me wild. The hard velvet anatomy I'd traced with my fingers. The steel studs of his piercings I'd mapped with my tongue.

Touch created an erotic image in my mind, but it wouldn't be the same as seeing him. And now, I realized the power he'd had over me all those weeks—and the strength it would've taken to resist wanting me like he had.

He swore at the first brush of my hands as I worked open the waist of his pants and carefully dragged them, along with his boxer briefs, to the ground.

Oh my...

My jaw sagged at the sight. It was everything my touch had charted in my mind, but more. His huge cock hung heavy in front of him, dark hair curled at the root. To think I'd fit that in my mouth, all the way to my throat...I gulped, letting my eyes trace the web of veins that ran along the thick length all the way to the blunt tip.

His studded tip.

To see the metal balls, knowing they were the ends of the metal bars running like a cross through his cock...knowing I'd felt them deep inside me. Knowing that being inside me moved something inside of him.

My mouth went completely dry.

"I feel it," he croaked, standing like a Roman god come to life. "I feel your eyes. The heat of your stare when you look at me." It wasn't a charge, it was awe and pleasure and humility. "Did you feel it, too?"

It took a moment for words to work again. "Yes." I'd felt every second of his stare on me, even when I couldn't see it. It was like the wind—invisible but palpable. *And made of fire.*

"Athena..."

"On your knees."

I drank in the sight of his perfectly carved and scarred body lower to the ground, one knee and then the other, his cock bobbing heavily in front of him.

"My imagination is killing me," he confessed hoarsely, his chin tipped up like a beggar pleading for sight.

I bent forward and sealed my lips to his, his reaction instantaneous. His mouth wanted to level the playing field—wanted to put me at his mercy. He licked and stroked, tangled his tongue with mine in a dance I couldn't quit. I felt his hand find the side of my calf and start to slide higher.

"Darius..." I pulled back.

Hunger was etched across his features. The crease of his mouth. The thump of his pulse.

"I need you," he rasped.

I shivered and straightened, needing him too. But there, my plan faltered. Seeing the strain on his face and those full lips so close to my chest...

"Open your mouth," I instructed, the huskiness of my voice making it both unrecognizable and utterly honest.

His torturous lips peeled apart, aching for whatever morsel I was willing to feed him.

I cupped my own breast and inched forward, presenting his waiting mouth with the hard, aching peak of my nipple. Time tiptoed forward and then stopped for a split second at the moment he sensed there was something for him to taste. He couldn't see, couldn't feel, but there was a flicker—a twitch over the muscles of his brow.

His lips latched down with hard pressure, making me gasp as an instant bolt of heat shot between my thighs.

"Darius," I moaned, my hand sliding to his cheek—his head—and clutching him to me as he devoured my nipple with boundless hunger.

I arched my back, my head tipping toward the star-studded sky and felt closer to heaven than I'd ever imagined. He made me feel safe. Wanted. Powerful and protected. And loved. In spite of everything we'd gone through—everything that had kept us apart—there was no one I'd ever felt as close to.

Dare groaned into my skin, the flick of his tongue and the pull of his lips sending my mind into a tangle of sensations, each stronger than the last until I swore my legs were going to give out. Until I couldn't think—couldn't breathe—couldn't...

"*Darius.*" My loud gasp pierced the still night air as his fingers slid between my thighs, and his deep groan made the trees shiver.

"I need you," he rumbled, biting gently on my nipple as his thumb worked over my clit.

I couldn't recover from the wave of pleasure fast enough before he doused me with another. Two fingers sinking deep inside my sex and curling into that spot that would have me collapse.

I'd never felt vulnerable with a man before. Never trusted so implicitly. So unwaveringly. Never loved so wholly as I did this man.

"So, fucking warm and soft and wet." His heavy breaths tortured my sensitive flesh in the space between the strokes of his tongue. "I want to live inside you."

Oh god.

"Every day, I want to put some part of me inside you." His fingers moved in painfully and pleasurably slow strokes, reeling me closer and closer to the peak of release. "Every day."

"Darius..." This wasn't how this was supposed to go. I was supposed to be guiding him, and instead, I was clutched to the blindfolded man on his knees, whose mouth and fingers were my undoing.

"Every day until one day..." He trailed off, biting down on my nipple as he curled his fingers into my front wall and then furiously stroked over my clit, the sensation like adding accelerant directly onto a fire. "Until one day when I put a baby inside you."

"*Dare!*" I cried out, the edge of my release clawing for me like a tornado through my core, and I didn't want it. *No,* I did want it, but not like this.

I grabbed his wrist and pulled myself back, panting as I stood a just-unreachable distance from the god on his knees.

"Fuck, Athena." His chest heaved. "*Fuck.*"

My eyes lowered, and I wondered how it was possible that he was even bigger. Thicker and longer. The whole length pulsing drops of precum to his tip.

His ragged groan snapped my attention back to his mouth, which was currently filled with his fingers that had been stuffed inside me.

My core clenched, my climax clawing to be set free.

"I could come from the taste of you, Angel," he said with a low voice, dragging his tongue along the edges of his fingers to make sure he got every last drop.

I moved back in front of him, cupping his face and bringing that mouth of his to mine. He gave his whole focus to the kiss as I lowered to my knees. His hands found my waist, holding my body flush to his until his mouth made my head feel light.

"I need you," I said against his lips. "I've always needed you."

Covering his hands with my own, I turned slowly in front of him until my back was to his front. He shuddered again, kissing along the edge of my shoulder as one of his palms skated up my quivering stomach to my breast. I bit my lip, savoring the feel for a moment, before I tipped forward and reached between my legs, taking hold of his thick length and relishing his deep groan.

"*Fuck.*" His rough voice swirled around me.

I couldn't help but stroke him. I wanted to feel his hard heat just for a second—wanted to hear the rough strain of pleasure seep from his chest and paint an audible picture of his lust.

"You're killing me, Angel," he hissed, his hold on my hip tightening to the point where it planted a delicious hope I'd wake up with his fingerprints on me in the morning.

I smiled and smeared the bead of moisture all over the head of his cock, coating the ends of his piercings in the process.

His head dropped to the corner of my neck, his teeth latching to my skin before he groaned, "Save me. Please, fucking save me."

I shuddered, the words more powerful than even an *I love you* would've been. My breath latched in my chest like it had claws, holding there as I arched back until I felt him notched at my core. A little more, and my exhale spilled out when his blunt tip pushed inside me. There, I held him.

"Save me, too," I murmured and slid my hand free to lay on top of his, my message clear. *Take me. All of me.*

And he did.

His growl was the kind that belonged outside. In the forest. With the animals. Because that was how he claimed me. Like a blinded beast, he held me steady and buried himself to the hilt in one thrust.

Pleasure and fullness and pure bliss consumed me. Our cries wove together with the sounds of our bodies. The hard slap of his hips as he drove into me.

I felt everything like I'd lost every sensation except touch. I felt the press of his balls to my swollen clit when he sank deep. I felt the thickness of him stretch my body to make himself at home. I felt the hard, unyielding stroke of his piercings inside me, rubbing over my G-spot like it was made to do.

With every thrust, I bent farther forward, wanting him deeper and harder and faster. Soon, I was on my hands and knees, doing everything I could to brace against his savage thrusts. His massive palm splayed on my lower back, branding my skin as surely as he branded my sex.

For a moment, it felt like my consciousness floated above our bodies—around us—soaking in the sight of him driving into my prone body from behind, claiming me in a feral, animalistic way that belonged in the forest. That belonged underneath the stars.

He groaned over and over. My name. Praises. Curses. And everything in between.

Desire spiraled. Coiled. Twisted and arced. A lightning bolt brought to life in the depths of my body. My knees spread wider, and I went to my elbows, letting him stroke deeper until I swore I felt the thickness of him reach my stomach...and that spot deep inside me where his piercings felt like dynamite tossed into a bonfire.

"Darius!" I came with a cry that split my chest, my hips jerking uncontrollably as my release ravaged me.

I saw stars as though they were pinned to the ground rather than the sky. My body orgasmed so fast and so violently, my brain couldn't keep up. Like my cells and senses moved without direction or restraint, exploding into tiny, brilliant bits like my climax had turned me into his very own constellation.

Behind me, Dare swore and thrust through my clenching muscles. He buried himself deep, my sex taking every inch, feeling every swell and every pulse. The way he thickened was like fire crawling down a fuse, all the way to the base before he exploded. And then, with a roar, he moved again, pumping through his release as warmth filled me. Soaked me. Leaked from me.

Time didn't exist in the aftermath. When he pulled me back up against him, my arms and shoulders protested, giving some sense of how long I'd been propped forward.

His hand slid around my waist to my stomach, holding there for a moment like he could feel himself still inside me before sliding his hand up to my neck. I shivered when his fingers turned my head so he could find my lips.

"Let's go inside," he murmured, pressing soft kisses to my lips.

I hummed, not really wanting to move at all right now.

"I'm going to sleep inside you again, Angel."

The Villain

I shivered, and my eyes fluttered open. I'd thought maybe the other night was different. It was the first time he'd had sex with someone in a long time. The buildup. The need. I wondered if it would only be a one-night thing...and how to ask for it every night.

How to tell him I wanted a part of him inside me at all times, too.

"Darius..."

"I'll rest on my good shoulder, I promise," he rumbled, his mouth stamping kisses along the side of my neck. "Just need to sleep with my cock inside you. Feels like the only way I'll know this is real...that you're really mine."

A warm shiver consumed me, the heat of an unspoken confession charging through me with unexpected force.

I was really his. I always would be. *Because I loved him.*

Instead, the response that came out was, "Okay."

Tomorrow.

Tomorrow I'd tell him how I loved him and hope it would erase the last fears of his past from ever hurting him again.

Chapter Twenty-One

Dare

Bang. Bang. Bang.

I jolted against the warmth tucked to my front, Athena's bare body curled against mine. *Around mine.* A groan awoke in my chest, my body tucked into the heat of her pussy. It only took a second for my dick to turn from semi-hard to steel and for all of me to regret having to move from this spot.

I'd waited...a lifetime for last night. A lifetime of trials and triumphs and loss. A lifetime of thinking our paths had diverged and that door would be forever closed.

I'd waited a lifetime to love Athena Holman, and I didn't want to wait a second more to tell her.

But I would have to because someone needed me.

"*Darius?*" It was Rob knocking.

Athena made a soft noise that didn't help my body's growing reaction.

"Dammit." Gritting my teeth, I quickly pulled my body from hers and pressed a kiss to her bare shoulder. "Stay here."

The Villain

I rose from the bed, finding my sweatpants on the floor where I'd discarded them when we came inside last night. Pulling them on, I looked around for the wrap for my arm and realized it was still outside. *Oh well.*

Rob must've heard my commotion because she didn't knock or say anything more, instead waiting for me to come to her.

I opened the door quietly, finding my sister reclined against the wall. "What is it?"

I stepped into the stairwell, closing the door behind me, but not before Rob saw enough over my shoulder. I watched something flicker in her gaze—a bright happiness that appeared for a second through the clouds that normally shrouded her.

"Sorry to wake you." She looked genuinely apologetic.

"I'm assuming it's important." I folded my arms, giving support to my shoulder.

"We found the shooter."

"What?" I reeled. "Who? Where is he?" There was hardly room for the two of us on the small landing, but still, I advanced a step toward her. "I want to talk to him."

"Not going to happen," she said, and I stilled. "He's dead."

"Fuck!" I spat the word, reaching to drive a hand through my hair and realizing too late it was my injured arm. I pulled it down with a wince and a more effusive curse that ended abruptly when the door opened again.

"Dare?" Athena's voice settled me even though I wished we hadn't woken her. "Hey, Rob," she greeted my sister when she realized who was with me.

"Sorry for the interruption." Rob looked at me, knowing it was my decision how to handle this conversation.

I exhaled slowly. "Let's go back inside." There was no need to stay cramped in the hallway anymore.

Rob's information hung like a cloud of uncertainty over my shoulders as we went into the kitchen. Athena went directly to the coffee machine, filling the tank with water and letting it start to heat.

"What's going on?"

Again, Rob looked at me, and my jaw tightened. I wanted to protect Athena from this, but that would always be my downfall—wanting to protect her from things that were out of my control.

"Rob said they found the shooter, but he's dead," I rasped.

It should be a good thing—it was a good thing. But my gut told me his death was just one more in this string that was going to leave us with more questions than answers. It was strikingly suspicious that everyone who'd tried to kill Athena ended up dead before we could interrogate them.

"Dead?" Athena gaped and looked at Rob. "Who is he? What happened?"

Rob sighed. "Last night, Monterey police got a call about an accident on the highway. A car veered off the road and down the embankment; the driver was pronounced dead at the scene."

"And the driver is our guy? How do you know? How are you sure?"

"Well, it was the car. Black Mercedes with tinted windows. License plate 4GR03T3," Rob said, her eyes flicking to Athena as she poured three cups of coffee. "Police got to the scene, ran the plate, and that pinged the nets Ty set up. Harm reached out to Rorik, who went up there early this morning to offer his assistance on the autopsy. Harm just called Ty with the update."

"And Ty sent you?"

"No one else wanted to disturb..." She trailed off, biting the corner of her lip to stop a smile as Athena fumbled with one of the mugs, saving it before coffee sloshed everywhere and giving it to my sister.

The Villain

"Do they have an ID on the body?" And a reason to believe he was our guy?

"Alan Brady." Rob lifted the mug and took a sip. "His ID had another name, but AFIS matched his prints to his real identity. He was investigated for involvement in several homicides about a decade ago, but nothing stuck. And after that, it looks like he was living under aliases."

Our gazes met, the reason passing between them: *Brady was a fixer.*

"What else?" The guy might be a criminal, but that didn't make him the criminal responsible for shooting me.

She paused for only a second. "They found the gun in the trunk of the car. It was wrapped in a black garbage bag. He was probably going to toss it. They matched ballistics to the slug Rorik pulled from your shoulder."

"I see." I took the mug Athena offered me, murmuring my thanks as I let my fingers brush over hers. Less than ten minutes away from her body, and I was craving her touch more than I wanted coffee.

"There's more," she said, and I looked back at her. "Ty checked into his accounts. There was a fifty-thousand-dollar deposit made from the same account that paid Athena's ex."

"So, Ivans paid Brandon. When Brandon didn't succeed and got arrested, Ivans helped him escape custody and then killed him because he could implicate him."

"But he still wanted Athena dead."

"So, he hired Brady to fix it." My grip on the mug tightened, wishing it was around the dead man's throat.

Rob nodded. "I talked to Ty and Harm. We think Brady sprung Brandon from custody and brought him back to Ivans to question him. Meanwhile, Ivans gave Brady Brandon's original task of..."

"Killing me," Athena filled in softly.

"Brady left to track you down. At some point, Ivans and Brandon ended up killing each other, and by the time Brady returned, you and Ty were on scene. We think he didn't realize Ivans had been killed, too, and that's why he continued to go after Athena, thinking the man who paid him was still alive."

"And then he died."

With that, the conversation stilled for a beat, but I couldn't leave it there. "Cause of death?"

"Blunt force trauma from the accident. The car went off the side of the road and then off a cliff."

"Right." The hot coffee settled with bitter familiarity on my tongue. Just like the sense of unease and doubt in my chest. "And the reason he crashed?"

"His blood alcohol level was off the charts," she replied, her eyes narrowing. "What are you thinking?"

I gritted my teeth. "I'm thinking that the people who keep trying to harm Athena conveniently keep turning up dead."

Rob stiffened, the movement slight but strong enough to ripple the silence.

"What is it? What are you thinking?" I asked steadily.

"Nothing," she answered too quickly, her fingers tensing around the ring on her necklace.

"You think it's Remington, don't you?"

"No." Again, the answer was too quick to be anything but a false denial.

Why?

Why would the former FBI agent, who now sat at the top of his previous employer's Most Wanted list, be involved in our business?

Yes, there was a moment last year when Rob told one of her friends to impersonate the infamous criminal to save the woman he loved. Looking back now, that moment seemed like a

The Villain

siren. A warning flare. The very first domino that toppled all the rest. He'd been involved in helping Harm save Daria. He'd sent the photo of Athena and Ivans to me. He was everywhere. Alright, not everywhere. But everywhere he shouldn't be.

"Why would Remington want to help us?"

There were plenty of things Rob did on her own. Plenty of secrets she kept from the rest of us. And that was fine, unless it was a man like Remington who had her in his sights.

"He wouldn't," she declared. "And your first mistake would be to think anything he does is to help anyone but himself. So, if he did play some role in this, it would be to serve his own purpose. Regardless, whichever way you look at this, Remington or accident, it means Athena is safe."

I stiffened, anger rushing through me. I wish she wouldn't have said that. It didn't feel like Athena was safe. It felt like we didn't know enough to be certain that all the bad guys were offed by a benevolent villain, let alone to declare Athena safe.

"So, it's over?" Athena asked hesitantly. "I can go home? Go to my art show in two weeks?"

The owner of the gallery assured Athena that the show would go on whether or not it was safe for Athena to be there. She wanted to support her—wanted her success. But Athena really wanted to be present. Wanted to see her dream—her future—finally come to life.

"Rorik's running additional tox screens on the body, but I can't think of any reason not to. Can you?" Rob looked at me.

I pushed an exhale through my tight lips, wanting to say yes. Wanting to insist that Athena needed to stay here for a few more days until we could be certain. *But certain of what?*

"I don't know," I ground out, my voice turning hoarse. There was no reason—no one else who would want to hurt her. *Then why did it make me feel uneasy?*

Maybe it was because I thought I'd have a few more days with her here before we talked about what happened next. It wasn't that I was uncertain of what I wanted with her—which was nothing short of everything—but she was the one who'd been married. Betrayed. She was the one who was just starting over, and I was afraid to admit I wanted to start with everything—afraid that what I wanted might be too much too fast and I'd lose her all over again.

"Well, I'll leave you two to decide that." Rob leaned over the counter and set her mug in the sink. "I'll let you know if we find out anything else." *But she wasn't planning on it.*

I walked my sister to the door, following her into the hall to give us some privacy.

"Do you really think she's safe?" I rasped, not caring how vulnerable I sounded.

Rob tipped her head, her sharp stare softening. "I think she's not the one you're afraid to let out of here."

I'd lived here for so long—secluded myself for so long. To not only find someone and be with them but to now venture out...was that the thing that made my chest tight?

"You deserve a life, Dare." She put her hand on my arm and then pulled me in for a hug.

It was there I realized I'd started to believe it.

Guilt was a bad habit, started by trauma and strengthened by solitude, but I was going to break it. I had a reason to break it now.

"So do you," I reminded her as she went to pull away.

"I have a life," she said and smiled at me. "I have my people. My purpose."

"And love?"

Her smile flickered but recovered quickly. "Love? If I fall, who's left to take care of Ty? He's getting up there."

I chuckled and glanced around, saying, "If he hears you say that..."

"A good debate is good for the soul."

"I don't think Ty would agree with that either."

"Maybe he needs a little disagreement in his life."

After finishing with Rob, I returned inside the cabin, my eyes hooked to the floor, until the door was shut and I heard her voice.

"Dare." The expectation in her voice told me everything. She wanted to leave. She wanted to go home. She wanted to go back to normal. *But did she want to do it with me?* "Come home with me."

I stilled. "Athena..."

She moved in front of me. "You don't have to," she murmured, sliding her tongue over her bottom lip as she flicked her eyes around the room. "Not if this is where you want to be."

Hell no.

I reached for her cheek, turning her head up. "It's not," I confessed, lowering my lips toward hers. "I think it's been a safe house for me, too."

All these years, I've felt sheltered here. Protected. Cocooned from the harsh reminders of the world and what I'd done. But the cabin had been nothing more than a limbo. A protected purgatory I deemed myself destined to spend the rest of my days in. But from the day I'd brought her here, it was as though her presence had shined a light in my darkness, and I could finally see.

I could see the empty space and bare walls. I could see the lack of a life as though it were carved into the foundation.

"Then come home with me."

I let loose an exhale when my forehead touched hers.

"Okay."

Chapter Twenty-Two

Athena

"You're incredible."

I turned, smiling as Darius approached, his gaze flicking to all of my paintings decorating the walls of the gallery.

Landscapes from here to Sacramento. Bright, bold colors claiming every inch of the canvasses, beckoning the viewers into a vivid escape.

"We're about to find out," I murmured, tipping my head back as his arms came around me.

"I already know, Angel." Dare cupped my cheek and lowered his mouth to mine, sweeping me into a kiss that instantly calmed my nerves.

Over the course of two weeks, fear of more danger had slowly and steadily been replaced by anxiety over my show. Wanting everything to be perfect. Worrying that it wouldn't be. And Dare had been by my side in every way.

For me, starting over didn't happen in a day. It didn't

happen the instant I moved to a different town and into Mom's house. My new life had been built day by day since I'd moved home. Box by box. Painting by painting. Connection by connection. All leading to this.

It wasn't until we'd left Sherwood that it hit me what my gallery show had started to represent. My rebirth.

After months of becoming reacquainted with myself after Brandon, returning to my first love of art, and then finding Darius again, it was like digging up all the pieces of my heart and soul that had been methodically buried by an insecure, weak man who wanted to make me feel like nothing.

But standing here, surrounded by the paintings I'd spent countless hours creating and supported by the man who'd do anything for me, I was the person I'd always wanted to be. And I was Dare's everything.

"Though I'm still nervous about the portrait," he murmured, ending the kiss and tilting his head to the portrait I was standing in front of. The only portrait in the gallery. *Ryan's.*

There was no color, only pencil and charcoal. A man brought to life in shades of gray—like many soldiers who experienced war. Some parts of them shining bright, other parts too dark to ignore.

I'd started the portrait from a photo Dare had shown me the night we'd left Sherwood for the second time, and I surprised him with the finished drawing two days ago. He'd cried; we both had. And then he protested when I told him I wanted it hanging in the center of the gallery.

"You're not responsible for his death," I'd reminded him. *"But you are responsible for keeping his story alive."*

I wasn't the only one starting over and breaking free from the things that had held me down.

"Don't be nervous. Just tell them how he made you smile. Laugh. Live."

The drawing wasn't for sale; it was for the story. Ryan's story. A black-and-white reminder of the sacrifice of soldiers so the rest of us could live in color. And Darius was here to tell it.

He made a low noise and lowered his head to my neck, whispering in my ear, "They're going to love you."

"And if they don't?"

"Then fuck them," he rasped, and my heart fluttered. "If they don't buy your paintings, I'll buy all of them."

"What? No." I shook my head and laughed. "You can't—"

"There's nothing I wouldn't do—no price I wouldn't pay—to know how you spent every moment in the years we've been apart."

It had been so long, and yet, decades felt like nothing more than a drop in the ocean. Like no time had passed from the first time he lifted me onto my kitchen counter and kissed me senseless to the second time.

It made me wonder if the idea of time was more art than science. An interpretation of the world around us the way it could bend and stretch, quicken and slow, relative to its surroundings. Like a blank canvas altered by the paint of perception.

And around Dare, the time we'd been apart folded in on itself until it seemed so small compared to the time we'd been back together.

"Darius..." My lips parted, the words I'd lived with for weeks but hadn't said no longer met a barrier of fear. This was my new beginning. And I wanted it to start with loving him. "I—"

"Athena! Are you ready? The parking lot is filling up," Glenn interrupted gleefully, tossing her bright orange scarf over her shoulder as she joined us.

"It is?"

"Come see." She ushered me eagerly with her.

"I'll be right here," Dare murmured as he stepped back, his admiration urging me to step into my future as equally as the love in his eyes promised I'd find him there waiting.

"Excuse me, Ms. Holman. I'd like to purchase a painting."

I didn't think twice about the cold shiver that went through me; the air conditioning was on full blast. I didn't think twice as I turned toward the deep voice that wanted one of my works; there was a huge crowd here to see my paintings. One that had awed and overwhelmed and consumed me.

And when I faced him, I didn't think; *I remembered.*

My jaw went slack, the last blank frames of my memory from the morning of the explosion etched into place by this man's pointed chin, narrow eyes, and dark hair. And then I caught the slow gesture of his hand as he moved his jacket to the side, revealing his right hand tucked underneath and holding a gun.

"We're going to walk nice and easy to the back like you want to show me something." His jacket flapped shut, concealing the danger underneath.

Without thought, my gaze searched for Dare. I was the one who told him I was fine. Who assured him he didn't have to hover—

"Don't even think about screaming or making a scene unless you want someone to die."

I looked back at the dark eyes glaring at me, and the air in my lungs went up in smoke. I nodded, not trusting myself to

The Villain

speak, and turned, plastering my best attempt at a smile like everyone else's life depended on it.

Breathe, Athena. Dare will realize. Dare will find you.

The man's presence loomed behind me like a spider coming for his prey. I followed his instructions because if I wasn't careful—if I didn't think about how to get out of this—I'd only end up more tangled in his web.

We walked around the last displays in the gallery, and somehow I managed to give off no sign of concern to the few people we passed. The door that led to the warehouse space in the back swung open just before we reached it, and Glenn appeared. I tensed, and my captor made a low noise to remind me of the consequences of straying from his will.

"Oh, Athena." My friend beamed. "There's someone asking about the soldier—"

"It's not for sale."

"But you should hear the offer—"

"Not at any price," I insisted.

"If you say so." Glenn sighed, and then seemingly noticed the man behind me. Instantly, she was skeptical. "Do you need something? Is everything okay?"

"Oh yes." I nodded effusively. "Mr. Henry is a former client, and he wants one of the landscapes I don't have out on display." The lie came easily when it was the only thing protecting her life.

Glenn instantly relaxed. "Oh, how nice." She stepped to the side and held the door open. "Well, don't be too long. I think you should hear this offer."

I shook my head and walked by her, holding my breath that she didn't notice anything off about the man behind me—or what was hidden underneath his jacket.

I jumped when the door closed loudly in the big open

space, the clang of metal ricocheting off the walls like a knock inside a coffin.

"Mr. Henry?"

I spun and banded my arms over my chest, staring at his arched brow. "What do you want from me?"

"Keep walking." His chin jerked in the direction of the back door.

My throat tightened, and I slowed my pace, hoping he wouldn't notice. "You were at Richard's house the other morning."

The less he realized I knew, the better, so I kept my knowledge of Ivans's real identity to myself.

"Yes." He chuckled. "Richard."

As for the man with the gun to my back, his identity I didn't know. But I recognized him. The instant I saw him, I remembered his face. I remembered Richard—Ray—escorting me through the house that morning. He wanted the paintings in the living room and begged me to tell him where to hang them.

Suddenly, pain seared through my head. I gasped and pressed a hand to my temple, bowing over in pain and knocking something off the table next to me.

"Dammit. Keep moving." His orders came with the press of his gun to my back, the whole of me stumbling forward like I was made out of a single block of stone, my joints forgetting how to bend for a split second.

And then I saw what I'd knocked over—a tube of paint. One that I proceeded to step on when he'd pushed me to move, sending yellow paint squirting over the floor.

Yellow. *Follow me.*

I planted my next step squarely in the yellow acrylic, trying to get as much as I could on my shoe so I could leave a trail.

"You came over while I was there..." I murmured to hold

The Villain

onto the memory and to distract him from the intentional trail of yellow footprints I now left on the concrete floor.

"I did."

The memory didn't come back in pieces, it came back like threads. Strand after strand. Images. Sounds. Smells. That all had to be woven together.

Ray had just led me to the living room when there'd been a knock at the door. He'd left me with a smile and a plea to use my artist's touch to decide where the paintings should go.

I'd never been more grateful for Glenn's massive warehouse. Storage space. Studio space. And right now, a safe space, since it was clear my captor had no intention of killing me here.

"Unfortunately for you, Richard was a fool."

I held onto my reply, instead clinging to the threads of my memory and weaving more of that morning.

"We have to talk." A voice I hadn't recognized echoed into the living room after Richard opened the door—*my captor's voice.*

"Not now."

"You don't get a damn choice." There was anger—rage even in the tone—and I remembered staring blankly at the painting in my hand, too preoccupied with Richard's visitor to think about where it should hang.

"Then in here." Their steps went from loud to quiet as they walked to the other side of the house, their voices disappearing out of earshot.

I'd felt unsettled. Uncomfortable. Like the bubble surrounding my fledgling relationship with Richard had been pricked. I'd propped the paintings, one against each wall, without much thought and headed for the front door; it was nothing but pure instinct that told me I should get out of there.

My hand was on the doorknob when I realized I could hear their voices again.

"She shouldn't be here." The stranger's voice was louder.

She... he was talking about me.

"It changes nothing." I heard Richard's reply as I moved toward the voices.

"For a doctor, you can be pretty damn idiotic."

Doctor? Richard wasn't a doctor.

"It changes nothing. I'll take care of her when the time comes." Richard could've meant a thousand things by those words, but my brain would only let me believe he meant one thing. One unbelievable thing.

"Outside," the rough voice behind me demanded, dragging my thoughts back to the present.

We'd reached the back of the warehouse and the exit to the small parking area out back. My fingers trembled, pushing the bar as I remembered the last thing I'd heard.

"I don't trust your track record, Ray. I'm having it handled."

Ray. He'd called him Ray.

"I'm not jeopardizing anything. You forget, Wenner, I'm the one who lost a decade of my life to protect Belmont. What I'm owed is worth far more than a pretty blond's fuck."

I couldn't restrain my gasp. The slightest sound of shock snapped the man's attention to the door, letting me see his face.

Wenner. I knew that name.

I turned on the pavement, shocking Lloyd Wenner with my about-face. "You work for GrowTech..." I said slowly, suddenly seeing the man in a whole new light. His expensive suit. His air of authority.

But according to Dare, GrowTech was trying to get rid of Ivans.

His eyes flashed. "I see you've learned a little something since your imbecile husband failed at his singular task."

I ignored the barb. "Ex," I said, and he glared at me. "Ex-husband."

He pulled the gun from his jacket. "Get in the car, Ms. Holman."

Stubbornness propped my chin higher. "What do you want from me?"

"I think that should be pretty obvious," he said and shook his head. "You saw me. You know too much. And I've been planning Belmont's downfall for too long to let the whole thing go to shit because of Ivans. Now, get in the car."

Planning... Suddenly, all the pieces formed a fuzzy picture. Wenner was the missing link. He was the invisible string that knotted everything together and explained the unexplainable. Who killed Ivans. Why a GrowTech account paid Brandon and then the other man who'd shot Dare. It was all Wenner's setup. A frame job to pin my death on Belmont because I'd met him the night of the gala.

I didn't understand the depths or intricacies of their vendetta, but I understood that I'd become the sacrificial pawn in their game.

"Or what?"

He reached into his pocket, and dread wrapped its cold fingers around my throat. "Or I kill you." He lifted his hand, some kind of switch in his fingers with a toggle and a button. He flipped the toggle, and in the corner of my eyes, I saw a red light flicker.

A red light tucked into the frame of Dare's motorcycle.

"And then I'll kill the man who thinks he has a chance at saving you."

The earth opened up beneath me and swallowed me whole. Wenner had planted a bomb on Dare's bike, and if I didn't drive us away from here, he'd make it look like I did, and as soon as he knew Dare was following...

Adrenaline injected like fire into my veins. Or maybe it was pure fear. Not of my own death, but of his.

Dare hadn't lived in so long because of a death and because of a woman...and he'd risked everything to protect me. Now I would do the same.

"Alright." I let my chin fall.

"Get in. You're driving." He waved me to the driver's side with the gun. "And remember whose life you're risking if you try anything stupid."

Chapter Twenty-Three

Dare

There was a man in a black jacket I didn't like.

Everything about him, from the way he walked into the gallery to how he left his sunglasses on his face. And when he looked at the paintings on the wall, it was like he was staring right through them—*as though they weren't what he was looking for.*

Athena had asked for space, and I understood. My hovering while she was trying to share her inspiration and process with guests interested in her paintings wasn't ideal. I was growly, broody, and protective, but I couldn't help myself. Especially because this guy made me skin crawl from the moment he'd walked into the gallery.

The room was a decent size. Large enough to keep a couple feet and a few people between us. He'd veered to the right inside the door, and I maneuvered myself into his shadow. One painting and then the next.

Maybe he was here because he loved art. He certainly took

his time in front of each of Athena's landscapes to give that impression. He stood and stared...and stared. But something still didn't feel right about him. As he moved to the next one, my stare flicked to Athena. She was at the back of the gallery, chatting with an older woman, a blissful smile on her face—and I hoped like hell this was nothing more than me being paranoid.

He moved again, working his way closer to Athena. *But also moving along the perimeter.*

I looked for Harm, wishing I could tell him to go stand by Athena for a few minutes—*or ask him if I was going crazy*. But he was on the other side of the room, and I wasn't willing to put even that short distance between me and this guy.

Another couple steps and the dark-haired stranger went to the next painting. The third before he'd reach the back of the room. And Athena.

I cleared my throat, my eyes flicking around the room, the crowd and closed space suddenly starting to feel like an ambush. My chest tightened, requiring a sudden strength to keep my breathing steady.

She was going to be fine.

What other danger could there be?

I repeated the questions in my mind the way I'd said them aloud a hundred times over the last two weeks. I didn't care how many men were dead, it still felt like there was something missing. A loose thread taunting me, but I couldn't find it to pull.

I thought—fucking hoped—this would've been easier. A week at Athena's house—our house—without incident should've eased my fears. Maybe not completely, but more than this.

Sunglass guy stepped back and then easily glided around a small group of people to the next painting. Even the way he

The Villain

walked didn't seem normal. Like he was used to moving undetected through crowds.

I didn't like this. Not a fucking bit. *Two more until he was at Athena.* My pulse picked up. *Fuck this.* I was going to stop him and introduce myself. Figure out what the hell his deal was. *And why he was staring at artwork through those damn sunglasses.*

The second I turned, letting my attention settle on him in an obvious as fuck way, he spun in my direction. My hand went for my weapon and then fell to my side when he strolled casually by me toward the door.

Absolutely not.

I followed him. I gave him the lead through the gallery, wanting to avoid any kind of scene inside for Athena's sake. His disappeared through the front door, and it had almost shut by the time I pushed it open again.

I stopped short, zeroing in on him as he unlocked a black Mercedes. *He was leaving...and I was overreacting.* I let out a heavy exhale, about to head back inside when he looked up at me—directly fucking at me. And smiled.

Fuck.

I whipped the door back open, my gaze snapping toward where I'd last seen Athena. *She wasn't there.* I scanned the room. Fucking people everywhere—even the older woman Athena had been talking to—but no sign of my woman.

I moved like a tidal wave through the crowd toward my brother.

"Have you seen Athena?" I interrupted my brother's conversation with a stranger I didn't care about.

"What?" He looked over his shoulder. "She was just—"

"Yeah, she was just," I snapped low. "Double-check the gallery. I'm going to the back."

My footfalls felt heavy enough to dent the floor as I went to the back of the room where the door led to the private part of the building.

"Glenn." I grabbed the gallery owner's arm, releasing it when I saw her wince. "I'm sorry, have you seen Athena?"

She blinked and then nodded. "Yeah, she just went to the back," she said, and my shoulders sagged. "A previous client of hers stopped in to purchase some other paintings he'd seen before."

"Before?" A chill gripped my heart.

"Yes. A Mr. Henry."

Mr. Henry. *Ryan Henry.*

I stilled. The only reason Athena would give that name was because she was in trouble. The man in the sunglasses had been a distraction for whoever had approached Athena and forced her to go with him. *And she'd given him Ryan's name to warn me.*

"Tell my brother," I ordered and bolted for the back.

Glenn's voice followed me as I yanked open the door labeled *Private,* pulling out my weapon as I hurried into the space. *Empty.* It was my first instinct, but my eyes whipped around the space.

"Athena?" I called, scanning the room over the barrel of my gun.

And then I saw it. The spilled yellow paint—and the footsteps leading to the back door. Two sets of them.

I took off, charging through the space in seconds and throwing open the door. As soon as I was outside, I saw her.

She was in a black sedan—*driving*—with Lloyd Wenner.

A thousand questions landed like a blitz. *Wenner? How? Why? What had we missed?* But their answers didn't matter until she was safe.

"*Athena!*" I shouted, breaking into a sprint for the car.

"*No!*" I saw her mouth move—her expression—and it was

The Villain

like I could actually hear her scream before Wenner clearly shouted at her to drive.

She hit the gas, the sedan burning rubber onto the asphalt as she turned right in front of me and pulled out of the lot, heading out of town.

"Fuck." I didn't have time to get my brother. Didn't have time to call Ty. I didn't have time for any-fucking-thing except to go after her.

I headed for my bike. In seconds, gravel kicked behind the wheels as I tore out onto the road, my heart pounding in my chest. The wind burned my skin as I tipped over a hundred on the speedometer to catch up to them. My head craned at every passing road, afraid they'd turn off before I reached them, and with every second that passed that I wasn't reaching the car, I worried I'd lost them.

I lowered the bike, taking the next turn dangerously fast in my frustration.

And then I saw her.

Jesus. The needle pierced one-hundred-fifteen on the gauge for me to catch them. *She was flying.*

My mind scrambled to figure out why. She knew I was coming for her. Wenner wouldn't risk shooting her since she was the one driving. *So why the hell was she speeding like she was trying to get away from me?*

I picked up speed to catch them, but so did she, speeding to keep a distance between us. *What. The. Fuck.* I let off a little, settling at a hundred, and she slowed, too.

"Slow down," I muttered, my hot exhales of frustration filling my helmet.

I tried to slow again, but this time, she maintained her speed, so I quickly revved my bike to catch my original position. This stretch of highway ran along the ocean, so there was no way I'd consider shooting out a tire to stop the car when it risked sending her over the guardrail—and over a cliff.

Wenner must be telling her she had to drive this fast—to keep a certain distance. Or maybe she was afraid if I got close enough that Wenner would shoot me.

I wished I could tell her I didn't care about getting shot again. I'd take every bullet that came my way if it got her out of his grasp.

Fear injected into my veins when we bared to the left and I saw the turns in the upcoming road. There was no way she could take them at the speed she was. She would have to slow down.

Except she didn't.

The car careened around the first curve, the tires protesting with a squeal, and I swore violently.

Suddenly, the car lurched as she pressed on the brakes. It was only for a second. A second that brought me much closer. A second that I saw her gaze in the rearview. A second for me to recognize the look in her eyes—it was the same one she'd had that night under the stars.

Trust me.

Trust her for—*fuck!*

I let off the gas as she swerved wildly toward the center of the two-lane road. *Jesus Christ.* The car practically drifted around the upcoming sharp turn, disappearing from my sight for an instant. I floored the gas, racing around the hard left to catch up, and as soon as the car came back into sight, all I saw was red.

A red brake light and the smoke of burning rubber.

The car careened for the rock wall on the left, tires squealing to stop in time, and I was headed right toward them.

"*Fuck!*" I shouted, and instinct took over. If I tried to brake and avoid a crash, I'd end up over the handlebars. The only thing I could do was evacuate.

I launched myself from my seat, pulling my arms close as I dove off my bike. Of course, it was my injured side that took the impact first. I shouted, pain slicing through my shoulder as it connected with the asphalt. The impact tore through the fabric of my skirt and then through my skin. I heard a crack and knew something had broken.

But none of that mattered. I had to get to Athena.

Rocks ate through my palms as I stopped myself from rolling. Only my right arm worked to push me onto my knees. I turned just as the car veered to the right, trying to turn away from the wall. The back corner slammed into the rocks, sending the whole thing lurching.

And then came my bike. Metal and sparks sprayed down the pavement as it skidded toward the vehicle.

I saw Wenner in the passenger window. He shouted and then looked out at the bike sliding toward him—and then at me. There was only pure fear in his eyes.

He knew I wasn't going to let him survive this.

I started to stand just as my motorcycle crashed into the back right tire of the car with impressive speed.

And then all I saw and heard and felt was the boom.

Everything was ringing. Spinning. Hot smoke filled my first deep breath and oxygenated my body with pure panic.

"Athena!" I shouted and sat up.

Everything hurt. Everything burned.

My bike was obliterated. The car was in deconstructed pieces strewn over the road.

A bomb.

My bike had been a bomb...and she'd forced me from it to save me.

My heart strained to beat. Its lumbering thuds were the only thing I could hear over the ringing in my ears from the blast.

I pushed myself upright. The world tilted with every step, threatening to open up and swallow me whole, but still I kept moving—stumbling to the wreckage.

This was why she'd kept her distance—to keep me out of range of the detonator.

My lungs worked not in breaths but only to inhale strength and shout her name. I needed her alive. I needed her to survive.

Half of the car was completely gone. Mostly the back and stretching to the passenger side where my bike had hit it. Small fires oozed destruction from various parts of the remaining frame, burning my nostrils with smoke.

She had to be alive.

I reached the car. In the passenger seat was Wenner. Still recognizable but definitely dead. In his hands were a gun and the half-melted remains of a detonator.

And in the driver's seat was Athena, slumped forward over the airbag, her arm limp like she'd tried to shield herself from the blast.

"Athena!" I called to her, realizing the only way to reach her was by climbing on top of the hood. The driver's door was pinned by the wall, and the passenger side was blocked by Wenner's body.

I scrambled to the front, seeing flashing lights and familiar bikes appearing from around the fateful turn.

"I'm coming, Angel." I climbed onto the hood, cursing my

left arm that was dislocated and fucking useless. "Athena." I crouched at the windshield, the glass completely shattered from the accident and explosion.

"Dare!" Harm shouted and rushed toward me.

I ignored him, reaching for Athena's wrist.

"Athena, please wake up," I begged, feeling for her pulse.

The soft flutter at her wrist was both everything and not enough. Alive but not awake.

"I'm going to get you out of here," I muttered. The broken glass cut into my shoulders and back as I squeezed through the windshield opening. I ripped the seat belt from its moorings and started to work my good arm under her torso.

"Jesus, Dare. You need—"

"To get her out of here. I have to get her out." I didn't even look at my brother, but I heard him climbing on the hood.

"I've got you," I murmured to Athena, hoping she could hear me. *Praying.*

A surge of pain broke through the adrenaline when I tried to lift her.

"Fuck," I hissed, wishing like all hell my left arm was injured any other way. Broken, bleeding, or burned, it would've still moved.

"Dare, I need you to grab her waist," Harm ordered, his tone like a whip the way it cracked me back to our unit days. And I obeyed. I always obeyed.

I moved my hand down her back while Harm grabbed underneath her shoulders.

"We lift on three," he said, and I fisted as much of her jeans in my one hand as I could, seeing the blood run down my arm. "One. Two. *Three—*"

I let out a roar, pulling with all my might. And then she was moving—gliding out of the car and up into my brother's strong hold.

"Athena," I murmured as soon as her weight was gone, each gasping breath like a hundred knives burying themselves in my lungs.

I didn't feel the cut of the glass when I climbed back out of the car. I moved off the hood, everything underneath me moving like a buoy in the middle of the storm. Tipping. Turning. Swaying.

My feet landed on the ground, and I looked for her. She had to be okay. That was all I needed. I could survive every other injury thrown at me except losing her again.

"*Dare!*" Harm was yelling. "*Look at me.*"

My vision swam, but I aimed for the sound of his voice, and there, through the blur, I saw Athena's blond hair and her red blouse in my brother's arms, the flickering ambulance lights behind him.

Thank God.

"Save her..." was all I managed before the world went dark.

Chapter Twenty-Four

Athena

There was an itch on my nose. I sighed and reached to scratch it, except I couldn't. Something was in my way. Something big and hard covered my finger and landed on the side of my nose instead of my finger. Something was attached to my hand, and I needed it off.

"Hey there, you have to keep that on," a deep voice rumbled from the darkness.

Darius. He was the first thing I registered. He would always be the first thing I registered. But it was the second thing that made me suck air into the giant pit in my stomach. *Darkness.*

Not again.

My eyes flung open, fear driving them wide. Too wide. Instantly, light blinded me, and I made a weak noise of pained relief. *There was light.*

And him.

"Darius." My voice didn't sound like my own, a familiar dryness in my throat as I carefully opened my eyes once more.

His beautiful face crystallized in front of me. The tense edge of his jaw. His full lips. The scar along his cheek. And those dark eyes—full of worry and hope and something infinitely more.

"I'm here, Angel." He pulled my hand to his mouth, pressing his lips to the back of my knuckles as he murmured, "I'm here."

Here. Bright lights. White walls. Sterile scent. *I was in the hospital.* And it was a sensor attached to my fingertip; that was what I was feeling—and hearing. The rhythmic beeps reached my ears from the monitors on the other side of the bed.

"What happened?" I croaked and tried to turn toward him, my entire body protesting with aches and pains, my memory a foggy equivalent.

He shifted, and I noticed his left arm was back in a sling—a new one. One that looked far more necessary than the last. *Along with the cast on his arm.*

"You saved me," he rasped. "You saved my life."

Saved... for a moment, I thought my memory might be lost again. How many times could I traumatize my brain and expect it to still function like normal? But then details started to float to the surface—details that seemed far too clear to be anything but real.

The gallery. The gun. *The detonator in Wenner's hand.* I gasped, the slight motion spreading pain through my chest.

"Careful. You have a few cracked ribs."

I ignored him and the pain. "There was a bomb—he put a bomb on your bike." Tears welled in my eyes, recalling the look on Dare's face when he'd seen me in the car. And when he'd chased us to try and save me, I swore I could feel his pain and confusion in my very bones.

The Villain

"I know—"

"I had to keep you away. Wenner said if you got too close, he'd kill you," I rambled, trying to blurt out all the things I hadn't been able to tell him as I drove away from him before. "He—" I sucked in a breath and then started over. "He told me to get in the car and drive."

The beeping beside me came faster, reliving brief flashes of those minutes held at gunpoint in the car. Told to drive faster. To lose him. The aching glances in the rearview mirror like I could reflect my plea all the way back to the man I loved.

"I didn't know what else to do. He was going to kill you. I"—my breath caught—"I had to get you off the bike."

"I know—"

"Are you okay?" My lip quivered. "I'm so sorry."

His eyes glimmered. "Don't be sorry, Angel. You saved my life."

I tried to swallow over the lump in my throat, tears pricking in the corners of my eyes. "You broke something." I nodded to the cast—an immovable one around his arm.

"We both did," he rumbled. "My arm. Collarbone. You cracked a few ribs. Cuts, scrapes, bruises, and burns. All survivable. All because of you."

I let out a shaky breath, curling my fingers a little tighter around his. "Dare—"

"I love you," he interrupted me, the words leaving his lungs with the force of a gale wind. "I love you, Athena Holman."

"Dare…"

"I love your kindness. Your compassion. Your talent and dedication. Your strength and bravery. But mostly, I love your generous, selfless spirit."

My chest shook, tears coming hot and fast down my cheeks.

"You more than saved my life, Athena. You saved my heart. My soul."

"I love you, too," I choked out, reaching for his cheek and pulling his face to mine.

Between the two of us, I was sure we were a sight. Battered and bruised and bandaged, but blissful. Completely blissful as his mouth claimed mine.

The kiss swallowed us up into our own little bubble. It pushed out the past and the dangers that had almost claimed my life and then his. It kept away the pain of betrayal and the fear of loss. It left only the two of us with what we'd had all the way at the beginning—each other.

And that was everything.

"Dare—"

The door to my room burst open, Harm filling the wide space, followed by Rob and one of the doctors, distinguished by his white coat and scrubs.

"I told you he'd be in here," Rob muttered and strolled around Harm with a loud sigh.

I looked at Dare. "Did you leave your room?"

"I had to see you."

I bit my lip, my heart feeling like it wanted to explode.

"You could've left a note," Harm grumbled, coming to stand beside Rob as he addressed me. "How are you feeling?"

"I'm okay. All things considered."

"Good." He let out a deep breath, his firm expression dissolving into pure emotion. "Thank you."

"Me?"

"For saving my brother's life." His voice cracked at the end, and the glimmer in his gaze revealed his own tears that threatened.

"That was a heck of a stunt you pulled off," Rob chimed in with a tipped smile of awe.

"Don't get any ideas," Dare growled at her. "We're taking a

break for danger. I think we've had more than enough for a while."

A break from danger. Did that mean...

"Is Wenner...is he..."

"Dead," he assured me before I even had to finish the question. "He can't hurt you anymore."

Tears slipped down my cheeks. I hadn't even felt them lining the edges of my eyes until they dripped free.

"He was at the house that morning," I said quietly, drawing the attention of the entire room.

Dare stiffened at my side, his fingers closing just a little tighter to remind me he was here. "You remembered."

I lowered my chin. "He came up to me in the gallery, and I remembered his face—I remembered the last of that morning."

Dare lifted my hand to his mouth, pressing kisses to the back of my hand and wrist like he could fix my hurt through sheer will.

"I went to drop off the paintings, and Wenner came to the house. He was clearly upset, so Rich—Ray—took him back to his office. I didn't feel...comfortable, so I was going to leave, but I heard them talking." I swallowed over the lump in my throat and pushed forward, the drugs in my system dulling the pain in my head I knew I would be feeling right about now. "I don't know why, but I went toward the room, and I heard him—heard Wenner say that they had to get rid of me. That he was taking care of it."

"Jesus," Harm muttered.

"I ran, but not before Wenner saw me through the door." My eyes closed then, retreating into the darkness for a moment where there was nothing else to focus on except that this nightmare was finally over.

"He'd already planned the bomb," Dare said low, breaking the silence. When I looked at him, he continued, "Wenner must've been working with Ivans to blackmail or overthrow Belmont. It was why the account tied to the house belonged to GrowTech. Why it was the same account that paid Brandon—"

"Why Brandon didn't recognize Ivans," Harm added. "It was Wenner who'd paid him."

"Wenner was pulling the strings the whole time. He was using Ivans to get them both what they wanted, and when Ivans became too much of a liability, he hired Brady to take him out, and then got rid of Brady for good measure."

"He's been cleaning up after Belmont for a decade," Rob said, her voice strained with anger. "If anyone knows how to cover his own tracks, it would be Wenner."

"I was the only piece left," I said softly.

"Because you saw him that morning. He didn't know you didn't remember."

"Or that I didn't even know his name."

The room settled into silence for several long seconds, everyone seemingly waiting to be sure that one more shoe didn't drop.

"It's over," Dare said low, finding my stare. "You'll be able to go home."

"We will," I corrected him.

There was a soft noise, and we both turned just as the door to my hospital room closed softly behind Rob.

"She'll be fine," Harm said quietly, the brothers sharing a look that spoke volumes; it was best to leave her alone right now. "I'm heading back to the garage. Ty and Rhys have been handling the police investigation."

"Thanks."

"Thank you." I released my breath when Dare and I were alone again. "I can't believe this is all over."

Strange how a few weeks could affect your life so

The Villain

completely, it felt like it had been years since things had been normal.

Dare cupped my cheek and brought his head back to mine. "It's not over," he murmured huskily. "This is just the beginning."

"I think this was the last one," Dare said, carefully breaking down what he'd declared as the last moving box we'd just finished unpacking.

I stood for a second, taking in the space now devoid of boxes. Taking in the filled shelves and decorated walls. Taking in all the photographs we'd hung of Mom and me, old photos of Darius and me, and photos of Darius and his family and his team. It was still Mom's old couches and her floral wallpaper, but it was also me now; *it was also us*.

It had been two weeks since we'd been released from the hospital, both of us a little worse for the wear, but happier for the future.

Gentle recuperation had been possible because of his family...my found family.

They'd kept us updated on how the dust settled after the accident; apparently, Belmont made a statement mourning the loss of his longtime friend and COO in a tragic car accident. If he knew about Wenner's discontent or the plot against him, there was no sign of it.

Ty made sure we were stocked on food. Tray after tray of his homemade frozen meals were delivered every few days, so all we had to do was microwave. Rorik came by to make sure we were healing well. Harm and Rhys and their partners, Daria and Merritt, would come over for dinner, after which Rhys would magically make his interesting-looking instrument—a hurdy-gurdy—appear, and we'd sing a few songs until the night ended. It was Rob, though, who visited the most. Helped us unpack at the beginning until we were a little more functional. Some days, it almost felt like she didn't come to see us but to escape...something.

"What did Harm want?"

His brother had stopped by half an hour ago, and the two of them had talked in my makeshift studio in the garage.

Dare's jaw tensed, and I went to him, resting a hand on his arm. My instinct as of late was to assume danger, but the pained look on his face didn't signal a threat.

I watched his throat bob and the way he had to coerce every muscle into coordination to speak.

"He wants me to take his bike."

My brow creased. Dare's motorcycle had been completely destroyed in the bomb, but why would Harm want to give him his?

"Why doesn't he want his own bike?"

"No." His exhale blew through his lips, his head swaying. "Not Harm's. My brother wants me to have Ryan's bike."

I felt my jaw slacken.

Dare nodded slowly. "It's covered in the back of the shop. It's an obnoxious yellow crotch rocket that we all bought after we came home. It was the one he always talked about, so we bought it for him...for his memory."

Tears collected in my eyes, and when he looked at me, I saw the same mirrored in his.

"Harm said it was a unanimous vote for me to have it."

"Oh, Darius..."

"I don't know if I can," he admitted low. "If I should."

"Maybe it deserves more than to be hidden, preserved

The Villain

under a cover and known only by the people closest to it," I said softly, framing his face. "Maybe it deserves to live its life now, too."

The tension released from his shoulders with a big shudder and groan just before he kissed me, long and deep and slow, before he drew back.

"I love you, Angel."

"I love you, too."

"We should go." He took my hand and started pulling me.

"Go where?" I balked but didn't do much to resist him as he led us right through the front door.

"There's a meteor shower tonight." His eyes twinkled when he told me, and my heart skipped in my chest.

"Darius, what are you doing?" I let out a sound between a laugh and a cry as he locked the front door from the inside and closed it—*locking us out*. "My purse is in there, and my keys—"

He pulled me into his arms, his lips finding the shell of my ear. "Good thing I know how to pick a lock."

Epilogue

Dare

Three months later...

"You need anything?" I leaned through the doorway.

"Nope." Ty didn't even look up from his computer. Lately, his work had claimed his focus with the same exacting precision as a knife through his chest.

With Ivans and Wenner gone, it was only Belmont left. Bernard Belmont. The man whose castle of cards was finally starting to crumble around him and who was battening down the hatches to shield himself from consequence.

Nodding, I grunted a goodbye and headed through the garage for the door.

I'd left Ryan's bike—*my bike*—parked outside since I'd only

The Villain

stopped by to grab a few things. No sense in opening up a whole bay.

I reached for the handle and swung the door wide and came face-to-face with a raised fist. Not intended for me—but to knock on the door.

The owner of the fist instantly lowered it, his startled expression holding him in silence.

"Can I help you?"

"I'm looking for Tynan Bates." The stranger pushed his narrow glasses higher and tried to look around me. "Is he here?"

My eyes narrowed, immediately assessing the man.

Everything about him was worn. From his voice to his frown to his tattered gray suit. Even the black sedan still running in the driveway was dirtied and scraped like it hadn't seen a wash in a decade.

"Who are you?" Like hell I was going to tell him if Ty was here or not before I even knew who the hell he was.

With a huff, he reached into his jacket pocket and pulled out a card, glancing over his shoulder in the process. This time, when I followed his line of sight back to his car, I saw a shadow move in the back seat.

He wasn't alone.

My spine tingled and my fingers twitched at my side, ready to reach for my weapon should this guy decide to do something stupid.

"Officer Daws."

"Officer?" I looked at the card. "*Parole* officer."

"Yes." He bristled, his sharp eyes narrowing further. "Is Mr. Bates here or not? I need to speak with him."

"What's this—"

"I'm here." Ty's voice boomed as he pushed me to the side, staring Mr. Daws down with a glare that I hadn't seen in a long time. "What do you want?"

"I'm here about Ms. Brant."

Daws was too nervous to notice how my friend's entire body tensed. I couldn't remember the last time Ty had been affected by any kind of news or anything...like this.

Who the hell was Ms. Brant?

Wait.

Brant.

The familiarity of the name hit me. Jon Brant had been Ty's mentor—his friend—in Special Forces. While the rest of us had come home emotionally and physically benched after our last mission and Ryan's death, Ty had gone back. One more mission at the request of his mentor, Jon. *One more brother lost.*

"I can handle this, Dare," he uttered his dismissal to me but didn't take his eyes from Daws.

"Are you—"

"Go."

I swallowed my protest and nodded. We all had things—times when questions were off the table. This was one of those times.

I walked away, but I went slow—slow enough to hear the last vestiges of their conversation.

"What about her?"

"She violated her parole again, so I'm remanding her to your custody."

"*What? No.*" Ty spoke with so much emotion I swore I felt the earth move.

"Either that or I report it and she goes to jail—real jail this time, Bates, not juvie."

"Dammit. What the hell did she do? I'll fix it."

"You need to fix *her*," the other man snarled, and even though I'd reached my bike, my head whipped when I heard the car door open.

Both men glared at the woman—*girl?*—who got out. If the

The Villain

dictionary were a picture book, I had a feeling this girl's picture would be under *trouble*. Jet-black hair. Piercings. Tattoos. But it was her give-no-shit swagger that really sold it for me.

"Uncle Tynan." Her voice was sarcastically sweet, especially on the word *uncle*. "So *good* to see you again."

I'd never seen Ty's jaw look like it was about to snap. The whole of him, really.

"Six weeks. Six weeks until her parole ends. Six weeks until I suggest you start letting her clean up her own messes," Daws said low, but the breeze carried his voice over to me.

Instantly, Ty was in the man's face, towering over him like a hungry ogre ready to bite his whole damn head off. "Get out."

Damn, Ty was pissed.

Flustered, Daws shook his head and rushed back to his car.

"Sutton."

Sutton Brant.

"You don't look very happy to see me." She pouted and then laughed.

"You shouldn't be here." My friend barreled his arms over his chest like a volcano about to erupt. For years, Ty had been our benchmark for emotionless, logical living. But emotion hadn't been absent; it had been dormant. And now he was on the verge of exploding. "What have you done, Sutton?"

"You heard the man, *Uncle Ty*." Her mocking tone was the loudest part of her words before she stepped forward, right in his face. "I'm your problem now."

Ty's angry glare followed her inside before it darted back to me. *Yeah, I wasn't getting involved in this.* I flipped my visor down and started my bike. I had other things to do today than watching Ty's cool composure erupt. Even though that did sound entertaining.

"Come outside with me," I begged, drawing her away from her latest canvas.

"But…"

I pressed a kiss to her neck. "It will be here tomorrow, but this…tonight can't wait."

Athena smiled and turned her head, and I couldn't resist a taste of her lips, dipping my tongue into her sweetness for long minutes before I groaned low, "That will have to wait, too."

She pouted adorably but stood.

"Trust me?"

Her nod was implicit.

"Good." I moved behind her and reached around her head, covering her eyes with my palms.

"Darius…" She shivered.

"Let me guide you," I said low, and I carefully walked us to the sliding back door that I'd already opened in preparation.

I only took us a few feet outside onto the grass before I peeled my hands away from her face.

"What…" She cupped my hands over her mouth, her eyes roaming over my handiwork.

A blanket on the ground, pillows placed on top of it. Battery-powered tea lights flickering along the edges.

"What is this?"

"We're stargazing." I led her to the blanket and tipped my head to the heavens.

"The Big Dipper." She pointed to the right.

"Orion's Belt." I pointed in front of her, slightly to the left.

Her gaze followed my hand, and as soon as her focus was

there, I dropped my arm and reached in my pocket for the box tucked inside it.

"There's one back here," I rumbled low and lowered down on one knee.

Her gasp of surprise was one of the most beautiful sights—one of the most beautiful memories I'd never forget.

"Darius..." Her lip quivered.

"This one's called the proposal," I said and opened the box, revealing the solitaire diamond ring nestled inside.

"Dare..."

"I love you, Athena. I love you more than the stars in the sky, and I don't want to spend any more of this lifetime without you."

Tears left a path that glistened down her cheeks as she stared at me. A second passed and then another, and then, to my surprise, her eyes drifted shut.

"Ask me again," she pleaded.

My brow creased. "I'll ask you as many times as it takes you to say yes, Angel, but...what are you doing?"

Her smile beamed wide as she explained, "This time, I want to feel your love."

I loved when she did this. When she went back to the darkness to remind herself she wasn't afraid of it—to remind her of all the things and perspectives it had given her. It was only in the darkness that we learned how to find the light.

My chest felt so tight, I thought it might crack as the words broke free. "Athena Holman, will you marry me?"

Her bright smile stretched wider. "Yes," she murmured, and I took her hand, sliding the ring along her narrow finger. "I love you."

"I love you, too."

. . .

The End.

The Vigilant

Tynan Bates always believed he had the skills to protect everyone he loved. Mission after mission proved his special forces unit was invincible. Until it wasn't, and he lost his friend and mentor. Years later, haunted by guilt, Tynan has no desire for anything more in life than to atone for his failure.

He thought atonement came in the form of Vigilante business—righting wrongs left unpunished by the law. As it turns out, it showed up in the form of his mentor's daughter at his front door. Along with her parole officer.

Sutton Brant has made some bad choices. If 'trouble' isn't her middle name, it should be. Now, she's under house arrest with a man fifteen years her senior. *Though her vague memories didn't prepare her for Ty's handsome yet broody appeal.*

Tasked to keep Sutton out of trouble for the next two months, Tynan is nothing if not vigilant when it comes to his duty. However, living in such close proximity with the woman who is

Dr. Rebecca Sharp

as beautiful as she is infuriating proves more difficult than he anticipated. But when she starts asking about his scars, that's where he draws the line... until Sutton's past catches up with her. Tynan will do anything to keep her safe because this time, he has everything to lose.

Download here.

Other Works by Dr. Rebecca Sharp

The Vigilantes

The Vendetta
The Verdict
The Villain
The Vigilant
The Vow

The Kinkades

The Woodsman
The Lightkeeper
The Candlemaker
The Innkeeper

Reynolds Protective

Archer
Hunter
Gunner
Ranger

Covington Security

Betrayed

Bribed

Beguiled

Burned

Branded

Broken

Believed

Bargained

Braved

Carmel Cove

Beholden

Bespoken

Besotted

Befallen

Beloved

Betrothed

The Odyssey Duet

The Fall of Troy

The Judgment of Paris

Country Love Collection

Tequila

Ready to Run

Fastest Girl in Town

Last Name

I'll Be Your Santa Tonight

Michigan for the Winter

Remember Arizona

Ex To See

A Cowboy for Christmas

Meant to Be

Accidentally on Purpose

The Winter Games

Up in the Air

On the Edge

Enjoy the Ride

In Too Deep

Over the Top

The Gentlemen's Guild

The Artist's Touch

The Sculptor's Seduction

The Painter's Passion

Passion & Perseverance Trilogy

(A Pride and Prejudice Retelling)

First Impressions

Second Chances

Third Time is the Charm

Standalones

Reputation

Redemption

Revolution

Hypothetically

Want to #staysharp with everything that's coming?

Join my newsletter!

About the Author

Rebecca Sharp is a contemporary romance author of over thirty published novels and dentist living in PA with her amazing husband, affectionately referred to as Mr. GQ.

She writes a wide variety of contemporary romance. From new adult to extreme sports romance, forbidden romance to romantic comedies, her books will always give you strong heroines, hot alphas, unique love stories, and always a happily ever after. When she's not writing or seeing patients, she loves to travel with her husband, snowboard, and cook.

She loves to hear from readers. You can find her on Facebook, Instagram, and Goodreads. And, of course, you can email her directly at author@drrebeccasharp.com.

If you want to be emailed with exclusive cover reveals, upcoming book news, etc. you can sign up for her mailing list on her website: www.drrebeccasharp.com

Happy reading!

xx

Rebecca

Made in the USA
Middletown, DE
06 April 2025